Between the Acts
and
A Room of One's Own

by

Virginia Woolf

Printed on acid free ANSI archival quality paper.
ISBN: 978-1-78139-497-7
© 2015 Benediction Classics, Oxford

Contents

Between the Acts

Between the Acts

It was a summer's night and they were talking, in the big room with the windows open to the garden, about the cesspool. The county council had promised to bring water to the village, but they hadn't.

Mrs. Haines, the wife of the gentleman farmer, a goosefaced woman with eyes protruding as if they saw something to gobble in the gutter, said affectedly: "What a subject to talk about on a night like this!"

Then there was silence; and a cow coughed; and that led her to say how odd it was, as a child, she had never feared cows, only horses. But, then, as a small child in a perambulator, a great cart-horse had brushed within an inch of her face. Her family, she told the old man in the arm-chair, had lived near Liskeard for many centuries. There were the graves in the churchyard to prove it.

A bird chuckled outside. "A nightingale?" asked Mrs. Haines. No, nightingales didn't come so far north. It was a daylight bird, chuckling over the substance and succulence of the day, over worms, snails, grit, even in sleep.

The old man in the arm-chair--Mr. Oliver, of the Indian Civil Service, retired--said that the site they had chosen for the cesspool was, if he had heard aright, on the Roman road. From an aeroplane, he said, you could still see, plainly marked, the scars made by the Britons; by the Romans; by the Elizabethan manor house; and by the plough, when they ploughed the hill to grow wheat in the Napoleonic wars.

"But you don't remember . . ." Mrs. Haines began. No, not that. Still he did remember--and he was about to tell them what, when there was a sound outside, and Isa, his son's wife, came in with her hair in pigtails; she was wearing a dressing-gown with faded peacocks on it. She came in like a swan swimming its way; then was checked and stopped; was surprised to find people there; and lights burning. She had been sitting with her little boy who wasn't well, she apologized. What had they been saying?

"Discussing the cesspool," said Mr. Oliver.

"What a subject to talk about on a night like this!" Mrs. Haines exclaimed again.

What had *he* said about the cesspool; or indeed about anything? Isa wondered, inclining her head towards the gentleman farmer, Rupert Haines. She had met him at a Bazaar; and at a tennis party. He had handed her a cup and a racquet--that was all. But in his ravaged face she always felt mystery; and in his silence, passion. At the tennis party she had felt this, and at the Bazaar. Now a third time, if anything more strongly, she felt it again.

"I remember," the old man interrupted, "my mother. . . ." Of his mother he remembered that she was very stout; kept her tea-caddy locked; yet had given him in that very room a copy of Byron. It was over sixty years ago, he told them, that his mother had given him the works of Byron in that very room. He paused.

"She walks in beauty like the night," he quoted.

Then again:

"So we'll go no more a-roving by the light of the moon."

Isa raised her head. The words made two rings, perfect rings, that floated them, herself and Haines, like two swans down stream. But his snow-white breast was circled with a tangle of dirty duckweed; and she too, in her webbed feet was entangled, by her husband, the stockbroker. Sitting on her three-cornered chair she swayed, with her dark pigtails hanging, and her body like a bolster in its faded dressing-gown.

Mrs. Haines was aware of the emotion circling them, excluding her. She waited, as one waits for the strain of an organ to die out before leaving church. In the car going home to the red villa in the cornfields, she would destroy it, as a thrush pecks the wings off a butterfly. Allowing ten seconds to intervene, she rose; paused; and then, as if she had heard the last strain die out, offered Mrs. Giles Oliver her hand.

But Isa, though she should have risen at the same moment that Mrs. Haines rose, sat on. Mrs. Haines glared at her out of goose-like eyes, gobbling, "Please, Mrs. Giles Oliver, do me the kindness to recognize my existence. . . ." which she was forced to do, rising at last from her chair, in her faded dressing-gown, with the pigtails falling over each shoulder.

Pointz Hall was seen in the light of an early summer morning to be a middle-sized house. It did not rank among the houses that are mentioned in guide books. It was too homely. But this whitish house with the grey roof, and the wing thrown out at right angles, lying unfortunately low on the meadow with a fringe of trees on the bank above it so that smoke curled up to the nests of the rooks, was a desirable house to live in. Driving past, people said to each other: "I wonder if that'll ever come into the market?" And to the chauffeur: "Who lives there?"

The chauffeur didn't know. The Olivers, who had bought the place something over a century ago, had no connection with the Warings, the Elveys, the Mannerings or the Burnets; the old families who had all intermarried, and lay in their deaths intertwisted, like the ivy roots, beneath the churchyard wall.

Only something over a hundred and twenty years the Olivers had been there. Still, on going up the principal staircase--there was another, a mere ladder at the back for the servants--there was a portrait. A length of yellow brocade was visible half-way up; and, as one reached the top, a small powdered face, a great head-dress slung with pearls, came into view; an ancestress of sorts. Six or seven bedrooms opened out of the corridor. The butler had been a soldier; had married a lady's maid; and, under a glass case there was a watch that had stopped a bullet on the field of Waterloo.

It was early morning. The dew was on the grass. The church clock struck eight times. Mrs. Swithin drew the curtain in her bedroom--the faded white chintz that so agreeably from the outside tinged the window with its green lining. There with her old hands on the hasp, jerking it open, she stood: old Oliver's married sister; a widow. She always meant to set up a house of her own; perhaps in Kensington, perhaps at Kew, so that she could have the benefit of the gardens. But she stayed on all through the summer; and when winter wept its damp upon the panes, and choked the gutters with dead leaves, she said: "Why, Bart, did they build the house in the hollow, facing north?" Her brother said, "Obviously to escape from nature. Weren't four horses needed to drag the family coach through the mud?" Then he told her the famous story of the great eighteenth-century winter; when for a whole month the house had been blocked by snow. And the trees had fallen. So every year, when winter came, Mrs. Swithin retired to Hastings.

But it was summer now. She had been waked by the birds. How they sang! attacking the dawn like so many choir boys attacking an iced cake. Forced to listen, she had stretched for her favourite reading--an Outline of History--and had spent the hours between three and five thinking of rhododendron forests in Piccadilly; when the entire continent, not then, she understood, divided by a channel, was all one; populated, she understood, by elephant-bodied, seal-necked, heaving, surging, slowly writhing, and, she supposed, barking monsters; the iguanodon, the mammoth, and the mastodon; from whom presumably, she thought, jerking the window open, we descend.

It took her five seconds in actual time, in mind time ever so much longer, to separate Grace herself, with blue china on a tray, from the leather-covered grunting monster who was about, as the door opened, to demolish a whole tree in the green steaming undergrowth of the primeval forest. Naturally, she jumped, as Grace put the tray down and said: "Good morning, Ma'am." "Batty," Grace called her, as she felt on her face the divided glance that was half meant for a beast in a swamp, half for a maid in a print frock and white apron.

"How those birds sing!" said Mrs. Swithin, at a venture. The window was open now; the birds certainly were singing. An obliging thrush hopped across the lawn; a coil of pinkish rubber twisted in its beak. Tempted by the sight to continue her imaginative reconstruction of the past, Mrs. Swithin paused; she was given to increasing the bounds of the moment by flights into past or future; or sidelong down corridors and alleys; but she remembered her mother--her mother in that very room rebuking her. "Don't stand gaping, Lucy, or the wind'll change . . ." How often her mother had rebuked her in that very room--"but in a very different world," as her brother would remind her. So she sat down to morning tea, like any other old lady with a high nose, thin cheeks, a ring on her finger and the usual trappings of rather shabby but gallant old age, which included in her case a cross gleaming gold on her breast.

The nurses after breakfast were trundling the perambulator up and down the terrace; and as they trundled they were talking--not shaping pellets of information or handing ideas from one to another, but rolling words, like sweets on their tongues; which, as they thinned to transparency, gave off pink, green, and sweetness. This morning that sweetness was: "How cook had told 'im off about the asparagus; how when she rang I said: how it was a sweet costume with blouse to match;" and that was leading to something about a feller as they walked up and down the terrace rolling sweets, trundling the perambulator.

It was a pity that the man who had built Pointz Hall had pitched the house in a hollow, when beyond the flower garden and the vegetables there was this stretch of high ground. Nature had provided a site for a house; man had built his house in a hollow. Nature had provided a stretch of turf half a mile in length and level, till it suddenly dipped to the lily pool. The terrace was broad enough to take the entire shadow of one of the great trees laid flat. There you could walk up and down, up and down, under the shade of the trees. Two or three grew close together; then there were gaps. Their roots broke the turf, and among those bones were green waterfalls and cushions of grass in which violets grew in spring or in summer the wild purple orchis.

Amy was saying something about a feller when Mabel, with her hand on the pram, turned sharply, her sweet swallowed. "Leave off grubbing," she said sharply. "Come along, George."

The little boy had lagged and was grouting in the grass. Then the baby, Caro, thrust her fist out over the coverlet and the furry bear was jerked overboard. Amy had to stoop. George grubbed. The flower blazed between the angles of the roots. Membrane after membrane was torn. It blazed a soft yellow, a lambent light under a film of velvet; it filled the caverns behind the eyes with light. All that inner darkness became a hall, leaf smelling, earth smelling of yellow light. And the tree was beyond the flower; the grass, the flower and the tree were entire. Down on his knees grubbing he held the flower complete. Then there was a roar and a hot breath and a stream of coarse grey hair rushed between him and the flower. Up he leapt, toppling in his fright, and saw coming towards him a terrible peaked eyeless monster moving on legs, brandishing arms.

"Good morning, sir," a hollow voice boomed at him from a beak of paper.

The old man had sprung upon him from his hiding-place behind a tree.

"Say good morning, George; say 'Good morning, Grandpa,'" Mabel urged him, giving him a push towards the man. But George stood gaping. George stood gazing. Then Mr. Oliver crumpled the paper which he had cocked into a snout and appeared in person. A very tall old man, with gleaming eyes, wrinkled cheeks, and a head with no hair on it. He turned.

"Heel!" he bawled, "heel, you brute!" And George turned; and the nurses turned holding the furry bear; they all turned to look at Sohrab the Afghan hound bounding and bouncing among the flowers.

"Heel!" the old man bawled, as if he were commanding a regiment. It was impressive, to the nurses, the way an old boy of his age could still bawl and make a brute like that obey him. Back came the Afghan hound, sidling, apologetic. And as he cringed at the old man's feet, a string was slipped over his collar; the noose that old Oliver always carried with him.

"You wild beast . . . you bad beast," he grumbled, stooping. George looked at the dog only. The hairy flanks were sucked in and out; there was a blob of foam on its nostrils. He burst out crying.

Old Oliver raised himself, his veins swollen, his cheeks flushed; he was angry. His little game with the paper hadn't worked. The boy was a cry-baby. He nodded and sauntered on, smoothing out the crumpled paper and muttering, as he tried to find his line in the column, "A cry-baby--a cry-baby." But the breeze blew the great sheet out; and over the edge he surveyed the landscape--flowing fields, heath and woods. Framed, they became a picture. Had he been a painter, he would have fixed his easel here, where the country, barred by trees, looked like a picture. Then the breeze fell.

"M. Daladier," he read finding his place in the column, "has been successful in pegging down the franc. . . ."

Mrs. Giles Oliver drew the comb through the thick tangle of hair which, after giving the matter her best attention, she had never had shingled or bobbed; and lifted the heavily embossed silver brush that had been a wedding present and had its uses in impressing chambermaids in hotels. She lifted it and stood in front of the three-folded mirror, so that she could see three separate versions of her rather heavy, yet handsome, face; and also, outside the glass, a slip of terrace, lawn and tree tops.

Inside the glass, in her eyes, she saw what she had felt overnight for the ravaged, the silent, the romantic gentleman farmer. "In love," was in her eyes. But outside, on the washstand, on the dressing-table, among the silver boxes and tooth-brushes, was the other love; love for her husband, the stockbroker--"The father of my children," she added, slipping into the cliché conveniently provided by fiction. Inner love was in the eyes; outer love on the dressing-table. But what feeling was it that stirred in her now when above the looking-glass, out of doors, she saw coming across the lawn the perambulator; two nurses; and her little boy George, lagging behind?

She tapped on the window with her embossed hairbrush. They were too far off to hear. The drone of the trees was in their ears; the chirp of birds; other incidents of garden life, inaudible, invisible to her in the bedroom, absorbed them. Isolated on a green island, hedged about with snowdrops, laid with a counterpane of puckered silk, the innocent island floated under her window. Only George lagged behind.

She returned to her eyes in the looking-glass. "In love," she must be; since the presence of his body in the room last night could so affect her; since the words he said, handing her a teacup, handing her a tennis racquet, could so attach themselves to a certain spot in her; and thus lie between them like a wire, tingling, tangling, vibrating--she groped, in the depths of the looking-glass, for a word to fit the infinitely quick vibrations of the aeroplane propeller that she had seen once at dawn at Croydon. Faster, faster, faster, it whizzed, whirred, buzzed, till all the flails became one flail and up soared the plane away and away. . . .

"Where we know not, where we go not, neither know nor care," she hummed. "Flying, rushing through the ambient, incandescent, summer silent . . ."

The rhyme was "air." She put down her brush. She took up the telephone.

"Three, four, eight, Pyecombe," she said.

"Mrs. Oliver speaking. . . . What fish have you this morning? Cod? Halibut? Sole? Plaice?"

"There to lose what binds us here," she murmured. "Soles. Filleted. In time for lunch please," she said aloud. "With a feather, a blue feather . . . flying mounting through the air . . . there to lose what binds us here . . ." The words weren't worth writing in the book bound like an account book in case Giles suspected. "Abortive," was the word that expressed her. She never came out of a shop, for example, with the clothes she admired; nor did her figure, seen against the dark roll of trousering in a shop window, please her. Thick of waist, large of limb, and, save for her hair, fashionable in the tight modern way, she never looked like Sappho, or one of the beautiful young men whose photographs adorned the weekly papers. She looked what she was: Sir Richard's daughter; and niece of the two old ladies at Wimbledon who were so proud, being O'Neils, of their descent from the Kings of Ireland.

A foolish, flattering lady, pausing on the threshold of what she once called "the heart of the house," the threshold of the library, had once said: "Next to the kitchen, the library's always the nicest room in the house." Then she added, stepping across the threshold: "Books are the mirrors of the soul."

In this case a tarnished, a spotted soul. For as the train took over three hours to reach this remote village in the very heart of England, no one ventured so long a journey, without staving off possible mind-hunger, without buying a book on a bookstall. Thus the mirror that reflected the soul sublime, reflected also the soul bored. Nobody could pretend, as they looked at the shuffle of shilling shockers that week-enders had dropped, that the looking-glass always reflected the anguish of a Queen or the heroism of King Harry.

At this early hour of a June morning the library was empty. Mrs. Giles had to visit the kitchen. Mr. Oliver still tramped the terrace. And Mrs. Swithin was of course at church. The light but variable breeze, foretold by the weather expert, flapped the yellow curtain, tossing light, then shadow. The fire greyed, then glowed, and the tortoiseshell butterfly beat on the lower pane of the window; beat, beat, beat; repeating that if no human being ever came, never, never, never, the books would be mouldy, the fire out and the tortoiseshell butterfly dead on the pane.

Heralded by the impetuosity of the Afghan hound, the old man entered. He had read his paper; he was drowsy; and so sank down into the chintz-covered chair with the dog at his feet--the Afghan hound. His nose on his paws, his haunches drawn up, he looked a stone dog, a crusader's dog, guarding even in the realms of death the sleep of his master. But the master was not dead; only dreaming; drowsily, seeing as in a glass, its lustre spotted, himself, a young man helmeted; and a cascade falling. But no water; and the hills, like grey stuff pleated; and in the sand a hoop of ribs; a bullock maggot-eaten in the sun; and in the shadow of the rock, savages; and in his hand a gun. The dream hand clenched; the real hand lay on the chair arm, the veins swollen but only with a brownish fluid now.

The door opened.

"Am I," Isa apologized, "interrupting?"

Of course she was--destroying youth and India. It was his fault, since she had persisted in stretching his thread of life so fine, so far. Indeed he was grateful to her, watching her as she strolled about the room, for continuing.

Many old men had only their India--old men in clubs, old men in rooms off Jermyn Street. She in her striped dress continued him, murmuring, in front of the book cases: "The moor is dark beneath the moon, rapid clouds have drunk the last pale beams of even. . . . I have ordered the fish," she said aloud, turning, "though whether it'll be fresh or not I can't promise. But veal is dear, and everybody in the house is sick of beef and mutton. . . . Sohrab," she said, coming to a standstill in front of them, "What's *he* been doing?"

His tail never wagged. He never admitted the ties of domesticity. Either he cringed or he bit. Now his wild yellow eyes gazed at her, gazed at him. He could outstare them both. Then Oliver remembered:

"Your little boy's a cry-baby," he said scornfully.

"Oh," she sighed, pegged down on a chair arm, like a captive balloon, by a myriad of hair-thin ties into domesticity. "What's been happening?"

"I took the newspaper," he explained, "so . . ."

He took it and crumpled it into a beak over his nose. "So," he had sprung out from behind a tree on to the children.

"And he howled. He's a coward, your boy is."

She frowned. He was not a coward, her boy wasn't. And she loathed the domestic, the possessive; the maternal. And he knew it and did it on purpose to tease her, the old brute, her father-in-law.

She looked away.

"The library's always the nicest room in the house," she quoted, and ran her eyes along the books. "The mirror of the soul" books were. *The Faerie Queene* and Kinglake's *Crimea;* Keats and the *Kreutzer Sonata.* There they were, reflecting. What? What remedy was there for her at her age--the age of the century, thirty-nine--in books? Book-shy she was, like the rest of her generation; and gun-shy too. Yet as a person with a raging tooth runs her eye in a chemist shop over green bottles with gilt scrolls on them lest one of them may contain a cure, she considered: Keats and Shelley; Yeats and Donne. Or perhaps not a poem; a life. The life of Garibaldi. The life of Lord Palmerston. Or perhaps not a person's life; a county's. *The Antiquities of Durham; The Proceedings of the Archæological Society of Nottingham.* Or not a life at all, but science--Eddington, Darwin, or Jeans.

None of them stopped her toothache. For her generation the newspaper was a book; and, as her father-in-law had dropped the *Times,* she took it and read: "A horse with a green tail . . ." which was fantastic. Next, "The guard at Whitehall . . ." which was romantic and then, building word upon word she read: "The troopers told her the horse had a green tail; but she found it was just an ordinary horse. And they dragged her up to the barrack room where she was thrown upon a bed. Then one of the troopers removed part of her clothing, and she screamed and hit him about the face. . . ."

That was real; so real that on the mahogany door panels she saw the Arch in Whitehall; through the Arch the barrack room; in the barrack room the bed, and on the bed the girl was screaming and hitting him about the face, when the door (for in fact it was a door) opened and in came Mrs. Swithin carrying a hammer.

She advanced, sidling, as if the floor were fluid under her shabby garden shoes, and, advancing, pursed her lips and smiled, sidelong, at her brother. Not a word passed between them as she went to the cupboard in the corner and replaced the hammer, which she had taken without asking leave; together--she unclosed her fist-- with a handful of nails.

"Cindy--Cindy," he growled, as she shut the cupboard door.

Lucy, his sister, was three years younger than he was. The name Cindy, or Sindy, for it could be spelt either way, was short for Lucy. It was by this name that he had called her when they were children; when she had trotted after him as he fished, and had made the meadow flowers into tight little bunches, winding one long grass stalk round and round and round. Once, she remembered, he had made her take the fish off the hook herself. The blood had shocked her--"Oh!" she had cried--

for the gills were full of blood. And he had growled: "Cindy!" The ghost of that morning in the meadow was in her mind as she replaced the hammer where it belonged on one shelf; and the nails where they belonged on another; and shut the cupboard about which, for he still kept his fishing tackle there, he was still so very particular.

"I've been nailing the placard on the Barn," she said, giving him a little pat on the shoulder.

The words were like the first peal of a chime of bells. As the first peals, you hear the second; as the second peals, you hear the third. So when Isa heard Mrs. Swithin say: "I've been nailing the placard to the Barn," she knew she would say next:

"For the pageant."

And he would say:

"Today? By Jupiter! I'd forgotten!"

"If it's fine," Mrs. Swithin continued, "they'll act on the terrace . . ."

"And if it's wet," Bartholomew continued, "in the Barn."

"And which will it be?" Mrs. Swithin continued. "Wet or fine?"

Then, for the seventh time in succession, they both looked out of the window.

Every summer, for seven summers now, Isa had heard the same words; about the hammer and the nails; the pageant and the weather. Every year they said, would it be wet or fine; and every year it was--one or the other. The same chime followed the same chime, only this year beneath the chime she heard: "The girl screamed and hit him about the face with a hammer."

"The forecast," said Mr. Oliver, turning the pages till he found it, "says: Variable winds; fair average temperature; rain at times."

He put down the paper, and they all looked at the sky to see whether the sky obeyed the meteorologist. Certainly the weather was variable. It was green in the garden; grey the next. Here came the sun--an illimitable rapture of joy, embracing every flower, every leaf. Then in compassion it withdrew, covering its face, as if it forebore to look on human suffering. There was a fecklessness, a lack of symmetry and order in the clouds, as they thinned and thickened. Was it their own law, or no law, they obeyed? Some were wisps of white hair merely. One, high up, very distant, had hardened to golden alabaster; was made of immortal marble. Beyond that was blue, pure blue, black blue; blue that had never filtered down; that had escaped registration. It never fell as sun, shadow, or rain upon the world, but disregarded the little coloured ball of earth entirely. No flower felt it; no field; no garden.

Mrs. Swithin's eyes glazed as she looked at it. Isa thought her gaze was fixed because she saw God there, God on his throne. But as a shadow fell next moment on the garden Mrs. Swithin loosed and lowered her fixed look and said:

"It's very unsettled. It'll rain, I'm afraid. We can only pray," she added, and fingered her crucifix.

"And provide umbrellas," said her brother.

Lucy flushed. He had struck her faith. When she said "pray," he added "umbrellas." She half covered the cross with her fingers. She shrank; she cowered; but next moment she exclaimed:

"Oh there they are--the darlings!"

The perambulator was passing across the lawn.

Isa looked too. What an angel she was--the old woman! Thus to salute the children; to beat up against those immensities and the old man's irreverences her skinny hands, her laughing eyes! How courageous to defy Bart and the weather!

"He looks blooming," said Mrs. Swithin.

"It's astonishing how they pick up," said Isa.

"He ate his breakfast?" Mrs. Swithin asked.

"Every scrap," said Isa.

"And baby? No sign of measles?"

Isa shook her head. "Touch wood," she added, tapping the table.

"Tell me, Bart," said Mrs. Swithin turning to her brother, "what's the origin of that? Touch wood . . . Antaeus, didn't he touch earth?"

She would have been, he thought, a very clever woman, had she fixed her gaze. But this led to that; that to the other. What went in at this ear, went out at that. And all were circled, as happens after seventy, by one recurring question. Hers was, should she live at Kensington or at Kew? But every year, when winter came, she did neither. She took lodgings at Hastings.

"Touch wood; touch earth; Antaeus," he muttered, bringing the scattered bits together. Lempriere would settle it; or the Encyclopædia. But it was not in books the answer to his question--why, in Lucy's skull, shaped so much like his own, there existed a prayable being? She didn't, he supposed, invest it with hair, teeth or toe-nails. It was, he supposed more of a force or a radiance, controlling the thrush and the worm; the tulip and the hound; and himself, too, an old man with swollen veins. It got her out of bed on a cold morning and sent her down the muddy path to worship it, whose mouthpiece was Streatfield. A good fellow, who smoked cigars in the vestry. He needed some solace, doling out preachments to asthmatic elders, perpetually repairing the perpetually falling steeple, by means of placards nailed to Barns. The love, he was thinking, that they should give to flesh and blood they give to the church . . . when Lucy rapping her fingers on the table said:

"What's the origin--the origin--of that?"

"Superstition," he said.

She flushed, and the little breath too was audible that she drew in as once more he struck a blow at her faith. But, brother and sister, flesh and blood was not a barrier, but a mist. Nothing changed their affection; no argument; no fact; no truth. What she saw he didn't; what he saw she didn't--and so on, *ad infinitum*.

"Cindy," he growled. And the quarrel was over.

The Barn to which Lucy had nailed her placard was a great building in the farmyard. It was as old as the church, and built of the same stone, but it had no steeple. It was raised on cones of grey stone at the corners to protect it from rats and damp. Those who had been to Greece always said it reminded them of a temple. Those who had never been to Greece--the majority--admired it all the same. The roof was weathered red-orange; and inside it was a hollow hall, sun-shafted, brown, smelling of corn, dark when the doors were shut, but splendidly illuminated when the doors at the end stood open, as they did to let the wagons in--the long low wagons, like ships of the sea, breasting the corn, not the sea, returning in the evening shagged with hay. The lanes caught tufts where the wagons had passed.

Now benches were drawn across the floor of the Barn. If it rained, the actors were to act in the Barn; planks had been laid together at one end to form a stage. Wet or fine, the audience would take tea there. Young men and women--Jim, Iris, David, Jessica--were even now busy with garlands of red and white paper roses left over from the Coronation. The seeds and the dust from the sacks made them sneeze. Iris had a handkerchief bound round her forehead; Jessica wore breeches. The young men worked in shirt sleeves. Pale husks had stuck in their hair, and it was easy to run a splinter of wood into the fingers.

"Old Flimsy" (Mrs. Swithin's nickname) had been nailing another placard on the Barn. The first had been blown down, or the village idiot, who always tore down what had been nailed up, had done it, and was chuckling over the placard under the shade of some hedge. The workers were laughing too, as if old Swithin had left a wake of laughter behind her. The old girl with a wisp of white hair flying, knobbed shoes as if she had claws corned like a canary's, and black stockings wrinkled over the ankles, naturally made David cock his eye and Jessica wink back, as she handed him a length of paper roses. Snobs they were; long enough stationed that is in that one corner of the world to have taken indelibly the print of some three hundred years of customary behaviour. So they laughed; but respected. If she wore pearls, pearls they were.

"Old Flimsy on the hop," said David. She would be in and out twenty times, and finally bring them lemonade in a great jug and a plate of sandwiches. Jessie held the garland; he hammered. A hen strayed in; a file of cows passed the door; then a sheep dog; then the cowman, Bond, who stopped.

He contemplated the young people hanging roses from one rafter to another. He thought very little of anybody, simples or gentry. Leaning, silent, sardonic, against the door he was like a withered willow, bent over a stream, all its leaves shed, and in his eyes the whimsical flow of the waters.

"Hi--huh!" he cried suddenly. It was cow language presumably, for the parti-coloured cow, who had thrust her head in at the door lowered her horns, lashed her tail and ambled off. Bond followed after.

"That's the problem," said Mrs. Swithin. While Mr. Oliver consulted the Encyclopædia searching under Superstition for the origin of the expression "Touch Wood," she and Isa discussed fish: whether, coming from a distance, it would be fresh.

They were so far from the sea. A hundred miles away, Mrs. Swithin said; no, perhaps a hundred and fifty. "But they do say," she continued, "one can hear the waves on a still night. After a storm, they say, you can hear a wave break. . . . I like that story," she reflected. "Hearing the waves in the middle of the night he saddled a horse and rode to the sea. Who was it, Bart, who rode to the sea?"

16

He was reading.

"You can't expect it brought to your door in a pail of water," said Mrs. Swithin, "as I remember when we were children, living in a house by the sea. Lobsters, fresh from the lobster pots. How they pinched the stick cook gave them! And salmon. You know if they're fresh because they have lice in their scales."

Bartholomew nodded. A fact that was. He remembered, the house by the sea. And the lobster.

They were bringing up nets full of fish from the sea; but Isa was seeing--the garden, variable as the forecast said, in the light breeze. Again, the children passed, and she tapped on the window and blew them a kiss. In the drone of the garden it went unheeded.

"Are we really," she said, turning round, "a hundred miles from the sea?"

"Thirty-five only," her father-in-law said, as if he had whipped a tape measure from his pocket and measured it exactly.

"It seems more," said Isa. "It seems from the terrace as if the land went on for ever and ever."

"Once there was no sea," said Mrs. Swithin. "No sea at all between us and the continent. I was reading that in a book this morning. There were rhododendrons in the Strand; and mammoths in Piccadilly."

"When we were savages," said Isa.

Then she remembered; her dentist had told her that savages could perform very skilful operations on the brain. Savages had false teeth, he said. False teeth were invented, she thought he said, in the time of the Pharaohs.

"At least so my dentist told me," she concluded.

"Which man d'you go to now?" Mrs. Swithin asked her.

"The same old couple; Batty and Bates in Sloane Street."

"And Mr. Batty told you they had false teeth in the time of the Pharaohs?" Mrs. Swithin pondered.

"Batty? Oh not Batty. Bates," Isa corrected her.

Batty, she recalled, only talked about Royalty. Batty, she told Mrs. Swithin, had a patient a Princess.

"So he kept me waiting well over an hour. And you know, when one's a child, how long that seems."

"Marriages with cousins," said Mrs. Swithin, "can't be good for the teeth."

Bart put his finger inside his mouth and projected the upper row outside his lips. They were false. Yet, he said, the Olivers hadn't married cousins. The Olivers couldn't trace their descent for more than two or three hundred years. But the Swithins could. The Swithins were there before the Conquest.

"The Swithins," Mrs. Swithin began. Then she stopped. Bart would crack another joke about Saints, if she gave him the chance. And she had had two jokes cracked at her already; one about an umbrella; another about superstition.

So she stopped and said, "How did we begin this talk?" She counted on her fingers. "The Pharaohs. Dentists. Fish . . . Oh yes, you were saying, Isa, you'd ordered fish; and you were afraid it wouldn't be fresh. And I said 'That's the problem. . . .'"

The fish had been delivered, Mitchell's boy, holding them in a crook of his arm, jumped off his motor bike. There was no feeding the pony with lumps of sugar at the kitchen door, nor time for gossip, since his round had been increased. He had to deliver right over the hill at Bickley; also go round by Waythorn, Roddam, and Pyeminster, whose names, like his own, were in Domesday Book. But the cook--Mrs. Sands she was called, but by old friends Trixie--had never in all her fifty years been over the hill, nor wanted to.

He dabbed them down on the kitchen table, the filleted soles, the semi-transparent boneless fish. And before Mrs. Sands had time to peel the paper off, he was gone, giving a slap to the very fine yellow cat who rose majestically from the basket chair and advanced superbly to the table, winding the fish.

Were they a bit whiffy? Mrs. Sands held them to her nose. The cat rubbed itself this way, that way against the table legs, against her legs. She would save a slice for Sunny--his drawing-room name Sung-Yen had undergone a kitchen change into Sunny. She took them, the cat attendant, to the larder, and laid them on a plate in that semi-ecclesiastical apartment. For the house before the Reformation, like so many houses in that neighbourhood, had a chapel; and the chapel had become a larder, changing, like the cat's name, as religion changed. The Master (his drawing-room name; in the kitchen they called him Bartie) would bring gentlemen sometimes to see the larder--often when cook wasn't dressed. Not to see the hams that hung from hooks, or the butter on a blue slate, or the joint for tomorrow's dinner, but to see the cellar that opened out of the larder and its carved arch. If you tapped--one gentleman had a hammer--there was a hollow sound; a reverberation; undoubtedly, he said, a concealed passage where once somebody had hid. So it might be. But Mrs. Sands wished they wouldn't come into her kitchen telling stories with the girls about. It put ideas into their silly heads. They heard dead men rolling barrels. They saw a white lady walking under the trees. No one would cross the terrace after dark. If a cat sneezed, "There's the ghost!"

Sunny had his little bit off the fillet. Then Mrs. Sands took an egg from the brown basket full of eggs; some with yellow fluff sticking to the shells; then a pinch of flour to coat those semi-transparent slips; and a crust from the great earthenware crock full of crusts. Then, returning to the kitchen, she made those quick movements at the oven, cinder raking, stoking, damping, which sent strange echoes through the house, so that in the library, the sitting-room, the dining-room, and the nursery, whatever they were doing, thinking, saying, they knew, they all knew, it was getting on for breakfast, lunch, or dinner.

"The sandwiches . . ." said Mrs. Swithin, coming into the kitchen. She refrained from adding "Sands" to "sandwiches," for Sand and sandwiches clashed. "Never play," her mother used to say, "on people's names." And Trixie was not a name that suited, as Sands did, the thin, acid woman, red-haired, sharp and clean, who never dashed off masterpieces, it was true; but then never dropped hairpins in the soup.

"What in the name of Thunder?" Bart had said, raising a hairpin in his spoon, in the old days, fifteen years ago, before Sands came, in the time of Jessie Pook.

Mrs. Sands fetched bread; Mrs. Swithin fetched ham. One cut the bread; the other the ham. It was soothing, it was consolidating, this handwork together. The cook's hands cut, cut, cut. Whereas Lucy, holding the loaf, held the knife up. Why's stale bread, she mused, easier to cut than fresh? And so skipped, sidelong, from yeast to alcohol; so to fermentation; so to inebriation; so to Bacchus; and lay under purple lamps in a vineyard in Italy, as she had done, often; while Sands heard the clock tick; saw the cat; noted a fly buzz; and registered, as her lips showed, a grudge she mustn't speak against people making work in the kitchen while they had a high old time hanging paper roses in the barn.

"Will it be fine?" asked Mrs. Swithin, her knife suspended. In the kitchen they humoured old Mother Swithin's fancies.

"Seems like it," said Mrs. Sands, giving her sharp look-out of the kitchen window.

"It wasn't last year," said Mrs. Swithin. "D'you remember what a rush we had--when the rain came--getting in the chairs?" She cut again. Then she asked about Billy, Mrs. Sands's nephew, apprenticed to the butcher.

"He's been doing," Mrs. Sands said, "what boys shouldn't; cheeking the master."

"That'll be all right," said Mrs. Swithin, half meaning the boy, half meaning the sandwich, as it happened a very neat one, trimmed, triangular.

"Mr. Giles may be late," she added, laying it, complacently, on top of the pile.

For Isa's husband, the stockbroker, was coming from London. And the local train, which met the express train, arrived by no means punctually, even if he caught the early train which was by no means certain. In which case it meant--but what it meant to Mrs. Sands, when people missed their trains, and she, whatever she might want to do, must wait, by the oven, keeping meat hot, no one knew.

"There!" said Mrs. Swithin, surveying the sandwiches, some neat, some not, "I'll take 'em to the barn." As for the lemonade, she assumed, without a flicker of doubt, that Jane the kitchenmaid would follow after.

Candish paused in the dining-room to move a yellow rose. Yellow, white, carnation red--he placed them. He loved flowers, and arranging them, and placing the green sword or heart shaped leaf that came, fitly, between them. Queerly, he loved them, considering his gambling and drinking. The yellow rose went there. Now all was ready--silver and white, forks and napkins, and in the middle the splashed bowl of variegated roses. So, with one last look, he left the dining-room.

Two pictures hung opposite the window. In real life they had never met, the long lady and the man holding his horse by the rein. The lady was a picture, bought by Oliver because he liked the picture; the man was an ancestor. He had a name. He held the rein in his hand. He had said to the painter:

"It you want my likeness, dang it sir, take it when the leaves are on the trees." There were leaves on the trees. He had said: "Ain't there room for Colin as well as Buster?" Colin was his famous hound. But there was only room for Buster. It was, he seemed to say, addressing the company not the painter, a damned shame to leave out Colin whom he wished buried at his feet, in the same grave, about 1750; but that skunk the Reverend Whatshisname wouldn't allow it.

He was a talk producer, that ancestor. But the lady was a picture. In her yellow robe, leaning, with a pillar to support her, a silver arrow in her hand, and a feather in her hair, she led the eye up, down, from the curve to the straight, through glades of greenery and shades of silver, dun and rose into silence. The room was empty.

Empty, empty, empty; silent, silent, silent. The room was a shell, singing of what was before time was; a vase stood in the heart of the house, alabaster, smooth, cold, holding the still, distilled essence of emptiness, silence.

Across the hall a door opened. One voice, another voice, a third voice came wimpling and warbling: gruff--Bart's voice; quavering--Lucy's voice; middle-toned-- Isa's voice. Their voices impetuously, impatiently, protestingly came across the hall saying: "The train's late"; saying: "Keep it hot"; saying: "We won't, no Candish, we won't wait."

Coming out from the library the voices stopped in the hall. They encountered an obstacle evidently; a rock. Utterly impossible was it, even in the heart of the country, to be alone? That was the shock. After that, the rock was raced round, embraced. If it was painful, it was essential. There must be society. Coming out of the library it was painful, but pleasant, to run slap into Mrs. Manresa and an unknown young man with tow-coloured hair and a twisted face. No escape was possible; meeting was inevitable. Uninvited, unexpected, droppers-in, lured off the high road by the very same instinct that caused the sheep and the cows to desire propinquity, they had come. But they had brought a lunch basket. Here it was.

"We couldn't resist when we saw the name on the signpost," Mrs. Manresa began in her rich fluty voice. "And this is a friend--William Dodge. We were going to sit all alone in a field. And I said: 'Why not ask our dear friends,' seeing the signpost, 'to shelter us?' A seat at the table--that's all we want. We have our grub. We have our glasses. We ask nothing but--" society apparently, to be with her kind.

And she waved her hand upon which there was a glove, and under the glove it seemed rings, at old Mr. Oliver.

He bowed deep over her hand; a century ago, he would have kissed it. In all this sound of welcome, protestation, apology and again welcome, there was an element of silence, supplied by Isabella, observing the unknown young man. He was of course a gentleman; witness socks and trousers; brainy--tie spotted, waistcoat undone; urban, professional, that is putty coloured, unwholesome; very nervous, exhibiting a twitch at this sudden introduction, and fundamentally infernally conceited, for he deprecated Mrs. Manresa's effusion, yet was her guest.

Isa felt antagonised, yet curious. But when Mrs. Manresa added, to make all shipshape: "He's an artist," and when William Dodge corrected her: "I'm a clerk in an office"--she thought he said Education or Somerset House--she had her finger on the knot which had tied itself so tightly, almost to the extent of squinting, certainly of twitching, in his face.

Then they went in to lunch, and Mrs. Manresa bubbled up, enjoying her own capacity to surmount, without turning a hair, this minor social crisis--this laying of two more places. For had she not complete faith in flesh and blood? and aren't we all flesh and blood? and how silly to make bones of trifles when we're all flesh and blood under the skin--men and women too! But she preferred men--obviously.

"Or what are your rings for, and your nails, and that really adorable little straw hat?" said Isabella addressing Mrs. Manresa silently and thereby making silence add its unmistakable contribution to talk. Her hat, her rings, her finger nails red as roses, smooth as shells, were there for all to see. But not her life history. That was only scraps and fragments to all of them, excluding perhaps William Dodge, whom she called "Bill" publicly--a sign perhaps that he knew more than they did. Some of the things that he knew--that she strolled the garden at midnight in silk pyjamas, had the loud speaker playing jazz, and a cocktail bar, of course they knew also. But nothing private; no strict biographical facts.

She had been born, but it was only gossip said so, in Tasmania: her grandfather had been exported for some hanky-panky mid-Victorian scandal; malversation of trusts was it? But the story got no further the only time Isabella heard it than "exported," for the husband of the communicative lady--Mrs. Blencowe of the Grange--took exception, pedantically, to "exported," said "expatriated" was more like it, but not the right word, which he had on the tip of his tongue, but couldn't get at. And so the story dwindled away. Sometimes she referred to an uncle, a Bishop. But he was thought to have been a Colonial Bishop only. They forgot and forgave very easily in the Colonies. Also it was said her diamonds and rubies had been dug out of the earth with his own hands by a "husband" who was not Ralph Manresa. Ralph, a Jew, got up to look the very spit and image of the landed gentry, supplied from directing City companies--that was certain--tons of money; and they had no child. But surely with George the Sixth on the throne it was old fashioned, dowdy, savoured of moth-eaten furs, bugles, cameos and black-edged notepaper, to go ferreting into people's pasts?

"All I need," said Mrs. Manresa ogling Candish, as if he were a real man, not a stuffed man, "is a corkscrew." She had a bottle of champagne, but no corkscrew.

"Look, Bill," she continued, cocking her thumb--she was opening the bottle--"at the pictures. Didn't I tell you you'd have a treat?"

Vulgar she was in her gestures, in her whole person, over-sexed, over-dressed for a picnic. But what a desirable, at least valuable, quality it was--for everybody felt, directly she spoke, "She's said it, she's done it, not I," and could take advantage of the breach of decorum, of the fresh air that blew in, to follow like leaping dolphins in the wake of an ice-breaking vessel. Did she not restore to old Bartholomew his spice islands, his youth?

"I told him," she went on, ogling Bart now, "that he wouldn't look at our things" (of which they had heaps and mountains) "after yours. And I promised him you'd show him the--the--" here the champagne fizzed up and she insisted upon filling Bart's glass first. "What is it all you learned gentlemen rave about? An arch? Norman? Saxon? Who's the last from school? Mrs. Giles?"

She ogled Isabella now, conferring youth upon her; but always when she spoke to women, she veiled her eyes, for they, being conspirators, saw through it.

So with blow after blow, with champagne and ogling, she staked out her claim to be a wild child of nature, blowing into this--she did give one secret smile--

sheltered harbour; which did make her smile, after London; yet it did, too, challenge London. For on she went to offer them a sample of her life; a few gobbets of gossip; mere trash; but she gave it for what it was worth; how last Tuesday she had been sitting next so and so; and she added, very casually a Christian name; then a nickname; and he'd said--for, as a mere nobody they didn't mind what they said to her--and "in strict confidence, I needn't tell you," she told them. And they all pricked their ears. And then, with a gesture of her hands as if tossing overboard that odious crackling-under-the-pot London life--so--she exclaimed "There! . . . And what's the first thing I do when I come down here?" They had only come last night, driving through June lanes, alone with Bill it was understood, leaving London, suddenly become dissolute and dirty, to sit down to dinner. "What do I do? Can I say it aloud? Is it permitted, Mrs. Swithin? Yes, everything can be said in this house. I take off my stays" (here she pressed her hands to her sides--she was stout) "and roll in the grass. Roll--you'll believe that . . ." She laughed wholeheartedly. She had given up dealing with her figure and thus gained freedom.

"That's genuine," Isa thought. Quite genuine. And her love of the country too. Often when Ralph Manresa had to stay in town she came down alone; wore an old garden hat; taught the village women *not* how to pickle and preserve; but how to weave frivolous baskets out of coloured straw. Pleasure's what they want she said. You often heard her, if you called, yodelling among the hollyhocks "Hoity te doity te ray do . . ."

A thorough good sort she was. She made old Bart feel young. Out of the corner of his eye, as he raised his glass, he saw a flash of white in the garden. Someone passing.

The scullery maid, before the plates came out, was cooling her cheeks by the lily pond.

There had always been lilies there, self-sown from wind-dropped seed, floating red and white on the green plates of their leaves. Water, for hundreds of years, had silted down into the hollow, and lay there four or five feet deep over a black cushion of mud. Under the thick plate of green water, glazed in their self-centred world, fish swam--gold, splashed with white, streaked with black or silver. Silently they manoeuvred in their water world, poised in the blue patch made by the sky, or shot silently to the edge where the grass, trembling, made a fringe of nodding shadow. On the water-pavement spiders printed their delicate feet. A grain fell and spiralled down; a petal fell, filled and sank. At that the fleet of boat-shaped bodies paused; poised; equipped; mailed; then with a waver of undulation off they flashed.

It was in that deep centre, in that black heart, that the lady had drowned herself. Ten years since the pool had been dredged and a thigh bone recovered. Alas, it was a sheep's, not a lady's. And sheep have no ghosts, for sheep have no souls. But, the servants insisted, they must have a ghost; the ghost must be a lady's; who had drowned herself for love. So none of them would walk by the lily pool at night, only now when the sun shone and the gentry still sat at table.

The flower petal sank; the maid returned to the kitchen; Bartholomew sipped his wine. Happy he felt as a boy; yet reckless as an old man; an unusual, an agreeable sensation. Fumbling in his mind for something to say to the adorable lady, he chose the first thing that came handy; the story of the sheep's thigh. "Servants," he said, "must have their ghost." Kitchenmaids must have their drowned lady.

"But so must I!" cried the wild child of nature, Mrs. Manresa. She became, of a sudden, solemn as an owl. She *knew*, she said, pinching a bit of bread to make this emphatic, that Ralph, when he was at the war, couldn't have been killed without her seeing him--"wherever I was, whatever I was doing," she added, waving her hands so that the diamonds flashed in the sun.

"I don't feel that," said Mrs. Swithin, shaking her head.

"No," Mrs. Manresa laughed. "You wouldn't. None of you would. You see I'm on a level with . . ." she waited till Candish had retired, "the servants. I'm nothing like so grown up as you are."

She preened, approving her adolescence. Rightly or wrongly? A spring of feeling bubbled up through her mud. They had laid theirs with blocks of marble. Sheep's bones were sheep's bones to them, not the relics of the drowned Lady Ermyntrude.

"And which camp," said Bartholomew turning to the unknown guest, "d'you belong to? The grown, or the ungrown?"

Isabella opened her mouth, hoping that Dodge would open his, and so enable her to place him. But he sat staring. "I beg your pardon, sir?" he said. They all looked at him. "I was looking at the pictures."

The picture looked at nobody. The picture drew them down the paths of silence.

Lucy broke it.

"Mrs. Manresa, I'm going to ask you a favour--If it comes to a pinch this afternoon, will you sing?"

This afternoon? Mrs. Manresa was aghast. Was it the pageant? She had never dreamt it was this afternoon. They would never have thrust themselves in--had they known it was this afternoon. And, of course, once more the chime pealed. Isa heard the first chime; and the second; and the third--If it was wet, it would be in the Barn; if it was fine on the terrace. And which would it be, wet or fine? And they all looked out of the window. Then the door opened. Candish said Mr. Giles had come. Mr. Giles would be down in a moment.

Giles had come. He had seen the great silver-plated car at the door with the initials R. M. twisted so as to look at a distance like a coronet. Visitors, he had concluded, as he drew up behind; and had gone to his room to change. The ghost of convention rose to the surface, as a blush or a tear rises to the surface at the pressure of emotion; so the car touched his training. He must change. And he came into the dining-room looking like a cricketer, in flannels, wearing a blue coat with brass buttons; though he was enraged. Had he not read, in the morning paper, in the train, that sixteen men had been shot, others prisoned, just over there, across the gulf, in the flat land which divided them from the continent? Yet he changed. It was Aunt Lucy, waving her hand at him as he came in, who made him change. He hung his grievances on her, as one hangs a coat on a hook, instinctively. Aunt Lucy, foolish, free; always, since he had chosen, after leaving college, to take a job in the city, expressing her amazement, her amusement, at men who spent their lives, buying and selling--ploughs? glass beads was it? or stocks and shares?--to savages who wished most oddly--for were they not beautiful naked?--to dress and live like the English? A frivolous, a malignant statement hers was of a problem which, for he had no special gift, no capital, and had been furiously in love with his wife--he nodded to her across the table--had afflicted him for ten years. Given his choice, he would have chosen to farm. But he was not given his choice. So one thing led to another; and the conglomeration of things pressed you flat; held you fast, like a fish in water. So he came for the week-end, and changed.

"How d'you do?" he said all round; nodded to the unknown guest; took against him; and ate his fillet of sole.

He was the very type of all that Mrs. Manresa adored. His hair curled; far from running away, as many chins did, his was firm; the nose straight, if short; the eyes, of course, with that hair, blue; and finally to make the type complete, there was something fierce, untamed, in the expression which incited her, even at forty-five, to furbish up her ancient batteries.

"He is my husband," Isabella thought, as they nodded across the bunch of many-coloured flowers. "The father of my children." It worked, that old cliché; she felt pride; and affection; then pride again in herself, whom he had chosen. It was a shock to find, after the morning's look in the glass, and the arrow of desire shot through her last night by the gentleman farmer, how much she felt when he came in, not a dapper city gent, but a cricketer, of love; and of hate.

They had met first in Scotland, fishing--she from one rock, he from another. Her line had got tangled; she had given over, and had watched him with the stream rushing between his legs, casting, casting--until, like a thick ingot of silver bent in the middle, the salmon had leapt, had been caught, and she had loved him.

Bartholomew too loved him; and noted his anger--about what? But he remembered his guest. The family was not a family in the presence of strangers. He must, rather laboriously, tell them the story of the pictures at which the unknown guest had been looking when Giles came in.

"That," he indicated the man with a horse, "was my ancestor. He had a dog. The dog was famous. The dog has his place in history. He left it on record that he wished his dog to be buried with him."

They looked at the picture.

"I always feel," Lucy broke the silence, "he's saying: 'Paint my dog.'"

"But what about the horse?" said Mrs. Manresa.

"The horse," said Bartholomew, putting on his glasses. He looked at the horse. The hindquarters were not satisfactory.

But William Dodge was still looking at the lady.

"Ah," said Bartholomew who had bought that picture because he liked that picture, "you're an artist."

Dodge denied it, for the second time in half an hour, or so Isa noted.

What for did a good sort like the woman Manresa bring these half-breeds in her trail? Giles asked himself. And his silence made its contribution to talk--Dodge that is, shook his head. "I like that picture." That was all he could bring himself to say.

"And you're right," said Bartholomew. "A man--I forget his name--a man connected with some Institute, a man who goes about giving advice, gratis, to descendants like ourselves, degenerate descendants, said . . . said . . ." He paused. They all looked at the lady. But she looked over their heads, looking at nothing. She led them down green glades into the heart of silence.

"Said it was by Sir Joshua?" Mrs. Manresa broke the silence abruptly.

"No, no," William Dodge said hastily, but under his breath.

"Why's he afraid?" Isabella asked herself. A poor specimen he was; afraid to stick up for his own beliefs--just as she was afraid, of her husband. Didn't she write her poetry in a book bound like an account book lest Giles might suspect? She looked at Giles.

He had finished his fish; he had eaten quickly, not to keep them waiting. Now there was cherry tart. Mrs. Manresa was counting the stones.

"Tinker, tailor, soldier, sailor, apothecary, ploughboy . . . that's me!" she cried, delighted to have it confirmed by the cherry stones that she was a wild child of nature.

"You believe," said the old gentleman, courteously chaffing her, "in that too?"

"Of course, of course I do!" she cried. Now she was on the rails again. Now she was a thorough good sort again. And they too were delighted; now they could follow in her wake and leave the silver and dun shades that led to the heart of silence.

"I had a father," said Dodge beneath his breath to Isa who sat next him, "who loved pictures."

"Oh, I too!" she exclaimed. Flurriedly, disconnectedly, she explained. She used to stay when she was a child, when she had the whooping cough, with an uncle, a clergyman; who wore a skull cap; and never did anything; didn't even preach; but made up poems, walking in his garden, saying them aloud.

"People thought him mad," she said. "I didn't. . . ."

She stopped.

"Tinker, tailor, soldier, sailor, apothecary, ploughboy. . . . It appears," said old Bartholomew, laying down his spoon, "that I am a thief. Shall we take our coffee in the garden?" He rose.

Isa dragged her chair across the gravel, muttering: "To what dark antre of the unvisited earth, or wind-brushed forest, shall we go now? Or spin from star to star and dance in the maze of the moon? Or. . . ."

She held her deck chair at the wrong angle. The frame with the notches was upside down.

"Songs my uncle taught me?" said William Dodge, hearing her mutter. He unfolded the chair and fixed the bar into the right notch.

She flushed, as if she had spoken in an empty room and someone had stepped out from behind a curtain.

"Don't you, if you're doing something with your hands, talk nonsense?" she stumbled. But what did he do with his hands, the white, the fine, the shapely?

Giles went back to the house and brought more chairs and placed them in a semi-circle, so that the view might be shared, and the shelter of the old wall. For by some lucky chance a wall had been built continuing the house, it might be with the intention of adding another wing, on the raised ground in the sun. But funds were lacking; the plan was abandoned, and the wall remained, nothing but a wall. Later, another generation had planted fruit trees, which in time had spread their arms widely across the red orange weathered brick. Mrs. Sands called it a good year if she could make six pots of apricot jam from them--the fruit was never sweet enough for dessert. Perhaps three apricots were worth enclosing in muslin bags. But they were so beautiful, naked, with one flushed cheek, one green, that Mrs. Swithin left them naked, and the wasps burrowed holes.

The ground sloped up, so that to quote Figgis's Guide Book (1833), "it commanded a fine view of the surrounding country. . . . The spire of Bolney Minster, Rough Norton woods, and on an eminence rather to the left, Hogben's Folly, so called because. . . ."

The Guide Book still told the truth. 1833 was true in 1939. No house had been built; no town had sprung up. Hogben's Folly was still eminent; the very flat, field-parcelled land had changed only in this--the tractor had to some extent superseded the plough. The horse had gone; but the cow remained. If Figgis were here now, Figgis would have said the same. So they always said when in summer they sat there to drink coffee, if they had guests. When they were alone, they said nothing. They looked at the view; they looked at what they knew, to see if what they knew might perhaps be different today. Most days it was the same.

"That's what makes a view so sad," said Mrs. Swithin, lowering herself into the deck-chair which Giles had brought her. "And so beautiful. It'll be there," she nodded at the strip of gauze laid upon the distant fields, "when we're not."

Giles nicked his chair into position with a jerk. Thus only could he show his irritation, his rage with old fogies who sat and looked at views over coffee and cream when the whole of Europe--over there--was bristling like. . . . He had no command of metaphor. Only the ineffective word "hedgehog" illustrated his vision of Europe, bristling with guns, poised with planes. At any moment guns would rake that land into furrows; planes splinter Bolney Minster into smithereens and blast the Folly. He, too, loved the view. And blamed Aunt Lucy, looking at views, instead of--doing what? What she had done was to marry a squire now dead; she had borne two children, one in Canada, the other, married, in Birmingham. His father, whom he loved, he exempted from censure; as for himself, one thing followed another; and so he sat, with old fogies, looking at views.

"Beautiful," said Mrs. Manresa, "beautiful . . ." she mumbled. She was lighting a cigarette. The breeze blew out her match. Giles hollowed his hand and lit another. She too was exempted--why, he could not say.

"Since you're interested in pictures," said Bartholomew, turning to the silent guest, "why, tell me, are we, as a race, so incurious, irresponsive and insensitive"--the champagne had given him a flow of unusual three-decker words--"to that noble art, whereas, Mrs. Manresa, if she'll allow me my old man's liberty, has her Shakespeare by heart?"

"Shakespeare by heart!" Mrs. Manresa protested. She struck an attitude. "To be, or not to be, that is the question. Whether 'tis nobler . . . Go on!" she nudged Giles, who sat next her.

"Fade far away and quite forget what thou amongst the leaves hast never known . . ." Isa supplied the first words that came into her head by way of helping her husband out of his difficulty.

"The weariness, the torture, and the fret . . ." William Dodge added, burying the end of his cigarette in a grave between two stones.

"There!" Bartholomew exclaimed, cocking his forefinger aloft. "That proves it! What springs touched, what secret drawer displays its treasures, if I say"--he raised more fingers--"Reynolds! Constable! Crome!"

"Why called 'Old'?" Mrs. Manresa thrust in.

"We haven't the words--we haven't the words," Mrs. Swithin protested. "Behind the eyes; not on the lips; that's all."

"Thoughts without words," her brother mused. "Can that be?"

"Quite beyond me!" cried Mrs. Manresa, shaking her head. "Much too clever! May I help myself? I know it's wrong. But I've reached the age--and the figure--when I do what I like."

She took the little silver cream jug and let the smooth fluid curl luxuriously into her coffee, to which she added a shovel full of brown sugar candy. Sensuously, rhythmically, she stirred the mixture round and round.

"Take what you like! Help yourself!" Bartholomew exclaimed. He felt the champagne withdrawing and hastened, before the last trace of geniality was withdrawn, to make the most of it, as if he cast one last look into a lit-up chamber before going to bed.

The wild child, afloat once more on the tide of the old man's benignity, looked over her coffee cup at Giles, with whom she felt in conspiracy. A thread united them--visible, invisible, like those threads, now seen, now not, that unite trembling grass blades in autumn before the sun rises. She had met him once only, at a cricket match. And then had been spun between them an early morning thread before the twigs and leaves of real friendship emerge. She looked before she drank. Looking was part of drinking. Why waste sensation, she seemed to ask, why waste a single drop that can be pressed out of this ripe, this melting, this adorable world? Then she drank. And the air round her became threaded with sensation. Bartholomew felt it; Giles felt it. Had he been a horse, the thin brown skin would have twitched, as if a fly had settled. Isabella twitched too. Jealousy, anger pierced her skin.

"And now," said Mrs. Manresa, putting down her cup, "about this entertainment--this pageant, into which we've gone and butted"--she made it, too, seem ripe like the apricot into which the wasps were burrowing--"Tell me, what's it to be?" She turned. "Don't I hear?" She listened. She heard laughter, down among the bushes, where the terrace dipped to the bushes.

Beyond the lily pool the ground sank again, and in that dip of the ground, bushes and brambles had mobbed themselves together. It was always shady; sun-flecked in summer, dark and damp in winter. In the summer there were always butterflies; fritillaries darting through; Red Admirals feasting and floating; cabbage whites, unambitiously fluttering round a bush, like muslin milkmaids, content to spend a life there. Butterfly catching, for generation after generation, began there; for Bartholomew and Lucy; for Giles; for George it had began only the day before yesterday, when, in his little green net, he had caught a cabbage white.

It was the very place for a dressing-room, just as, obviously, the terrace was the very place for a play.

"The very place!" Miss La Trobe had exclaimed the first time she came to call and was shown the grounds. It was a winter's day. The trees were leafless then.

"That's the place for a pageant, Mr. Oliver!" she had exclaimed. "Winding in and out between the trees. . . ." She waved her hand at the trees standing bare in the clear light of January.

"There the stage; here the audience; and down there among the bushes a perfect dressing-room for the actors."

She was always all agog to get things up. But where did she spring from? With that name she wasn't presumably pure English. From the Channel Islands perhaps? Only her eyes and something about her always made Mrs. Bingham suspect that she had Russian blood in her. "Those deep-set eyes; that very square jaw" reminded her--not that she had been to Russia--of the Tartars. Rumour said that she had kept a tea shop at Winchester; that had failed. She had been an actress. That had failed. She had bought a four-roomed cottage and shared it with an actress. They had quarrelled. Very little was actually known about her. Outwardly she was swarthy, sturdy and thick set; strode about the fields in a smock frock; sometimes with a cigarette in her mouth; often with a whip in her hand; and used rather strong language--perhaps, then, she wasn't altogether a lady? At any rate, she had a passion for getting things up.

The laughter died away.

"Are they going to act?" Mrs. Manresa asked.

"Act; dance; sing; a little bit of everything," said Giles.

"Miss La Trobe is a lady of wonderful energy," said Mrs. Swithin.

"She makes everyone do something," said Isabella.

"Our part," said Bartholomew, "is to be the audience. And a very important part too."

"Also, we provide the tea," said Mrs. Swithin.

"Shan't we go and help?" said Mrs. Manresa. "Cut up bread and butter?"

"No, no," said Mr. Oliver. "We are the audience."

"One year we had *Gammer Gurton's Needle,*" said Mrs. Swithin. "One year we wrote the play ourselves. The son of our blacksmith--Tony? Tommy?--had the loveliest voice. And Elsie at the Crossways--how she mimicked! Took us all off. Bart; Giles; Old Flimsy--that's me. People are gifted--very. The question is--how to bring it out? That's where she's so clever--Miss La Trobe. Of course, there's the whole of English literature to choose from. But how can one choose? Often on a wet day I begin counting up; what I've read; what I haven't read."

"And leaving books on the floor," said her brother. "Like the pig in the story; or was it a donkey?"

She laughed, tapping him lightly on the knee.

"The donkey who couldn't choose between hay and turnips and so starved," Isabella explained, interposing--anything--between her aunt and her husband, who hated this kind of talk this afternoon. Books open; no conclusion come to; and he sitting in the audience.

"We remain seated"--"We are the audience." Words this afternoon ceased to lie flat in the sentence. They rose, became menacing and shook their fists at you. This afternoon he wasn't Giles Oliver come to see the villagers act their annual pageant; manacled to a rock he was, and forced passively to behold indescribable horror. His face showed it; and Isa, not knowing what to say, abruptly, half purposely, knocked over a coffee cup.

William Dodge caught it as it fell. He held it for a moment. He turned it. From the faint blue mark, as of crossed daggers, in the glaze at the bottom he knew that it was English, made perhaps at Nottingham; date about 1760. His expression, considering the daggers, coming to this conclusion, gave Giles another peg on which to hang his rage as one hangs a coat on a peg, conveniently. A toady; a lickspittle; not a downright plain man of his senses; but a teaser and twitcher; a fingerer of sensations; picking and choosing; dillying and dallying; not a man to have straightforward love for a woman--his head was close to Isa's head--but simply a ----
At this word, which he could not speak in public, he pursed his lips; and the signet-ring on his little finger looked redder, for the flesh next it whitened as he gripped the arm of his chair.

"Oh what fun!" cried Mrs. Manresa in her fluty voice. "A little bit of everything. A song; a dance; then a play acted by the villagers themselves. Only," here she turned with her head on one side to Isabella, "I'm sure *she's* written it. Haven't you, Mrs. Giles?"

Isa flushed and denied it.

"For myself," Mrs. Manresa continued, "speaking plainly, I can't put two words together. I don't know how it is--such a chatterbox as I am with my tongue, once I hold a pen--" She made a face, screwed her fingers as if she held a pen in them. But the pen she held thus on the little table absolutely refused to move.

"And my handwriting--so huge--so clumsy--" She made another face and dropped the invisible pen.

Very delicately William Dodge set the cup in its saucer. "Now *he,*" said Mrs. Manresa, as if referring to the delicacy with which he did this, and imputing to him the same skill in writing, "writes beautifully. Every letter perfectly formed."

Again they all looked at him. Instantly he put his hands in his pockets.

Isabella guessed the word that Giles had not spoken. Well, was it wrong if he was that word? Why judge each other? Do we know each other? Not here, not now. But somewhere, this cloud, this crust, this doubt, this dust--She waited for a rhyme, it failed her; but somewhere surely one sun would shine and all, without a doubt, would be clear.

She started. Again, sounds of laughter reached her.

"I think I hear them," she said. "They're getting ready. They're dressing up in the bushes."

Miss La Trobe was pacing to and fro between the leaning birch trees. One hand was deep stuck in her jacket pocket; the other held a foolscap sheet. She was reading what was written there. She had the look of a commander pacing his deck. The leaning graceful trees with black bracelets circling the silver bark were distant about a ship's length.

Wet would it be, or fine? Out came the sun; and, shading her eyes in the attitude proper to an Admiral on his quarter-deck, she decided to risk the engagement out of doors. Doubts were over. All stage properties, she commanded, must be moved from the Barn to the bushes. It was done. And the actors, while she paced, taking all responsibility and plumping for fine, not wet, dressed among the brambles. Hence the laughter.

The clothes were strewn on the grass. Cardboard crowns, swords made of silver paper, turbans that were sixpenny dish cloths, lay on the grass or were flung on the bushes. There were pools of red and purple in the shade; flashes of silver in the sun. The dresses attracted the butterflies. Red and silver, blue and yellow gave off warmth and sweetness. Red Admirals gluttonously absorbed richness from dish cloths, cabbage whites drank icy coolness from silver paper. Flitting, tasting, returning, they sampled the colours.

Miss La Trobe stopped her pacing and surveyed the scene. "It has the makings . . ." she murmured. For another play always lay behind the play she had just written. Shading her eyes, she looked. The butterflies circling; the light changing; the children leaping; the mothers laughing--

"No, I don't get it," she muttered and resumed her pacing.

"Bossy" they called her privately, just as they called Mrs. Swithin "Flimsy." Her abrupt manner and stocky figure; her thick ankles and sturdy shoes; her rapid decisions barked out in guttural accents--all this "got their goat." No one liked to be ordered about singly. But in little troops they appealed to her. Someone must lead. Then too they could put the blame on her. Suppose it poured?

"Miss La Trobe!" they hailed her now. "What's the idea about this?"

She stopped. David and Iris each had a hand on the gramophone. It must be hidden; yet must be close enough to the audience to be heard. Well, hadn't she given orders? Where were the hurdles covered in leaves? Fetch them. Mr. Streatfield had said he would see to it. Where was Mr. Streatfield? No clergyman was visible. Perhaps he's in the Barn? "Tommy, cut along and fetch him." "Tommy's wanted in the first scene." "Beryl then . . ." The mothers disputed. One child had been chosen; another not. Fair hair was unjustly preferred to dark. Mrs. Ebury had forbidden Fanny to act because of the nettle-rash. There was another name in the village for nettle-rash.

Mrs. Ball's cottage was not what you might call clean. In the last war Mrs. Ball lived with another man while her husband was in the trenches. All this Miss La Trobe knew, but refused to be mixed up in it. She splashed into the fine mesh like a great stone into the lily pool. The criss-cross was shattered. Only the roots beneath water were of use to her. Vanity, for example, made them all malleable. The boys wanted the big parts; the girls wanted the fine clothes. Expenses had to be kept down. Ten pounds was the limit. Thus conventions were outraged. Swathed in conventions, they couldn't see, as she could, that a dish cloth wound round a head in the open looked much richer than real silk. So they squabbled; but she kept out of it. Waiting for Mr. Streatfield, she paced between the birch trees.

The other trees were magnificently straight. They were not too regular; but regular enough to suggest columns in a church; in a church without a roof; in an open-air cathedral, a place where swallows darting seemed, by the regularity of the trees, to make a pattern, dancing, like the Russians, only not to music, but to the unheard rhythm of their own wild hearts.

The laughter died away.

"We must possess our souls in patience," said Mrs. Manresa again. "Or could we help?" she suggested, glancing over her shoulder, "with those chairs?"

Candish, a gardener, and a maid were all bringing chairs--for the audience. There was nothing for the audience to do. Mrs. Manresa suppressed a yawn. They were silent. They stared at the view, as if something might happen in one of those fields to relieve them of the intolerable burden of sitting silent, doing nothing, in company. Their minds and bodies were too close, yet not close enough. We aren't free, each one of them felt separately to feel or think separately, nor yet to fall asleep. We're too close; but not close enough. So they fidgeted.

The heat had increased. The clouds had vanished. All was sun now. The view laid bare by the sun was flattened, silenced, stilled. The cows were motionless; the brick wall, no longer sheltering, beat back grains of heat. Old Mr. Oliver sighed profoundly. His head jerked; his hand fell. It fell within an inch of the dog's head on the grass by his side. Then up he jerked it again on to his knee.

Giles glared. With his hands bound tight round his knees he stared at the flat fields. Staring, glaring, he sat silent.

Isabella felt prisoned. Through the bars of the prison, through the sleep haze that deflected them, blunt arrows bruised her; of love, then of hate. Through other people's bodies she felt neither love nor hate distinctly. Most consciously she felt-- she had drunk sweet wine at luncheon--a desire for water. "A beaker of cold water, a beaker of cold water," she repeated, and saw water surrounded by walls of shining glass.

Mrs. Manresa longed to relax and curl in a corner with a cushion, a picture paper, and a bag of sweets.

Mrs. Swithin and William surveyed the view aloofly, and with detachment.

How tempting, how very tempting, to let the view triumph; to reflect its ripple; to let their own minds ripple; to let outlines elongate and pitch over--so--with a sudden jerk.

Mrs. Manresa yielded, pitched, plunged, then pulled herself up.

"What a view!" she exclaimed, pretending to dust the ashes of her cigarette, but in truth concealing her yawn. Then she sighed, pretending to express not her own drowsiness, but something connected with what she felt about views.

Nobody answered her. The flat fields glared green yellow, blue yellow, red yellow, then blue again. The repetition was senseless, hideous, stupefying.

"Then," said Mrs. Swithin, in a low voice, as if the exact moment for speech had come, as if she had promised, and it was time to fulfil her promise, "come, come and I'll show you the house."

She addressed no one in particular. But William Dodge knew she meant him. He rose with a jerk, like a toy suddenly pulled straight by a string.

"What energy!" Mrs. Manresa half sighed, half yawned. "Have I the courage to go too?" Isabella asked herself. They were going; above all things, she desired cold water, a beaker of cold water; but desire petered out, suppressed by the leaden duty she owed to others. She watched them go--Mrs. Swithin tottering yet tripping; and Dodge unfurled and straightened, as he strode beside her along the blazing tiles under the hot wall, till they reached the shade of the house.

A match-box fell--Bartholomew's. His fingers had loosed it; he had dropped it. He gave up the game; he couldn't be bothered. With his head on one side, his hand dangling above the dog's head he slept; he snored.

Mrs. Swithin paused for a moment in the hall among the gilt-clawed tables.

"This," she said, "is the staircase. And now--up we go."

She went up, two stairs ahead of her guest. Lengths of yellow satin unfurled themselves on a cracked canvas as they mounted.

"Not an ancestress," said Mrs. Swithin, as they came level with the head in the picture. "But we claim her because we've known her--O, ever so many years. Who was she?" she gazed. "Who painted her?" She shook her head. She looked lit up, as if for a banquet, with the sun pouring over her.

"But I like her best in the moonlight," Mrs. Swithin reflected, and mounted more stairs.

She panted slightly, going upstairs. Then she ran her hand over the sunk books in the wall on the landing, as if they were pan pipes.

"Here are the poets from whom we descend by way of the mind, Mr. . . ." she murmured. She had forgotten his name. Yet she had singled him out.

"My brother says, they built the house north for shelter, not south for sun. So they're damp in the winter." She paused. "And now what comes next?"

She stopped. There was a door.

"The morning room." She opened the door. "Where my mother received her guests."

Two chairs faced each other on either side of a fine fluted mantelpiece. He looked over her shoulder.

She shut the door.

"Now up, now up again." Again they mounted. "Up and up they went," she panted, seeing, it seemed, an invisible procession, "up and up to bed."

"A bishop; a traveller;--I've forgotten even their names. I ignore. I forget."

She stopped at a window in the passage and held back the curtain. Beneath was the garden, bathed in sun. The grass was sleek and shining. Three white pigeons were flirting and tiptoeing as ornate as ladies in ball dresses. Their elegant bodies swayed as they minced with tiny steps on their little pink feet upon the grass. Suddenly, up they rose in a flutter, circled, and flew away.

"Now," she said, "for the bedrooms." She tapped twice very distinctly on a door. With her head on one side, she listened.

"One never knows," she murmured, "if there's somebody there." Then she flung open the door.

He half expected to see somebody there, naked, or half dressed, or knelt in prayer. But the room was empty. The room was tidy as a pin, not slept in for months, a spare room. Candles stood on the dressing-table. The counterpane was straight. Mrs. Swithin stopped by the bed.

"Here," she said, "yes, here," she tapped the counterpane, "I was born. In this bed."

Her voice died away. She sank down on the edge of the bed. She was tired, no doubt, by the stairs, by the heat.

"But we have other lives, I think, I hope," she murmured. "We live in others, Mr. . . . We live in things."

She spoke simply. She spoke with an effort. She spoke as if she must overcome her tiredness out of charity towards a stranger, a guest. She had forgotten his name. Twice she had said "Mr." and stopped.

The furniture was mid-Victorian, bought at Maples, perhaps, in the forties. The carpet was covered with small purple dots. And a white circle marked the place where the slop pail had stood by the washstand.

Could he say "I'm William"? He wished to. Old and frail she had climbed the stairs. She had spoken her thoughts, ignoring, not caring if he thought her, as he had, inconsequent, sentimental, foolish. She had lent him a hand to help him up a steep place. She had guessed his trouble. Sitting on the bed he heard her sing, swinging her little legs, "Come and see my sea weeds, come and see my sea shells, come and see my dicky bird hop upon its perch"--an old child's nursery rhyme to help a child. Standing by the cupboard in the corner he saw her reflected in the glass. Cut off from their bodies, their eyes smiled, their bodiless eyes, at their eyes in the glass.

Then she slipped off the bed.

"Now," she said, "what comes next?" and pattered down the corridor. A door stood open. Everyone was out in the garden. The room was like a ship deserted by its crew. The children had been playing--there was a spotted horse in the middle of the carpet. The nurse had been sewing--there was a piece of linen on the table. The baby had been in the cot. The cot was empty.

"The nursery," said Mrs. Swithin.

Words raised themselves and became symbolical. "The cradle of our race," she seemed to say.

Dodge crossed to the fireplace and looked at the Newfoundland Dog in the Christmas Annual that was pinned to the wall. The room smelt warm and sweet; of clothes drying; of milk; of biscuits and warm water. "Good Friends" the picture was called. A rushing sound came in through the open door. He turned. The old woman had wandered out into the passage and leant against the window.

He left the door open for the crew to come back to and joined her.

Down in the courtyard beneath the window cars were assembling. Their narrow black roofs were laid together like the blocks of a floor. Chauffeurs were jumping down; here old ladies gingerly advanced black legs with silver-buckled shoes; old men striped trousers. Young men in shorts leapt out on one side; girls with skin-coloured legs on the other. There was a purring and a churning of the yellow gravel. The audience was assembling. But they, looking down from the window, were truants, detached. Together they leant half out of the window.

And then a breeze blew and all the muslin blinds fluttered out, as if some majestic goddess, rising from her throne among her peers, had tossed her amber-coloured raiment, and the other gods, seeing her rise and go, laughed, and their laughter floated her on.

Mrs. Swithin put her hands to her hair, for the breeze had ruffled it.

"Mr. . . ." she began.

"I'm William," he interrupted.

At that she smiled a ravishing girl's smile, as if the wind had warmed the wintry blue in her eyes to amber.

"I took you," she apologized, "away from your friends, William, because I felt wound tight here. . . ." She touched her bony forehead upon which a blue vein wriggled like a blue worm. But her eyes in their caves of bone were still lambent. He saw her eyes only. And he wished to kneel before her, to kiss her hand, and to say: "At school they held me under a bucket of dirty water, Mrs. Swithin; when I looked up, the world was dirty, Mrs. Swithin; so I married; but my child's not my child, Mrs. Swithin. I'm a half-man, Mrs. Swithin; a flickering, mind-divided little snake in the grass, Mrs. Swithin; as Giles saw; but you've healed me. . . ." So he wished to say; but said nothing; and the breeze went lolloping along the corridors, blowing the blinds out.

Once more he looked and she looked down on to the yellow gravel that made a crescent round the door. Pendant from her chain her cross swung as she leant out and the sun struck it. How could she weight herself down by that sleek symbol? How stamp herself, so volatile, so vagrant, with that image? As he looked at it, they were truants no more. The purring of the wheels became vocal. "Hurry, hurry, hurry," it seemed to say, "or you'll be late. Hurry, hurry, hurry, or the best seats'll be taken."

"O," cried Mrs. Swithin, "there's Mr. Streatfield!" And they saw a clergyman, a strapping clergyman, carrying a hurdle, a leafy hurdle. He was striding through the cars with the air of a person of authority, who is awaited, expected, and now comes.

"Is it time," said Mrs. Swithin, "to go and join--" She left the sentence unfinished, as if she were of two minds, and they fluttered to right and to left, like pigeons rising from the grass.

The audience was assembling. They came streaming along the paths and spreading across the lawn. Some were old; some were in the prime of life. There were children among them. Among them, as Mr. Figgis might have observed, were representatives of our most respected families--the Dyces of Denton; the Wickhams of Owlswick; and so on. Some had been there for centuries, never selling an acre. On the other hand there were new-comers, the Manresas, bringing the old houses up to date, adding bathrooms. And a scatter of odds and ends, like Cobbet of Cobbs Corner, retired, it was understood, on a pension from a tea plantation. Not an asset. He did his own housework and dug in his garden. The building of a car factory and of an aerodrome in the neighbourhood had attracted a number of unattached floating residents. Also there was Mr. Page, the reporter, representing the local paper. Roughly speaking, however, had Figgis been there in person and called a roll call, half the ladies and gentlemen present would have said: "*Adsum;* I'm here, in place of my grandfather or great-grandfather," as the case might be. At this very moment, half-past three on a June day in 1939 they greeted each other, and as they took their seats, finding if possible a seat next one another, they said: "That hideous new house at Pyes Corner! What an eyesore! And those bungalows!--have you seen 'em?"

Again, had Figgis called the names of the villagers, they too would have answered. Mrs. Sands was born Iliffe; Candish's mother was one of the Perrys. The green mounds in the churchyard had been cast up by their molings, which for centuries had made the earth friable. True, there were absentees when Mr. Streatfield called his roll call in the church. The motor bike, the motor bus, and the movies-- when Mr. Streatfield called his roll call, he laid the blame on them.

Rows of chairs, deck chairs, gilt chairs, hired cane chairs, and indigenous garden seats had been drawn up on the terrace. There were plenty of seats for everybody. But some preferred to sit on the ground. Certainly Miss La Trobe had spoken the truth when she said: "The very place for a pageant!" The lawn was as flat as the floor of a theatre. The terrace, rising, made a natural stage. The trees barred the stage like pillars. And the human figure was seen to great advantage against a background of sky. As for the weather, it was turning out, against all expectation, a very fine day. A perfect summer afternoon.

"What luck!" Mrs. Carter was saying. "Last year . . ." Then the play began. Was it, or was it not, the play? Chuff, chuff, chuff sounded from the bushes. It was the noise a machine makes when something has gone wrong. Some sat down hastily, others stopped talking guiltily. All looked at the bushes. For the stage was empty. Chuff, chuff, chuff the machine buzzed in the bushes. While they looked apprehensively and some finished their sentences, a small girl, like a rosebud in pink, advanced; took her stand on a mat, behind a conch, hung with leaves and piped:

Gentles and simples, I address you all . . .

So it was the play then. Or was it the prologue?

Come hither for our festival (she continued)
This is a pageant, all may see
Drawn from our island history.
England am I. . . .

"She's England," they whispered. "It's begun." "The prologue," they added, looking down at the programme.

"England am I," she piped again; and stopped.

She had forgotten her lines.

"Hear! Hear!" said an old man in a white waistcoat briskly. "Bravo! Bravo!"

"Blast 'em!" cursed Miss La Trobe, hidden behind the tree. She looked along the front row. They glared as if they were exposed to a frost that nipped them and fixed them all at the same level. Only Bond the cowman looked fluid and natural.

"Music!" she signalled. "Music!" But the machine continued: Chuff, chuff, chuff.

"A child new born . . ." she prompted.

"A child new born," Phyllis Jones continued,

> *Sprung from the sea*
> *Whose billows blown by mighty storm*
> *Cut off from France and Germany*
> *This isle.*

She glanced back over her shoulder. Chuff, chuff, chuff, the machine buzzed. A long line of villagers in shirts made of sacking began passing in and out in single file behind her between the trees. They were singing, but not a word reached the audience.

England am I, Phyllis Jones continued, facing the audience,

> *Now weak and small*
> *A child, as all may see . . .*

Her words peppered the audience as with a shower of hard little stones. Mrs. Manresa in the very centre smiled; but she felt as if her skin cracked when she smiled. There was a vast vacancy between her, the singing villagers and the piping child.

Chuff, chuff, chuff, went the machine like a corn-cutter on a hot day.

The villagers were singing, but half their words were blown away.

Cutting the roads . . . up to the hill top . . . we climbed. Down in the valley . . . sow, wild boar, hog, rhinoceros, reindeer . . . Dug ourselves in to the hill top . . . Ground roots between stones . . . Ground corn . . . till we too . . . lay under g--r--o--u--n--d . . .

The words petered away. Chuff, chuff, chuff, the machine ticked. Then at last the machine ground out a tune!

> *Armed against fate*
> *The valiant Rhoderick*

> *Armed and valiant*
> *Bold and blatant*
> *Firm elatant*
> *See the warriors--here they come . . .*

The pompous popular tune brayed and blared. Miss La Trobe watched from behind the tree. Muscles loosened; ice cracked. The stout lady in the middle began to beat time with her hand on her chair. Mrs. Manresa was humming:

> My home is at Windsor, close to the Inn.
> Royal George is the name of the pub.
> And boys you'll believe me,
> I don't want no asking . . .

She was afloat on the stream of the melody. Radiating royalty, complacency, good humour, the wild child was Queen of the festival. The play had begun.

But there was an interruption. "O," Miss La Trobe growled behind her tree, "the torture of these interruptions!"

"Sorry I'm so late," said Mrs. Swithin. She pushed her way through the chairs to a seat beside her brother.

"What's it all about? I've missed the prologue. England? That little girl? Now she's gone . . ."

Phyllis had slipped off her mat.

"And who's this?" asked Mrs. Swithin.

It was Hilda, the carpenter's daughter. She now stood where England had stood.

"O, England's grown . . ." Miss La Trobe prompted her.

"O, England's grown a girl now," Hilda sang out

("What a lovely voice!" someone exclaimed)

> *With roses in her hair,*
> *Wild roses, red roses,*
> *She roams the lanes and chooses*
> *A garland for her hair.*

"A cushion? Thank you so much," said Mrs. Swithin, stuffing the cushion behind her back. Then she leant forward.

"That's England in the time of Chaucer, I take it. She's been maying, nutting. She has flowers in her hair . . . But those passing behind her--" she pointed. "The Canterbury pilgrims? Look!"

All the time the villagers were passing in and out between the trees. They were singing; but only a word or two was audible ". . . *wore ruts in the grass . . . built the house in the lane . . .*" The wind blew away the connecting words of their chant, and then, as they reached the tree at the end they sang:

"To the shrine of the Saint . . . to the tomb . . . lovers . . . believers . . . we come . . ."

They grouped themselves together.

Then there was a rustle and an interruption. Chairs were drawn back. Isa looked behind her. Mr. and Mrs. Rupert Haines, detained by a breakdown on the road, had arrived. He was sitting to the right, several rows back, the man in grey.

Meanwhile the pilgrims, having done their homage to the tomb, were, it appeared, tossing hay on their rakes,

> *I kissed a girl and let her go,*
> *Another did I tumble,*
> *In the straw and in the hay . . .*

--that was what they were singing, as they scooped and tossed the invisible hay, when she looked round again.

"Scenes from English history," Mrs. Manresa explained to Mrs. Swithin. She spoke in a loud cheerful voice, as if the old lady were deaf. "Merry England."

She clapped energetically.

The singers scampered away into the bushes. The tune stopped. Chuff, chuff, chuff, the machine ticked. Mrs. Manresa looked at her programme. It would take till midnight unless they skipped. Early Briton; Plantagenets; Tudors; Stuarts--she ticked them off, but probably she had forgotten a reign or two.

"Ambitious, ain't it?" she said to Bartholomew, while they waited. Chuff, chuff, chuff went the machine. Could they talk? Could they move? No, for the play was going on. Yet the stage was empty; only the cows moved in the meadows; only the tick of the gramophone needle was heard. The tick, tick, tick seemed to hold them together, tranced. Nothing whatsoever appeared on the stage.

"I'd no notion we looked so nice," Mrs. Swithin whispered to William. Hadn't she? The children; the pilgrims; behind the pilgrims the trees, and behind them the fields--the beauty of the visible world took his breath away. Tick, tick, tick the machine continued.

"Marking time," said old Oliver beneath his breath.

"Which don't exist for us," Lucy murmured. "We've only the present."

"Isn't that enough?" William asked himself. Beauty--isn't that enough? But here Isa fidgetted. Her bare brown arms went nervously to her head. She half turned in her seat. "No, not for us, who've the future," she seemed to say. The future disturbing our present. Who was she looking for? William, turning, following her eyes, saw only a man in grey.

The ticking stopped. A dance tune was put on the machine. In time to it, Isa hummed: "What do I ask? To fly away, from night and day, and issue where--no partings are--but eye meets eye--and . . . O," she cried aloud: "Look at her!"

Everyone was clapping and laughing. From behind the bushes issued Queen Elizabeth--Eliza Clark, licensed to sell tobacco. Could she be Mrs. Clark of the village shop? She was splendidly made up. Her head, pearl-hung, rose from a vast ruff. Shiny satins draped her. Sixpenny brooches glared like cats' eyes and tigers' eyes; pearls looked down; her cape was made of cloth of silver--in fact swabs used to scour saucepans. She looked the age in person. And when she mounted the soap box in the centre, representing perhaps a rock in the ocean, her size made her appear gigantic. She could reach a flitch of bacon or haul a tub of oil with one sweep of her arm in the shop. For a moment she stood there, eminent, dominant, on the soap box with the blue and sailing clouds behind her. The breeze had risen.

> *The Queen of this great land . . .*

--those were the first words that could be heard above the roar of laughter and applause.

> *Mistress of ships and bearded men* (she bawled)
> *Hawkins, Frobisher, Drake,*
> *Tumbling their oranges, ingots of silver,*
> *Cargoes of diamonds, ducats of gold,*
> *Down on the jetty, there in the west land,--*
> (she pointed her fist at the blazing blue sky)
> *Mistress of pinnacles, spires and palaces--*
> (her arm swept towards the house)
> *For me Shakespeare sang--*
> (a cow mooed. A bird twittered)
> *The throstle, the mavis* (she continued)
> *In the green wood, the wild wood,*
> *Carolled and sang, praising England, the Queen,*
> *Then there was heard too*
> *On granite and cobble*
> *From Windsor to Oxford*
> *Loud laughter, low laughter*
> *Of warrior and lover,*
> *The fighter, the singer.*
> *The ashen haired babe*
> *(she stretched out her swarthy, muscular arm)*
> *Stretched his arm in contentment*
> *As home from the Isles came*
> *The sea faring men. . . .*

Here the wind gave a tug at her head dress. Loops of pearls made it top-heavy. She had to steady the ruffle which threatened to blow away.

"Laughter, loud laughter," Giles muttered. The tune on the gramophone reeled from side to side as if drunk with merriment. Mrs. Manresa began beating her foot and humming in time to it.

"Bravo! Bravo!" she cried. "There's life in the old dog yet!" And she trolloped out the words of the song with an abandonment which, if vulgar, was a great help to the Elizabethan age. For the ruff had become unpinned and great Eliza had forgotten her lines. But the audience laughed so loud that it did not matter.

"I fear I am not in my perfect mind," Giles muttered to the same tune. Words came to the surface--he remembered "a stricken deer in whose lean flank the world's harsh scorn has struck its thorn. . . . Exiled from its festival, the music turned ironical. . . . A churchyard haunter at whom the owl hoots and the ivy mocks tap-tap-tapping on the pane. . . . For they are dead, and I . . . I . . . I," he repeated, forgetting the words, and glaring at his Aunt Lucy who sat craned forward, her mouth gaping, and her bony little hands clapping.

What were they laughing at?

At Albert, the village idiot, apparently. There was no need to dress him up. There he came, acting his part to perfection. He came ambling across the grass, mopping and mowing.

> *I know where the tit nests*, he began
> *In the hedgerow. I know, I know--*
> *What don't I know?*
> *All your secrets, ladies,*
> *And yours too, gentlemen . . .*

He skipped along the front row of the audience, leering at each in turn. Now he was picking and plucking at Great Eliza's skirts. She cuffed him on the ear. He tweaked her back. He was enjoying himself immensely.

"Albert having the time of his life," Bartholomew muttered.

"Hope he don't have a fit," Lucy murmured.

"I know . . . I know . . ." Albert tittered, skipping round the soap box.

"The village idiot," whispered a stout black lady--Mrs. Elmhurst--who came from a village ten miles distant where they, too, had an idiot. It wasn't nice. Suppose he suddenly did something dreadful? There he was pinching the Queen's skirts. She half covered her eyes, in case he did do--something dreadful.

> *Hoppety, jiggety,* Albert resumed,
> *In at the window, out at the door,*
> *What does the little bird hear?* (he whistled on his fingers.)
> *And see! There's a mouse. . . .*
> (he made as if chasing it through the grass)
> *Now the clock strikes!*
> (he stood erect, puffing out his cheeks as if he were blowing a dandelion clock)
> *One, two, three, four. . . .*

And off he skipped, as if his turn was over.

"Glad that's over." said Mrs. Elmhurst, uncovering her face. "Now what comes next? A tableau. . . ?"

For helpers, issuing swiftly from the bushes, carrying hurdles, had enclosed the Queen's throne with screens papered to represent walls. They had strewn the ground with rushes. And the pilgrims who had continued their march and their chant in the background, now gathered round the figure of Eliza on her soap box as if to form the audience at a play.

Were they about to act a play in the presence of Queen Elizabeth? Was this, perhaps, the Globe theatre?

"What does the programme say?" Mrs. Herbert Winthrop asked, raising her lorgnettes.

She mumbled through the blurred carbon sheet. Yes; it was a scene from a play.

"About a false Duke; and a Princess disguised as a boy; then the long lost heir turns out to be the beggar, because of a mole on his cheek; and Carinthia--that's the Duke's daughter, only she's been lost in a cave--falls in love with Ferdinando who had been put into a basket as a baby by an aged crone. And they marry. That's I think what happens," she said, looking up from the programme.

"Play out the play," great Eliza commanded. An aged crone tottered forward.

("Mrs. Otter of the End House," someone murmured.)

She sat herself on a packing case, and made motions, plucking her dishevelled locks and rocking herself from side to side as if she were an aged beldame in a chimney corner.

("The crone, who saved the rightful heir," Mrs. Winthrop explained.)

> *'Twas a winter's night* (she croaked out)
> *I mind me that, I to whom all's one now, summer or winter.*
> *You say the sun shines? I believe you, Sir.*
> *'Oh but it's winter, and the fog's abroad'*
> *All's one to Elsbeth, summer or winter,*
> *By the fireside, in the chimney corner, telling her beads.*
> *I've cause to tell 'em.*
> *Each bead* (she held a bead between thumb and finger)
> *A crime!*
> *'Twas a winter's night, before cockcrow,*
> *Yet the cock did crow ere he left me--*
> *The man with a hood on his face, and the bloody hands*
> *And the babe in the basket.*
> *'Tee hee' he mewed, as who should say 'I want my toy'*
> *Poor witling!*
> *"Tee hee, tee hee!" I could not slay him!*
> *For that, Mary in Heaven forgive me*
> *The sins I've sinned before cockcrow!*
> *Down to the creek i' the dawn I slipped*
> *Where the gull haunts and the heron stands*
> *Like a stake on the edge of the marshes . . .*
> *Who's here?*
> (Three young men swaggered on to the stage and accosted her)
> *--"Are you come to torture me, Sirs?*
> *There is little blood in this arm,*

(she extended her skinny forearm from her ragged shift)
Saints in Heaven preserve me!

She bawled. They bawled. All together they bawled, and so loud that it was difficult to make out what they were saying: apparently it was: *Did she remember concealing a child in a cradle among the rushes some twenty years previously? A babe in a basket, crone! A babe in a basket?* they bawled. *The wind howls and the bittern shrieks,* she replied.

"There is little blood in my arm," Isabella repeated.

That was all she heard. There was such a medley of things going on, what with the beldame's deafness, the bawling of the youths, and the confusion of the plot that she could make nothing of it.

Did the plot matter? She shifted and looked over her right shoulder. The plot was only there to beget emotion. There were only two emotions: love; and hate. There was no need to puzzle out the plot. Perhaps Miss La Trobe meant that when she cut this knot in the centre?

Don't bother about the plot: the plot's nothing.

But what was happening? The Prince had come.

Plucking up his sleeve, the beldame recognized the mole; and, staggering back in her chair, shrieked:

My child! My child!

Recognition followed. The young Prince (Albert Perry) was almost smothered in the withered arms of the beldame. Then suddenly he started apart.

"Look where she comes!" he cried.

They all looked where she came--Sylvia Edwards in white satin.

Who came? Isa looked. The nightingale's song? The pearl in night's black ear? Love embodied.

All arms were raised; all faces stared.

"Hail, sweet Carinthia!" said the Prince, sweeping his hat off. And she to him, raising her eyes:

"My love! My lord!"

"It was enough. Enough. Enough," Isa repeated.

All else was verbiage, repetition.

The beldame meanwhile, because that was enough, had sunk back on her chair, the beads dangling from her fingers.

"Look to the beldame there--old Elsbeth's sick!"
(They crowded round her)
Dead, Sirs!

42

She fell back lifeless. The crowd drew away. Peace, let her pass. She to whom all's one now, summer or winter.

Peace was the third emotion. Love. Hate. Peace. Three emotions made the ply of human life. Now the priest, whose cotton wool moustache confused his utterance, stepped forward and pronounced benediction.

From the distaff of life's tangled skein, unloose her hands
(They unloosed her hands)
Of her frailty, let nothing now remembered be.
Call for the robin redbreast and the wren.
And roses fall your crimson pall.
(Petals were strewn from wicker baskets)
Cover the corpse. Sleep well.
(They covered the corpse)
On you, fair Sirs (he turned to the happy couple)
Let Heaven rain benediction!
Haste ere the envying sun
Night's curtain hath undone. Let music sound
And the free air of Heaven waft you to your slumber!
Lead on the dance!

The gramophone blared. Dukes, priests, shepherds, pilgrims and serving men took hands and danced. The idiot scampered in and out. Hands joined, heads knocking, they danced round the majestic figure of the Elizabethan age personified by Mrs. Clark, licensed to sell tobacco, on her soap box.

It was a mellay; a medley; an entrancing spectacle (to William) of dappled light and shade on half clothed, fantastically coloured, leaping, jerking, swinging legs and arms. He clapped till his palms stung.

Mrs. Manresa applauded loudly. Somehow she was the Queen; and he (Giles) was the surly hero.

"Bravo! Bravo!" she cried, and her enthusiasm made the surly hero squirm on his seat. Then the great lady in the bath chair, the lady whose marriage with the local peer had obliterated in his trashy title a name that had been a name when there were brambles and briars where the Church now stood--so indigenous was she that even her body, crippled by arthritis, resembled an uncouth, nocturnal animal, now nearly extinct--clapped and laughed loud--the sudden laughter of a startled jay.

"Ha, ha, ha!" she laughed and clutched the arms of her chair with ungloved twisted hands.

"A-maying, a-maying," they bawled. "In and out and round about, a-maying, a-maying. . . ."

It didn't matter what the words were; or who sang what. Round and round they whirled, intoxicated by the music. Then, at a sign from Miss La Trobe behind the tree, the dance stopped. A procession formed. Great Eliza descended from her soap box. Taking her skirts in her hand, striding with long strides, surrounded by Dukes and Princes, followed by the lovers arm in arm, with Albert the idiot playing in and out, and the corpse on its bier concluding the procession, the Elizabethan age passed from the scene.

"Curse! Blast! Damn 'em!" Miss La Trobe in her rage stubbed her toe against a root. Here was her downfall; here was the Interval. Writing this skimble-skamble stuff in her cottage, she had agreed to cut the play here; a slave to her audience,--to Mrs. Sands' grumble--about tea; about dinner;--she had gashed the scene here. Just as she had brewed emotion, she spilt it. So she signalled: Phyllis! And, summoned, Phyllis popped up on the mat again in the middle.

Gentles and simples, I address you all (she piped.)
Our act is done, our scene is over.
Past is the day of crone and lover.
The bud has flowered; the flower has fallen.
But soon will rise another dawning,
For time whose children small we be
Hath in his keeping, you shall see,
You shall see. . . .

Her voice petered out. No one was listening. Heads bent, they read "Interval" on the programme. And, cutting short her words, the megaphone announced in plain English: "An interval." Half an hour's interval, for tea. Then the gramophone blared out:

Armed against fate,
The valiant Rhoderick,
Bold and blatant,
Firm, elatant, etc., etc.

At that, the audience stirred. Some rose briskly; others stooped, retrieving walking-sticks, hats, bags. And then, as they raised themselves and turned about, the music modulated. The music chanted: *Dispersed are we*. It moaned: *Dispersed are we*. It lamented: *Dispersed are we,* as they streamed, spotting the grass with colour, across the lawns, and down the paths: *Dispersed are we.*

Mrs. Manresa took up the strain. *Dispersed are we.* "Freely, boldly, fearing no one" (she pushed a deck chair out of her way). "Youths and maidens" (she glanced behind her; but Giles had his back turned). "Follow, follow, follow me. . . . Oh Mr. Parker, what a pleasure to see *you* here! I'm for tea!"

"Dispersed are we," Isabella followed her, humming. "All is over. The wave has broken. Left us stranded, high and dry. Single, separate on the shingle. Broken is the three-fold ply . . . Now I follow" (she pushed her chair back . . . The man in grey was lost in the crowd by the ilex) "that old strumpet" (she invoked Mrs. Manresa's tight, flowered figure in front of her) "to have tea."

Dodge remained behind. "Shall I," he murmured, "go or stay? Slip out some other way? Or follow, follow, follow the dispersing company?"

Dispersed are we, the music wailed; *dispersed are we.* Giles remained like a stake in the tide of the flowing company.

"Follow?" He kicked his chair back. "Whom? Where?" He stubbed his light tennis shoes on the wood. "Nowhere. Anywhere." Stark still he stood.

Here Cobbet of Cobbs Corner, alone under the monkey puzzle tree, rose and muttered: "What was in her mind, eh? What idea lay behind, eh? What made her indue the antique with this glamour--this sham lure, and set 'em climbing, climbing, climbing up the monkey puzzle tree?"

Dispersed are we, the music wailed. *Dispersed are we.* He turned and sauntered slowly after the retreating company.

Now Lucy, retrieving her bag from beneath the seat, chirruped to her brother:

"Bart, my dear, come with me. . . . D'you remember, when we were children, the play we acted in the nursery?"

He remembered. Red Indians the game was; a reed with a note wrapped up in a pebble.

"But for us, my old Cindy"--he picked up his hat--"the game's over." The glare and the stare and the beat of the tom-tom, he meant. He gave her his arm. Off they strolled. And Mr. Page, the reporter, noted, "Mrs. Swithin: Mr. B. Oliver," then turning, added further "Lady Haslip, of Haslip Manor," as he spied that old lady wheeled in her chair by her footman winding up the procession.

To the valediction of the gramophone hid in the bushes the audience departed. *Dispersed,* it wailed, *Dispersed are we.*

Now Miss La Trobe stepped from her hiding. Flowing, and streaming, on the grass, on the gravel, still for one moment she held them together--the dispersing company. Hadn't she, for twenty-five minutes, made them see? A vision imparted was relief from agony . . . for one moment . . . one moment. Then the music petered out on the last word *we.* She heard the breeze rustle in the branches. She saw Giles Oliver with his back to the audience. Also Cobbet of Cobbs Corner. She hadn't made them see. It was a failure, another damned failure! As usual. Her vision escaped her. And turning, she strode to the actors, undressing, down in the hollow, where butterflies feasted upon swords of silver paper; where the dish cloths in the shadow made pools of yellow.

Cobbet had out his watch. Three hours till seven, he noted; then water the plants. He turned.

Giles, nicking his chair into its notch, turned too, in the other direction. He took the short cut by the fields to the Barn. This dry summer the path was hard as brick across the fields. This dry summer the path was strewn with stones. He kicked--a flinty yellow stone, a sharp stone, edged as if cut by a savage for an arrow. A barbaric stone; a pre-historic. Stone-kicking was a child's game. He remembered the rules. By the rules of the game, one stone, the same stone, must be kicked to the goal. Say a gate, or a tree. He played it alone. The gate was a goal; to be reached in ten. The first kick was Manresa (lust). The second, Dodge (perversion). The third himself (coward). And the fourth and the fifth and all the others were the same.

He reached it in ten. There, couched in the grass, curled in an olive green ring, was a snake. Dead? No, choked with a toad in its mouth. The snake was unable to swallow, the toad was unable to die. A spasm made the ribs contract; blood oozed. It was birth the wrong way round--a monstrous inversion. So, raising his foot, he stamped on them. The mass crushed and slithered. The white canvas on his tennis shoes was bloodstained and sticky. But it was action. Action relieved him. He strode to the Barn, with blood on his shoes.

The Barn, the Noble Barn, the barn that had been built over seven hundred years ago and reminded some people of a Greek temple, others of the middle ages, most people of an age before their own, scarcely anybody of the present moment, was empty.

The great doors stood open. A shaft of light like a yellow banner sloped from roof to floor. Festoons of paper roses, left over from the Coronation, drooped from the rafters. A long table, on which stood an urn, plates and cups, cakes and bread and butter, stretched across one end. The Barn was empty. Mice slid in and out of holes or stood upright, nibbling. Swallows were busy with straw in pockets of earth in the rafters. Countless beetles and insects of various sorts burrowed in the dry wood. A stray bitch had made the dark corner where the sacks stood a lying-in ground for her puppies. All these eyes, expanding and narrowing, some adapted to light, others to darkness, looked from different angles and edges. Minute nibblings and rustlings broke the silence. Whiffs of sweetness and richness veined the air. A blue-bottle had settled on the cake and stabbed its yellow rock with its short drill. A butterfly sunned itself sensuously on a sunlit yellow plate.

But Mrs. Sands was approaching. She was pushing her way through the crowd. She had turned the corner. She could see the great open door. But butterflies she never saw, mice were only black pellets in kitchen drawers; moths she bundled in her hands and put out of the window. Bitches suggested only servant girls misbehaving. Had there been a cat she would have seen it--any cat, a starved cat with a patch of mange on its rump opened the flood gates of her childless heart. But there was no cat. The Barn was empty. And so running, panting, set upon reaching the Barn and taking up her station behind the tea urn before the company came, she reached the Barn. And the butterfly rose and the bluebottle.

Following her in a scud came the servants and helpers--David, John, Irene, Lois. Water boiled. Steam issued. Cake was sliced. Swallows swooped from rafter to rafter. And the company entered.

"This fine old Barn . . ." said Mrs. Manresa, stopping in the doorway. It was not for her to press ahead of the villagers. It was for her, moved by the beauty of the Barn, to stand still; to draw aside; to gaze; to let other people come first.

"We have one, much like it, at Lathom," said Mrs. Parker, stopping, for the same reasons. "Perhaps," she added, "not quite so large."

The villagers hung back. Then, hesitating, dribbled past.

"And the decorations . . ." said Mrs. Manresa, looking round for someone to congratulate. She stood smiling, waiting. Then old Mrs. Swithin came in. She was gazing up too, but not at the decorations. At the swallows apparently.

"They come every year," she said, "the same birds." Mrs. Manresa smiled benevolently, humouring the old lady's whimsy. It was unlikely, she thought, that the birds were the same.

"The decorations, I suppose, are left over from the Coronation," said Mrs. Parker. "We kept ours too. We built a village hall."

Mrs. Manresa laughed. She remembered. An anecdote was on the tip of her tongue, about a public lavatory built to celebrate the same occasion, and how the Mayor . . . Could she tell it? No. The old lady, gazing at the swallows, looked too refined. "Refeened"--Mrs. Manresa qualified the word to her own advantage, thus confirming her approval of the wild child she was, whose nature was somehow "just human nature." Somehow she could span the old lady's "refeenment," also the boy's fun--Where was that nice fellow Giles? She couldn't see him; nor Bill either. The villagers still hung back. They must have someone to start the ball rolling.

"Well, I'm dying for my tea!" she said in her public voice; and strode forward. She laid hold of a thick china mug. Mrs. Sands giving precedence, of course, to one of the gentry, filled it at once. David gave her cake. She was the first to drink, the first to bite. The villagers still hung back. "It's all my eye about democracy," she concluded. So did Mrs. Parker, taking her mug too. The people looked to them. They led; the rest followed.

"What delicious tea!" each exclaimed, disgusting though it was, like rust boiled in water, and the cake fly-blown. But they had a duty to society.

"They come every year," said Mrs. Swithin, ignoring the fact that she spoke to the empty air. "From Africa." As they had come, she supposed, when the Barn was a swamp.

The Barn filled. Fumes rose. China clattered; voices chattered. Isa pressed her way to the table.

"Dispersed are we," she murmured. And held her cup out to be filled. She took it. "Let me turn away," she murmured, turning, "from the array"--she looked desolately round her--"of china faces, glazed and hard. Down the ride, that leads under the nut tree and the may tree, away, till I come to the wishing well, where the washerwoman's little boy--" she dropped sugar, two lumps, into her tea, "dropped a pin. He got his horse, so they say. But what wish should I drop into the well?" She looked round. She could not see the man in grey, the gentleman farmer; nor anyone known to her. "That the waters should cover me," she added, "of the wishing well."

The noise of china and chatter drowned her murmur. "Sugar for you?" they were saying. "Just a spot of milk? And you?" "Tea without milk or sugar. That's the way I like it." "A bit too strong? Let me add water."

"That's what I wished," Isa added, "when I dropped my pin. Water. Water . . ."

"I must say," the voice said behind her, "it's brave of the King and Queen. They're said to be going to India. She looks such a dear. Someone I know said his hair. . . ."

"There," Isa mused, "would the dead leaf fall, when the leaves fall, on the water. Should I mind not again to see may tree or nut tree? Not again to hear on the trembling spray the thrush sing, or to see, dipping and diving as if he skimmed waves in the air, the yellow woodpecker?"

She was looking at the canary yellow festoons left over from the Coronation.

"I thought they said Canada, not India," the voice said behind her back. To which the other voice answered: "D'you believe what the papers say? For instance, about the Duke of Windsor. He landed on the south coast. Queen Mary met him. She'd been buying furniture--that's a fact. And the papers say she met him . . ."

"Alone, under a tree, the withered tree that keeps all day, murmuring of the sea, and hears the Rider gallop . . ."

Isa filled in the phrase. Then she started. William Dodge was by her side.

He smiled. She smiled. They were conspirators; each murmuring some song my uncle taught me.

"It's the play," she said. "The play keeps running in my head."

"Hail, sweet Carinthia. My love. My life," he quoted.

"My lord, my liege," she bowed ironically.

She was handsome. He wanted to see her, not against the tea urn, but with her glass green eyes and thick body, the neck was broad as a pillar, against an arum lily or a vine. He wished she would say: "Come along. I'll show you the greenhouse, the pig sty, or the stable." But she said nothing, and they stood there holding their cups, remembering the play. Then he saw her face change, as if she had got out of one dress and put on another. A small boy battled his way through the crowd, striking against skirts and trousers as if he were swimming blindly.

"Here!" she cried raising her arm.

He made a bee-line for her. He was her little boy, apparently, her son, her George. She gave him cake; then a mug of milk. Then Nurse came up. Then again she changed her dress. This time, from the expression in her eyes it was apparently something in the nature of a strait waistcoat. Hirsute, handsome, virile, the young man in blue jacket and brass buttons, standing in a beam of dusty light, was her husband. And she his wife. Their relations, as he had noted at lunch, were as people say in novels "strained." As he had noted at the play, her bare arm had raised itself nervously to her shoulder when she turned--looking for whom? But here he was; and the muscular, the hirsute, the virile plunged him into emotions in which the mind had no share. He forgot how she would have looked against vine leaf in a greenhouse. Only at Giles he looked; and looked and looked. Of whom was he thinking as he stood with his face turned? Not of Isa. Of Mrs. Manresa?

Mrs. Manresa half-way down the Barn had gulped her cup of tea. How can I rid myself, she asked, of Mrs. Parker? If they were of her own class, how they bored her--her own sex! Not the class below--cooks, shopkeepers, farmers' wives; nor the class above--peeresses, countesses; it was the women of her own class that bored her. So she left Mrs. Parker, abruptly.

"Oh Mrs. Moore," she hailed the keeper's wife. "What did you think of it? And what did baby think of it?" Here she pinched baby. "I thought it every bit as good as anything I'd seen in London. . . . But we mustn't be outdone. We'll have a play of our own. In *our* Barn. We'll show 'em" (here she winked obliquely at the table; so many bought cakes, so few made at home) "how *we* do it."

Then cracking her jokes, she turned; saw Giles; caught his eye; and swept him in, beckoning. He came. And what--she looked down--had he done with his shoes? They were bloodstained. Vaguely some sense that he had proved his valour for her admiration flattered her. If vague it was sweet. Taking him in tow, she felt: I am the Queen, he my hero, my sulky hero.

"That's Mrs. Neale!" she exclaimed. "A perfect marvel of a woman, aren't you, Mrs. Neale! She runs our post office, Mrs. Neale. She can do sums in her head, can't you, Mrs. Neale? Twenty-five halfpenny stamps, two packets of stamped envelopes and a packet of postcards--how much does that come to, Mrs. Neale?"

Mrs. Neale laughed; Mrs. Manresa laughed; Giles too smiled, and looked down at his shoes.

She drew him down the Barn, in and out, from one to another. She knew 'em all. Every one was a thorough good sort. No, she wouldn't allow it, not for a moment--Pinsent's bad leg. "No, no. We're not going to take that for an excuse, Pinsent." If he couldn't bowl, he could bat. Giles agreed. A fish on a line meant the same to him and Pinsent; also jays and magpies. Pinsent stayed on the land; Giles went to an office. That was all. And she was a thorough good sort, making him feel less of an audience, more of an actor, going round the Barn in her wake.

Then, at the end by the door, they came upon the old couple, Lucy and Bartholomew, sitting on their Windsor chairs.

Chairs had been reserved for them. Mrs. Sands had sent them tea. It would have caused more bother than it was worth--asserting the democratic principle; standing in the crowd at the table.

"Swallows," said Lucy, holding her cup, looking at the birds. Excited by the company they were flitting from rafter to rafter. Across Africa, across France they had come to nest here. Year after year they came. Before there was a channel, when the earth, upon which the Windsor chair was planted, was a riot of rhododendrons, and humming birds quivered at the mouths of scarlet trumpets, as she had read that morning in her Outline of History, they had come . . . Here Bart rose from his chair.

But Mrs. Manresa absolutely refused to take his seat. "Go on sitting, go on sitting," she pressed him down again. "I'll squat on the floor." She squatted. The surly knight remained in attendance.

"And what did you think of the play?" she asked.

Bartholomew looked at his son. His son remained silent.

"And you Mrs. Swithin?" Mrs. Manresa pressed the old lady.

Lucy mumbled, looking at the swallows.

"I was hoping you'd tell me," said Mrs. Manresa. "Was it an old play? Was it a new play?"

No one answered.

"Look!" Lucy exclaimed.

"The birds?" said Mrs. Manresa, looking up.

There was a bird with a straw in its beak; and the straw dropped.

Lucy clapped her hands. Giles turned away. She was mocking him as usual, laughing.

"Going?" said Bartholomew. "Time for the next act?"

And he heaved himself up from his chair. Regardless of Mrs. Manresa and of Lucy, off he strolled too.

"Swallow, my sister, O sister swallow," he muttered, feeling for his cigar case, following his son.

Mrs. Manresa was nettled. What for had she squatted on the floor then? Were her charms fading? Both were gone. But, woman of action as she was, deserted by the male sex, she was not going to suffer tortures of boredom from the refeened old lady. Up she scrambled, putting her hands to hair as if it were high time that she went too, though it was nothing of the kind and her hair was perfectly tidy. Cobbet in his corner saw through her little game. He had known human nature in the East. It was the same in the West. Plants remained--the carnation, the zinnia, and the geranium. Automatically he consulted his watch; noted time to water at seven; and observed the little game of the woman following the man to the table in the West as in the East.

William at the table, now attached to Mrs. Parker and Isa, watched him approach. Armed and valiant, bold and blatant, firm elatant--the popular march tune rang in his head. And the fingers of William's left hand closed firmly, surreptitiously, as the hero approached.

Mrs. Parker was deploring to Isa in a low voice the village idiot.

"Oh that idiot!" she was saying. But Isa was immobile, watching her husband. She could feel the Manresa in his wake. She could hear in the dusk in their bedroom the usual explanation. It made no difference; his infidelity--but hers did.

"The idiot?" William answered Mrs. Parker for her. "He's in the tradition."

"But surely," said Mrs. Parker, and told Giles how creepy the idiot--"We have one in our village"--had made her feel. "Surely, Mr. Oliver, we're more civilized?"

"We?" said Giles. *"We?"* He looked, once, at William. He knew not his name; but what his left hand was doing. It was a bit of luck--that he could despise him, not himself. Also Mrs. Parker. But not Isa--not his wife. She had not spoken to him, not one word. Nor looked at him either.

"Surely," said Mrs. Parker, looking from one to the other. "Surely we are?"

Giles then did what to Isa was his little trick; shut his lips; frowned; and took up the pose of one who bears the burden of the world's woe, making money for her to spend.

"No," said Isa, as plainly as words could say it. "I don't admire you," and looked, not at his face, but at his feet. "Silly little boy, with blood on his boots."

Giles shifted his feet. Whom then did she admire? Not Dodge. That he could take for certain. Who else? Some man he knew. Some man, he was sure, in the Barn. Which man? He looked round him.

Then Mr. Streatfield, the clergyman, interrupted. He was carrying cups.

"So I shake hands with my heart!" he exclaimed, nodding his handsome, grizzled head and depositing his burden safely.

Mrs. Parker took the tribute to herself.

"Mr. Streatfield!" she exclaimed. "Doing all the work! While we stand gossiping!"

"Like to see the greenhouse?" said Isa suddenly, turning to William Dodge.

O not now, he could have cried. But had to follow, leaving Giles to welcome the approaching Manresa, who had him in thrall.

The path was narrow. Isa went ahead. And she was broad; she fairly filled the path, swaying slightly as she walked, and plucking a leaf here and there from the hedge.

"Fly then, follow," she hummed, "the dappled herds in the cedar grove, who, sporting, play, the red with the roe, the stag with the doe. Fly, away. I grieving stay. Alone I linger, I pluck the bitter herb by the ruined wall, the churchyard wall, and press its sour, its sweet, its sour, long grey leaf, so, twixt thumb and finger. . . ."

She threw away the shred of Old Man's Beard that she had picked in passing and kicked open the greenhouse door. Dodge had lagged behind. She waited. She picked up a knife from the plank. He saw her standing against the green glass, the fig tree, and the blue hydrangea, knife in hand.

"She spake," Isa murmured. "And from her bosom's snowy antre drew the gleaming blade. 'Plunge blade!' she said. And struck. 'Faithless!' she cried. Knife, too! It broke. So too my heart," she said.

She was smiling ironically as he came up.

"I wish the play didn't run in my head," she said. Then she sat down on a plank under the vine. And he sat beside her. The little grapes above them were green buds; the leaves thin and yellow as the web between birds' claws.

"Still the play?" he asked. She nodded. "That was your son," he said, "in the Barn?"

She had a daughter too, she told him, in the cradle.

"And you--married?" she asked. From her tone he knew she guessed, as women always guessed, everything. They knew at once they had nothing to fear, nothing to hope. At first they resented--serving as statues in a greenhouse. Then they liked it. For then they could say--as she did--whatever came into their heads. And hand him, as she handed him, a flower.

"There's something for your buttonhole, Mr. . . ." she said, handing him a sprig of scented geranium.

"I'm William," he said, taking the furry leaf and pressing it between thumb and finger.

"I'm Isa," she answered. Then they talked as if they had known each other all their lives; which was odd, she said, as they always did, considering she'd known him perhaps one hour. Weren't they, though, conspirators, seekers after hidden faces? That confessed, she paused and wondered, as they always did, why they could speak so plainly to each other. And added: "Perhaps because we've never met before, and never shall again."

"The doom of sudden death hanging over us," he said. "There's no retreating and advancing"--he was thinking of the old lady showing him the house--"for us as for them."

The future shadowed their present, like the sun coming through the many-veined transparent vine leaf; a criss-cross of lines making no pattern.

They had left the greenhouse door open, and now music came through it. A.B.C., A.B.C., A.B.C.--someone was practising scales. C.A.T. C.A.T. C.A.T. . . . Then the separate letters made one word "Cat." Other words followed. It was a simple tune, like a nursery rhyme--

> The King is in his counting house,
> Counting out his money,
> The Queen is in her parlour
> Eating bread and honey.

They listened. Another voice, a third voice, was saying something simple. And they sat on in the greenhouse, on the plank with the vine over them, listening to Miss La Trobe or whoever it was, practising her scales.

He could not find his son. He had lost him in the crowd. So old Bartholomew left the Barn, and went to his own room, holding his cheroot and murmuring:

> "O sister swallow, O sister swallow,
> How can thy heart be full of the spring?"

"How can my heart be full of the spring?" he said aloud, standing in front of the book case. Books: the treasured life-blood of immortal spirits. Poets; the legislators of mankind. Doubtless, it was so. But Giles was unhappy. "How can my heart, how can my heart," he repeated, puffing at his cheroot. "Condemned in life's infernal mine, condemned in solitude to pine . . ." Arms akimbo, he stood in front of his country gentleman's library. Garibaldi; Wellington; Irrigation Officers' Reports; and Hibbert on the Diseases of the Horse. A great harvest the mind had reaped; but for all this, compared with his son, he did not care one damn.

"What's the use, what's the use," he sank down into his chair muttering, "O sister swallow, O sister swallow, of singing your song?" The dog, who had followed him, flopped down on to the floor at his feet. Flanks sucked in and out, the long nose resting on his paws, a fleck of foam on the nostril, there he was, his familiar spirit, his Afghan hound.

The door trembled and stood half open. That was Lucy's way of coming in--as if she did not know what she would find. Really! It was her brother! And his dog! She seemed to see them for the first time. Was it that she had no body? Up in the clouds, like an air ball, her mind touched ground now and then with a shock of surprise. There was nothing in her to weight a man like Giles to the earth.

She perched on the edge of a chair like a bird on a telegraph wire before starting for Africa.

"Swallow, my sister, O sister swallow . . ." he murmured.

From the garden--the window was open--came the sound of someone practising scales. A.B.C. A.B.C. A.B.C. Then the separate letters formed one word "Dog." Then a phrase. It was a simple tune, another voice speaking.

"Hark hark, the dogs do bark
The beggars are coming to town . . ."

Then it languished and lengthened, and became a waltz. As they listened and looked--out into the garden--the trees tossing and the birds swirling seemed called out of their private lives, out of their separate avocations, and made to take part.

The lamp of love burns high, over the dark cedar groves,
The lamp of love shines clear, clear as a star in the sky. . . .

Old Bartholomew tapped his fingers on his knee in time to the tune.

Leave your casement and come, lady, I love till I die,

He looked sardonically at Lucy, perched on her chair. How, he wondered, had she ever borne children?

For all are dancing, retreating and advancing,
The moth and the dragon fly. . . .

She was thinking, he supposed, God is peace. God is love. For she belonged to the unifiers; he to the separatists.

Then the tune with its feet always on the same spot, became sugared, insipid; bored a hole with its perpetual invocation to perpetual adoration. Had it--he was ignorant of musical terms--gone into the minor key?

For this day and this dance and this merry, merry May
Will be over (he tapped his forefinger on his knee)
With the cutting of the clover this retreating and advancing--the swifts
seemed to have shot beyond their orbits--
Will be over, over, over,
And the ice will dart its splinter, and the winter,
O the winter, will fill the grate with ashes,
And there'll be no glow, no glow on the log.

He knocked the ash off his cheroot and rose.

"So we must," said Lucy; as if he had said aloud, "It's time to go."

The audience was assembling. The music was summoning them. Down the paths, across the lawns they were streaming again. There was Mrs. Manresa, with Giles at her side, heading the procession. In taut plump curves her scarf blew round her shoulders. The breeze was rising. She looked, as she crossed the lawn to the strains of the gramophone, goddess-like, buoyant, abundant, her cornucopia running over. Bartholomew, following, blessed the power of the human body to make the earth fruitful. Giles would keep his orbit so long as she weighted him to the earth. She stirred the stagnant pool of his old heart even--where bones lay buried, but the dragon flies shot and the grass trembled as Mrs. Manresa advanced across the lawn to the strains of the gramophone.

Feet crunched the gravel. Voices chattered. The inner voice, the other voice was saying: How can we deny that this brave music, wafted from the bushes, is expressive of some inner harmony? "When we wake" (some were thinking) "the day breaks us with its hard mallet blows." "The office" (some were thinking) "compels disparity. Scattered, shattered, hither thither summoned by the bell. 'Ping-ping-ping' that's the phone. 'Forward!' 'Serving!'--that's the shop." So we answer to the infernal, agelong and eternal order issued from on high. And obey. "Working, serving, pushing, striving, earning wages--to be spent--here? Oh dear no. Now? No, by and by. When ears are deaf and the heart is dry."

Here Cobbet of Cobbs Corner who had stooped--there was a flower--was pressed on by people pushing from behind.

For I hear music, they were saying. Music wakes us. Music makes us see the hidden, join the broken. Look and listen. See the flowers, how they ray their redness, whiteness, silverness and blue. And the trees with their many-tongued much syllabling, their green and yellow leaves hustle us and shuffle us, and bid us, like the starlings, and the rooks, come together, crowd together, to chatter and make merry while the red cow moves forward and the black cow stands still.

The audience had reached their seats. Some sat down; others stood a moment, turned, and looked at the view. The stage was empty; the actors were still dressing up among the bushes. The audience turned to one another and began to talk. Scraps and fragments reached Miss La Trobe where she stood, script in hand, behind the tree.

"They're not ready . . . I hear 'em laughing" (they were saying.) ". . . Dressing up. That's the great thing, dressing up. And it's pleasant now, the sun's not so hot . . . That's one good the war brought us--longer days . . . Where did we leave off? D'you remember? The Elizabethans . . . Perhaps she'll reach the present, if she skips. . . . D'you think people change? Their clothes, of course. . . . But I meant ourselves . . . Clearing out a cupboard, I found my father's old top hat. . . . But ourselves--do we change?"

"No, I don't go by politicians. I've a friend who's been to Russia. He says . . . And my daughter, just back from Rome, she says the common people, in the café's, hate Dictators. . . . Well, different people say different things. . . ."

"Did you see it in the papers--the case about the dog? D'you believe dogs can't have puppies? . . . And Queen Mary and the Duke of Windsor on the south coast? . . . D'you believe what's in the papers? I ask the butcher or the grocer . . . That's Mr. Streatfield, carrying a hurdle. . . . The good clergyman, I say, does more work for less pay than all the lot . . . It's the wives that make the trouble. . . ."

"And what about the Jews? The refugees . . . the Jews . . . People like ourselves, beginning life again . . . But it's always been the same. . . . My old mother, who's over eighty, can remember . . . Yes, she still reads without glasses. . . . How amazing! Well, don't they say, after eighty . . . Now they're coming . . . No, that's nothing. . . . I'd make it penal, leaving litter. But then, who's, my husband says, to collect the fines? . . . Ah there she is, Miss La Trobe, over there, behind that tree . . ."

Over there behind the tree Miss La Trobe gnashed her teeth. She crushed her manuscript. The actors delayed. Every moment the audience slipped the noose; split up into scraps and fragments.

"Music!" she signalled. "Music!"

"What's the origin," said a voice, "of the expression 'with a flea in his ear'?"

Down came her hand peremptorily. "Music, music," she signalled.

And the gramophone began A.B.C., A.B.C.

> *The King is in his counting house*
> *Counting out his money,*
> *The Queen is in her parlour*
> *Eating bread and honey. . . .*

Miss La Trobe watched them sink down peacefully into the nursery rhyme. She watched them fold their hands and compose their faces. Then she beckoned. And at last, with a final touch to her head dress, which had been giving trouble, Mabel Hopkins strode from the bushes, and took her place on the raised ground facing the audience.

Eyes fed on her as fish rise to a crumb of bread on the water. Who was she? What did she represent? She was beautiful--very. Her cheeks had been powdered; her colour glowed smooth and clear underneath. Her grey satin robe (a bedspread), pinned in stone-like folds, gave her the majesty of a statue. She carried a sceptre and a little round orb. England was she? Queen Anne was she? Who was she? She spoke too low at first; all they heard was

> *. . . reason holds sway.*

Old Bartholomew applauded.

"Hear! Hear!" he cried." Bravo! Bravo!"

Thus encouraged Reason spoke out.

Time, leaning on his sickle, stands amazed. While commerce from her Cornucopia pours the mingled tribute of her different ores. In distant mines the savage sweats; and from the reluctant earth the painted pot is shaped. At my behest, the armed warrior lays his shield aside; the heathen leaves the Altar steaming with unholy sacrifice. The violet and the eglantine over the riven earth their flowers entwine. No longer fears the unwary wanderer the poisoned snake. And in the helmet, yellow bees their honey make.

She paused. A long line of villagers in sacking were passing in and out of the trees behind her.

Digging and delving, ploughing and sowing they were singing, but the wind blew their words away.

Beneath the shelter of my flowing robe (she resumed, extending her arms) *the arts arise. Music for me unfolds her heavenly harmony. At my behest the miser leaves his hoard untouched; at peace the mother sees her children play. . . . Her children play . . .* she repeated, and, waving her sceptre, figures advanced from the bushes.

Let swains and nymphs lead on the play, while Zephyr sleeps, and the unruly tribes of Heaven confess my sway.

A merry little old tune was played on the gramophone. Old Bartholomew joined his finger tips; Mrs. Manresa smoothed her skirts about her knees.

> *Young Damon said to Cynthia*
> *Come out now with the dawn*
> *And don your azure tippet*
> *And cast your cares adown*
> *For peace has come to England,*
> *And reason now holds sway.*
> *What pleasure lies in dreaming*
> *When blue and green's the day?*
> *Now cast your cares behind you.*
> *Night passes: here is Day.*

Digging and delving, the villagers sang passing in single file in and out between the trees, *for the earth is always the same, summer and winter and spring; and spring and winter again; ploughing and sowing, eating and growing; time passes. . . .*

The wind blew the words away.

The dance stopped. The nymphs and swains withdrew. Reason held the centre of the stage alone. Her arms extended, her robes flowing, holding orb and sceptre, Mabel Hopkins stood sublimely looking over the heads of the audience. The audience gazed at her. She ignored the audience. Then while she gazed, helpers from the bushes arranged round her what appeared to be the three sides of a room. In the middle they stood a table. On the table they placed a china tea service. Reason surveyed this domestic scene from her lofty eminence unmoved. There was a pause.

"Another scene from another play, I suppose," said Mrs. Elmhurst, referring to her programme. She read out for the benefit of her husband, who was deaf: *"Where there's a Will there's a Way.* That's the name of the play. And the characters. . . ." She read out: "Lady Harpy Harraden, in love with Sir Spaniel Lilyliver. Deb, her maid. Flavinda, her niece, in love with Valentine. Sir Spaniel Lilyliver, in love with Flavinda. Sir Smirking Peace-be-with-you-all, a clergyman. Lord and Lady Fribble. Valentine, in love with Flavinda. What names for real people! But look--here they come!"

Out they came from the bushes--men in flowered waistcoats, white waistcoats and buckled shoes; women wearing brocades tucked up, hooped and draped; glass stars, blue ribands and imitation pearls made them look the very image of Lords and Ladies.

"The first scene," Mrs. Elmhurst whispered into her husband's ear, "is Lady Harraden's dressing-room. . . . That's her. . . ." She pointed. "Mrs. Otter, I think, from the End House; but she's wonderfully made up. And that's Deb her maid. Who she is, I don't know."

"Hush, hush, hush," someone protested.

Mrs. Elmhurst dropped her programme. The play had begun.

Lady Harpy Harraden entered her dressing-room, followed by Deb her maid.

LADY H. H. . . . *Give me the pounce-box. Then the patch. Hand me the mirror, girl. So. Now my wig. . . . A pox on the girl--she's dreaming!*

DEB . . . *I was thinking, my lady, what the gentleman said when he saw you in the Park.*

LADY H. H. (gazing in the glass) *So, so--what was it? Some silly trash! Cupid's dart-- hah, hah! lighting his taper--tush--at my eyes. . . . pooh! That was in milord's time, twenty years since. . . . But now--what'll he say of me now?* (She looks in the mirror) *Sir Spaniel Lilyliver, I mean . . .* (a rap at the door) *Hark! That's his chaise at the door. Run child. Don't stand gaping.*

DEB . . . (going to the door) *Say? He'll rattle his tongue as a gambler rattles dice in a box. He'll find no words to fit you. He'll stand like a pig in a poke. . . . Your servant, Sir Spaniel.*

Enter Sir Spaniel.

SIR S. L. . . . *Hail, my fair Saint! What, out o' bed so early? Methought, as I came along the Mall the air was something brighter than usual. Here's the reason. . . . Venus, Aphrodite, upon my word a very galaxy, a constellation! As I'm a sinner, a very Aurora Borealis!*

(He sweeps his hat off.)

LADY H. H. *Oh flatterer, flatterer! I know your ways. But come. Sit down. . . . A glass of Aqua Vitae. Take this seat, Sir Spaniel. I've something very private and particular to say to you. . . . You had my letter, Sir?*

SIR S. L. . . . *Pinned to my heart!*

(He strikes his breast.)

LADY H. H. . . . *I have a favour to ask of you, Sir.*

SIR S. L. . . . (singing) *What favour could fair Chloe ask that Damon would not get her? . . . A done with rhymes. Rhymes are still-a-bed. Let's speak prose. What can Asphodilla ask of her plain servant Lilyliver? Speak out, Madam. An ape with a ring in his nose, or a strong young jackanapes to tell tales of us when we're no longer here to tell truth about ourselves?*

LADY H. H. (flirting her fan) *Fie, fie, Sir Spaniel. You make me blush--you do indeed. But come closer.* (She shifts her seat nearer to him) *We don't want the whole world to hear us.*

SIR S. L. (aside) *Come closer? A pox on my life! The old hag stinks like a red herring that's been stood over head in a tar barrel!* (Aloud) *Your meaning, Madam? You were saying?*

LADY H. H. *I have a niece, Sir Spaniel, Flavinda by name.*

SIR S. L. (aside) *Why that's the girl I love, to be sure!* (Aloud) *You have a niece, madam? I seem to remember hearing so. An only child, left by your brother, so I've heard, in your Ladyship's charge--him that perished at sea.*

LADY H. H. *The very same Sir. She's of age now and marriageable. I've kept her close as a weevil, Sir Spaniel, wrapped in the sere cloths of her virginity. Only maids about her, never a man to my knowledge, save Clout the serving man, who has a wart on his nose and a face like a nutgrater. Yet some fool has caught her fancy. Some gilded fly--some Harry, Dick; call him what you will.*

SIR S. L. (aside) *That's young Valentine, I warrant. I caught 'em at the play together.* (Aloud) *Say you so, Madam?*

LADY H. H. *She's not so ill favoured, Sir Spaniel--there's beauty in our line--but that a gentleman of taste and breeding like yourself now might take pity on her.*

SIR S. L. *Saving your presence, Madam. Eyes that have seen the sun are not so easily dazzled by the lesser lights--the Cassiopeias, Aldebarans, Great Bears and so on--A fig for them when the sun's up!*

LADY H. H. (ogling him) *You praise my hair-dresser, Sir, or my ear-rings* (she shakes her head).

SIR S. L. (aside) *She jingles like a she-ass at a fair! She's rigged like a barber's pole of a May Day.* (Aloud) *Your commands, Madam?*

LADY H. H. *Well Sir, t'was this way Sir. Brother Bob, for my father was a plain country gentleman and would have none of the fancy names the foreigners brought with 'em--Asphodilla I call myself, but my Christian name's plain Sue--Brother Bob, as I was telling you, ran away to sea; and, so they say, became Emperor of the Indies; where the very stones are emeralds and the sheep-crop rubies. Which, for a tenderer-hearted man never lived, he would have brought back with him, Sir, to mend the family fortunes, Sir. But the brig, frigate or what they call it, for I've no head for sea terms, never crossed a ditch without saying the Lord's Prayer backwards, struck a rock. The Whale had him. But the cradle was by the bounty of Heaven washed ashore. With the girl in it; Flavinda here. What's more to the point, with the Will in it; safe and sound; wrapped in parchment. Brother Bob's Will. Deb there! Deb I say! Deb!*

(She hollas for Deb)

SIR S. L. (aside) *Ah hah! I smell a rat! A will, quotha! Where there's a Will there's a Way.*

LADY H. H. (bawling) *The Will, Deb! The Will! In the ebony box by the right hand of the escritoire opposite the window. . . . A pox on the girl! She's dreaming. It's these romances, Sir Spaniel--these romances. Can't see a candle gutter but its her heart that's melting, or snuff a wick without reciting all the names in Cupid's Calendar . . .*

(Enter Deb carrying a parchment)

LADY H. H. *So . . . Give it here. The Will. Brother Bob's Will* (she mumbles over the Will).

LADY H. H. *To cut the matter short, Sir, for these lawyers even at the Antipodes are a long-winded race--*

SIR S. L. *To match their ears, Ma'am--*

LADY H. H. *Very true, very true. To cut the matter short, Sir, my brother Bob left all he died possessed of to his only child Flavinda; with this proviso, mark ye. That she marry to her Aunt's liking. Her Aunt; that's me. Otherwise, mark ye, all--to wit ten bushels of diamonds; item of rubies; item two hundred square miles of fertile territory bounding the River Amazon to the Nor-Nor-East; item his snuff box; item his flageolet--he was always one to love a tune, sir, Brother Bob; item six Macaws and as many Concubines as he had with him at the time of his decease--all this with other trifles needless to specify he left, mark ye, should she fail to marry to her Aunt's liking-- that's me--to found a Chapel, Sir Spaniel, where six poor Virgins should sing hymns in perpetuity for the repose of his soul--which, to speak the truth, Sir Spaniel, poor Brother Bob stands in need of, perambulating the Gulf Stream as he is and consorting with Syrens. But take it; read the Will yourself, Sir.*

SIR S. L. (reading) *"Must marry to her Aunt's liking." That's plain enough.*

LADY H. H. *Her Aunt, Sir. That's me. That's plain enough.*

SIR S. L. (aside) *She speaks the truth there!* (Aloud) *You would have me understand, Madam. . . . ?*

LADY H. H. *Hist! Come closer. Let me whisper in your ear . . . You and I have long entertained a high opinion of one another, Sir Spaniel. Played at ball together. Bound our wrists with daisy chains together. If I mind aright, you called me little bride--'tis fifty years since. We might have made a match of it, Sir Spaniel, had fortune favoured. . . . You take my meaning, Sir?*

SIR S. L. *Had it been written in letters of gold, fifty feet high, visible from Paul's Churchyard to the Goat and Compasses at Peckham, it could have been no plainer. . . . Hist, I'll whisper it. I, Sir Spaniel Lilyliver, do hereby bind myself to take thee--what's the name of the green girl that was cast up in a lobster pot covered with seaweed? Flavinda, eh? Flavinda, so--to be my wedded wife . . . O for a lawyer to have it all in writing!*

LADY H. H. *On condition, Sir Spaniel.*

SIR S. L. *On condition, Asphodilla.*

(Both speak together)

That the money is shared between us.

LADY H. H. *We want no lawyer to certify that! Your hand on it, Sir Spaniel!*

SIR S. L. *Your lips Madam!*

(They embrace)

SIR S. L. *Pah! She stinks!*

"Ha! Ha! Ha!" laughed the indigenous old lady in her bathchair.

"Reason, begad! Reason!" exclaimed old Bartholomew, and looked at his son as if exhorting him to give over these womanish vapours and be a man, Sir.

Giles sat straight as a dart, his feet tucked under him.

Mrs. Manresa had out her mirror and lipstick and attended to her lips and nose.

The gramophone, while the scene was removed, gently stated certain facts which everybody knows to be perfectly true. The tune said, more or less, how Eve, gathering her robes about her, stands reluctant still to let her dewy mantle fall. The herded flocks, the tune continued, in peace repose. The poor man to his cot returns, and, to the eager ears of wife and child, the simple story of his toil relates: what yield the furrow bears; and how the team the plover on the nest has spared; while Wat her courses ran; and speckled eggs in the warm hollow lay. Meanwhile the good wife on the table spreads her simple fare; and to the shepherd's flute, from toil released, the nymphs and swains join hands and foot it on the green. Then Eve lets down her sombre tresses brown and spreads her lucent veil o'er hamlet, spire, and mead, etc., etc. And the tune repeated itself once more.

The view repeated in its own way what the tune was saying. The sun was sinking; the colours were merging; and the view was saying how after toil men rest from their labours; how coolness comes; reason prevails; and having unharnessed the team from the plough, neighbours dig in cottage gardens and lean over cottage gates.

The cows, making a step forward, then standing still, were saying the same thing to perfection.

Folded in this triple melody, the audience sat gazing; and beheld gently and approvingly without interrogation, for it seemed inevitable, a box tree in a green tub take the place of the ladies' dressing-room; while on what seemed to be a wall, was hung a great clock face; the hands pointing to three minutes to the hour; which was seven.

Mrs. Elmhurst roused herself from her reverie; and looked at her programme.

"Scene Two. The Mall," she read out. "Time; early morning. Enter Flavinda. Here she comes!"

Here came Millie Loder (shop assistant at Messrs. Hunt and Dicksons, drapery emporium), in sprigged satin, representing Flavinda.

FLAV. *Seven he said, and there's the clock's word for it. But Valentine--where's Valentine? La! How my heart beats! Yet it's not the time o' day, for I'm often afoot before the sun's up in the meadows . . . See--the fine folk passing! All a-tiptoeing like peacocks with spread tails! And I in my petticoat that looked so fine by my Aunt's cracked mirror. Why, here it's a dish clout . . . And they heap their hair up like a birthday cake stuck about with candles. . . . That's a diamond--that's a ruby . . . Where's Valentine? The Orange Tree in the Mall, he said. The tree--there. Valentine-- nowhere. That's a courtier, I'll warrant, that old fox with his tail between his legs. That's a serving wench out without her master's knowledge. That's a man with a broom to sweep paths for the fine ladies' flounces . . . La! the red in their cheeks! They never got that in the fields, I warrant! O faithless, cruel, hard-hearted Valentine. Valentine! Valentine!*

(She wrings her hands, turning from side to side.)

Didn't I leave my bed a-tiptoe and steal like a mouse in the wainscot for fear of waking Aunt? And lard my hair from her powder box? And scrub my cheeks to make 'em shine? And lie awake watching the stars climb the chimney pots? And give my gold guinea that Godfather hid behind the mistletoe last Twelfth Night to Deb so she shouldn't tell on me? And grease the key in the lock so that Aunt shouldn't wake and shriek Flavvy! Flavvy! Val, I say Val--That's him coming. . . . No, I could tell him a mile off the way he strides the waves like what d'you call him in the picture book. . . . That's not Val. . . . That's a cit; that's a fop; raising his glass, prithee, to have his fill of me . . . I'll be home then . . . No, I won't . . . That's to play the green girl again and sew samplers . . . I'm of age, ain't I, come Michaelmas? Only three turns of the moon and I inherit . . . Didn't I read it in the Will the day the ball bounced on top of the old chest where Aunt keeps her furbelows, and the lid opened? . . ." All I die possessed of to my Daughter . . ." So far I'd read when the old lady came tapping down the passage like a blind man in an alley. . . . I'm no castaway, I'd have you know, Sir; no fishtailed mermaid with a robe of sea weed, at your mercy. I'm a match for any of 'em--the chits you dally with, and bid me meet you at the Orange Tree when you're drowsing the night off spent in their arms. . . . Fie upon you, Sir, making sport with a poor girl so. . . . I'll not cry, I swear I won't. I'll not brew a drop of the salt liquid for a man who's served me so. . . . Yet to think on't--how we hid in the dairy the day the cat jumped. And read romances under the holly tree. La! how I cried when the Duke left poor Polly. . . . And my Aunt found me with eyes like red jellies. "What stung, niece?" says she. And cried "Quick Deb, the blue bag." I told ye . . . La, to think I read it all in a book and cried for another! . . . Hist, what's there among the trees? It's come--it's gone. The breeze is it? In the shade now--in the sun now. . . . Valentine on my life! It's he! Quick, I'll hide. Let the tree conceal me!

(Flavinda hides behind the tree.)

He's here . . . He turns . . . He casts about . . . He's lost the scent . . . He gazes--this way, that way. . . . Let him feast his eyes on the fine faces--taste 'em, sample 'em, say: "That's the fine lady I danced with . . . that I lay with . . . that I kissed under the mistletoe . . ." Ha! How he spews 'em out! Brave Valentine! How he casts his eyes upon the ground! How his frowns become him! "Where's Flavinda?" he sighs. "She I love like the heart in my breast." See him pull his watch out! "O faithless wretch!" he sighs. See how he stamps the earth! Now turns on his heel. . . . He sees me--no, the sun's in his eyes. Tears fill 'em . . . Lord, how he fingers his sword! He'll run it through his breast like the Duke in the story book! . . . Stop, Sir, stop!

(She reveals herself)

VALENTINE. . . . *O Flavinda, O!*

FLAVINDA. . . . *O Valentine, O!*

(They embrace)

The clock strikes nine.

"All that fuss about nothing!" a voice exclaimed. People laughed. The voice stopped. But the voice had seen; the voice had heard. For a moment Miss La Trobe behind her tree glowed with glory. The next, turning to the villagers who were passing in and out between the trees, she barked:

"Louder! Louder!"

For the stage was empty; the emotion must be continued; the only thing to continue the emotion was the song; and the words were inaudible.

"Louder! Louder!" She threatened them with her clenched fists.

Digging and delving (they sang), *hedging and ditching, we pass. . . . Summer and winter, autumn and spring return . . . All passes but we, all changes . . . but we remain forever the same . .* . (the breeze blew gaps between their words.)

"Louder, louder!" Miss La Trobe vociferated.

Palaces tumble down (they resumed), *Babylon, Nineveh, Troy . . . And Caesar's great house . . . all fallen they lie . . . Where the plover nests was the arch. . . . through which the Romans trod . . . Digging and delving we break with the share of the plough the clod . . . Where Clytemnestra watched for her Lord . . . saw the beacons blaze on the hills . . . we see only the clod . . . Digging and delving we pass. . . . and the Queen and the Watch Tower fall . . . for Agamemnon has ridden away. . . . Clytemnestra is nothing but. . . .*

The words died away. Only a few great names--Babylon, Nineveh, Clytemnestra, Agamemnon, Troy--floated across the open space. Then the wind rose, and in the rustle of the leaves even the great words became inaudible; and the audience sat staring at the villagers, whose mouths opened, but no sound came.

And the stage was empty. Miss La Trobe leant against the tree, paralyzed. Her power had left her. Beads of perspiration broke on her forehead. Illusion had failed. "This is death," she murmured, "death."

Then suddenly, as the illusion petered out, the cows took up the burden. One had lost her calf. In the very nick of time she lifted her great moon-eyed head and bellowed. All the great moon-eyed heads laid themselves back. From cow after cow came the same yearning bellow. The whole world was filled with dumb yearning. It was the primeval voice sounding loud in the ear of the present moment. Then the whole herd caught the infection. Lashing their tails, blobbed like pokers, they tossed their heads high, plunged and bellowed, as if Eros had planted his dart in their flanks and goaded them to fury. The cows annihilated the gap; bridged the distance; filled the emptiness and continued the emotion.

Miss La Trobe waved her hand ecstatically at the cows.

"Thank Heaven!" she exclaimed.

Suddenly the cows stopped; lowered their heads, and began browsing. Simultaneously the audience lowered their heads and read their programmes.

"The producer," Mrs. Elmhurst read out for her husband's benefit, "craves the indulgence of the audience. Owing to lack of time a scene has been omitted; and she begs the audience to imagine that in the interval Sir Spaniel Lilyliver has contracted an engagement with Flavinda; who had been about to plight her troth; when Valentine, hidden inside the grandfather's clock, steps forward; claims Flavinda as his bride; reveals the plot to rob her of her inheritance; and, during the confusion that ensues, the lovers fly together, leaving Lady Harpy and Sir Spaniel alone together."

"We're asked to imagine all that," she said, putting down her glasses.

"That's very wise of her," said Mrs. Manresa, addressing Mrs. Swithin. "If she'd put it all in, we should have been here till midnight. So we've got to imagine, Mrs. Swithin." She patted the old lady on the knee.

"Imagine?" said Mrs. Swithin. "How right! Actors show us too much. The Chinese, you know, put a dagger on the table and that's a battle. And so Racine . . ."

"Yes, they bore one stiff," Mrs. Manresa interrupted, scenting culture, resenting the snub to the jolly human heart. "T'other day I took my nephew--such a jolly boy at Sandhurst--to *Pop Goes the Weasel*. Seen it?" She turned to Giles.

"Up and down the City Road," he hummed by way of an answer.

"Did your Nanny sing that!" Mrs. Manresa exclaimed. "Mine did. And when she said 'Pop' she made a noise like a cork being drawn from a ginger-beer bottle. Pop!"

She made the noise.

"Hush, hush," someone whispered.

"Now I'm being naughty and shocking your aunt," she said. "We must be good and attend. This is Scene Three. Lady Harpy Harraden's Closet. The sound of horses' hooves is heard in the distance."

The sound of horses' hooves, energetically represented by Albert the idiot with a wooden spoon on a tray, died away.

LADY H. H. *Half-way to Gretna Green already! O my deceitful niece! You that I rescued from the brine and stood on the hearthstone dripping! O that the whale had swallowed you whole! Perfidious porpoise, O! Didn't the Horn book teach you Honour thy Great Aunt? How have you misread it and misspelt it, learnt thieving and cheating and reading of wills in old boxes and hiding of rascals in honest time-pieces that have never missed a second since King Charles's day! O Flavinda! Oporpoise, O!*

SIR S. L. (trying to pull on his jack boots) *Old--old--old. He called me "old"--"To your bed, old fool, and drink hot posset!"*

LADY H. H. *And she, stopping at the door and pointing the finger of scorn at me said "old" Sir--"woman" Sir--I that am in the prime of life and a lady!*

SIR S. L. (tugging at his boots) *But I'll be even with him. I'll have the law on' em! I'll run 'em to earth . . .*

(He hobbles up and down, one boot on, one boot off)

LADY H. H. (laying her hand on his arm) *Have mercy on your gout, Sir Spaniel. Bethink you, Sir--let's not run mad, we that are on the sunny side of fifty. What's this youth they prate on? Nothing but a goose feather blown on a north wind. Sit you down, Sir Spaniel. Rest your leg--so--*

(She pushes a cushion under his leg)

SIR S. L. *"Old" he called me . . . jumping from the clock like a jack-in-the-box . . . And she, making mock of me, points to my leg and cries "Cupid's darts, Sir Spaniel, Cupid's darts." O that I could braise 'em in a mortar and serve 'em up smoking hot on the altar of--O my gout, O my gout!*

LADY H. H. *This talk, Sir, ill befits a man of sense. Bethink you, Sir, only t'other day you were invoking--ahem--the Constellations. Cassiopeia, Aldebaran; the Aurora Borealis . . . It's not to be denied that one of 'em has left her sphere, has shot, has eloped, to put it plainly, with the entrails of a time-piece, the mere pendulum of a grandfather's clock. But, Sir Spaniel, there are some stars that--ahem--stay fixed; that shine, to put it in a nutshell, never so bright as by a sea-coal fire on a brisk morning.*

SIR S. L. *O that I were five and twenty with a sharp sword at my side!*

LADY H. H. (bridling) *I take your meaning, Sir. Te hee--To be sure, I regret it as you do. But youth's not all. To let you into a secret, I've passed the meridian myself. Am on t'other side of the Equator too. Sleep sound o' nights without turning. The dog days are over. . . . But bethink you, Sir. Where there's a will there's a way.*

SIR S. L. *God's truth Ma'am . . . ah my foot's like a burning, burning horseshoe on the devil's anvil ah!--what's your meaning?*

LADY H. H. *My meaning, Sir? Must I disrupt my modesty and unquilt that which has been laid in lavender since, my lord, peace be to his name--'tis twenty years since--was lapped in lead? In plain words, Sir, Flavinda's flown. The cage is empty. But we that have bound our wrists with cowslips might join 'em with a stouter chain. To have done with fallals and figures. Here am I, Asphodilla--but my plain name Sue. No matter what my name is--Asphodilla or Sue--here am I, hale and hearty, at your service. Now that the plot's out, Brother Bob's bounty must go to the virgins. That's plain. Here's Lawyer Quill's word for it. "Virgins . . . in perpetuity . . . sing for his soul" And I warrant you, he has need of it . . . But no matter. Though we have thrown that to the fishes that might have wrapped us in lamb's-wool, I'm no beggar. There's messuages; tenements; napery; cattle; my dowry; an inventory. I'll show you; engrossed on parchment; enough I'll warrant you to keep us handsomely, for what's to run of our time, as husband and wife.*

SIR S. L. *Husband and wife! So that's the plain truth of it! Why, Madam, I'd rather lash myself to a tar barrel, be bound to a thorn tree in a winter's gale. Faugh!*

LADY H. H. *. . . . A tar barrel, quotha! A thorn tree--quotha! You that were harping on galaxies and milky ways! You that were swearing I outshone 'em all! A pox on you--you faithless! You shark, you! You serpent in jack boots, you! So you won't have me? Reject my hand do you?*

(She proffers her hand; he strikes it from him.)

SIR S. L. *. . . . Hide your chalk stones in a woollen mit! pah! I'll none of 'em! Were they diamond, pure diamond, and half the habitable globe and all its concubines strung in string round your throat I'd none of it . . . none of it. Unhand me, scritch owl, witch, vampire! Let me go!*

LADY H. H. *. . . . So all your fine words were tinsel wrapped round a Christmas cracker!*

SIR S. L. . . . *Bells hung on an ass's neck! Paper roses on a barber's pole . . . O my foot, my foot . . . Cupid's darts, she mocked me . . . Old, old, he called me old . . .*

(He hobbles away)

LADY H. H. (left alone) *All gone. Following the wind. He's gone; she's gone; and the old clock that the rascal made himself into a pendulum for is the only one of 'em all to stop. A pox on 'em—turning an honest woman's house into a brothel. I that was Aurora Borealis am shrunk to a tar barrel. I that was Cassiopeia am turned to a she-ass. My head turns. There's no trusting man nor woman; nor fine speeches; nor fine looks. Off comes the sheep's skin; out creeps the serpent. Get ye to Gretna Green; couch on the wet grass and breed vipers. My head spins . . . Tar barrels, quotha. Cassiopeia . . . Chalk stones . . . Andromeda . . . Thorn trees. . . . Deb, I say, Deb* (She holloas) *Unlace me. I'm fit to burst . . . Bring me my green baize table and set the cards. . . . And my fur lined slippers, Deb. And a dish of chocolate. . . . I'll be even with 'em . . . I'll outlive 'em all. . . . Deb, I say! Deb! A pox on the girl! Can't she hear me? Deb, I say, you gipsy's spawn that I snatched from the hedge and taught to sew samplers! Deb! Deb!*

(She throws open the door leading to the maid's closet)

Empty! She's gone too! . . . Hist, what's that on the dresser?

(She picks up a scrap of paper and reads)

"*What care I for your goose-feather bed? I'm off with the raggle-taggle gipsies, O! Signed: Deborah, one time your maid.*" *So! She that I fed on apple parings and crusts from my own table, she that I taught to play cribbage and sew chemises . . . she's gone too. O ingratitude, thy name is Deborah! Who's to wash the dishes now; who's to bring me my posset now, suffer my temper and unlace my stays? . . . All gone. I'm alone then. Sans niece, sans lover; and sans maid.*

> *And so to end the play, the moral is,*
> *The God of love is full of tricks;*
> *Into the foot his dart he sticks,*
> *But the way of the will is plain to see;*
> *Let holy virgins hymn perpetually:*
> "*Where there's a will there's a way*"
> *Good people all, farewell,*
> (dropping a curtsey, Lady H. H. withdrew)

The scene ended. Reason descended from her plinth. Gathering her robes about her, serenely acknowledging the applause of the audience, she passed across the stage; while Lords and Ladies in stars and garters followed after; Sir Spaniel limping escorted Lady Harraden smirking; and Valentine and Flavinda arm in arm bowed and curtsied.

"God's truth!" cried Bartholomew catching the infection of the language. "There's a moral for you!"

He threw himself back in his chair and laughed, like a horse whinnying.

A moral. What? Giles supposed it was: Where there's a Will there's a Way. The words rose and pointed a finger of scorn at him. Off to Gretna Green with his girl; the deed done. Damn the consequences.

"Like to see the greenhouse?" he said abruptly, turning to Mrs. Manresa.

"Love to!" she exclaimed, and rose.

Was there an interval? Yes, the programme said so. The machine in the bushes went chuff, chuff, chuff. And the next scene?

"The Victorian age," Mrs. Elmhurst read out. Presumably there was time then for a stroll round the gardens, even for a look over the house. Yet somehow they felt--how could one put it--a little not quite here or there. As if the play had jerked the ball out of the cup; as if what I call myself was still floating unattached, and didn't settle. Not quite themselves, they felt. Or was it simply that they felt clothes conscious? Skimpy out-of-date voile dresses; flannel trousers; panama hats; hats wreathed with raspberry-coloured net in the style of the Royal Duchess's hat at Ascot seemed flimsy somehow.

"How lovely the clothes were," said someone, casting a last look at Flavinda disappearing. "Most becoming. I wish . . ."

Chuff, chuff, chuff went the machine in the bushes, accurately, insistently.

Clouds were passing across the sky. The weather looked a little unsettled. Hogben's Folly was for a moment ashen white. Then the sun struck the gilt vane of Bolney Minster.

"Looks a little unsettled," said someone.

"Up you get . . . Let's stretch our legs," said another voice. Soon the lawns were floating with little moving islands of coloured dresses. Yet some of the audience remained seated.

"Major and Mrs. Mayhew," Page the reporter noted, licking his pencil. As for the play, he would collar Miss Whatshername and ask for a synopsis. But Miss La Trobe had vanished.

Down among the bushes she worked like a nigger. Flavinda was in her petticoats. Reason had thrown her mantle on a holly hedge. Sir Spaniel was tugging at his jack boots. Miss La Trobe was scattering and foraging.

"The Victorian mantle with the bead fringe . . . Where is the damned thing? Chuck it here . . . Now the whiskers . . ."

Ducking up and down she cast her quick bird's eye over the bushes at the audience. The audience was on the move. The audience was strolling up and down. They kept their distance from the dressing-room; they respected the conventions. But if they wandered too far, if they began exploring the grounds, going over the house, then. . . . Chuff, chuff, chuff went the machine. Time was passing. How long would time hold them together? It was a gamble; a risk. . . . And she laid about her energetically, flinging clothes on the grass.

Over the tops of the bushes came stray voices, voices without bodies, symbolical voices they seemed to her, half hearing, seeing nothing, but still, over the bushes, feeling invisible threads connecting the bodiless voices.

"It all looks very black."

"No one wants it--save those damned Germans."

There was a pause.

"I'd cut down those trees . . ."

"How they get their roses to grow!"

"They say there's been a garden here for five hundred years . . ."

"Why even old Gladstone, to do him justice . . ."

Then there was silence. The voices passed the bushes. The trees rustled. Many eyes, Miss La Trobe knew, for every cell in her body was absorbent, looked at the view. Out of the corner of her eye she could see Hogben's Folly; then the vane flashed.

"The glass is falling," said a voice.

She could feel them slipping through her fingers, looking at the view.

"Where's that damned woman, Mrs. Rogers? Who's seen Mrs. Rogers?" she cried, snatching up a Victorian mantle.

Then, ignoring the conventions, a head popped up between the trembling sprays: Mrs. Swithin's.

"Oh Miss La Trobe!" she exclaimed; and stopped. Then she began again; "Oh Miss La Trobe, I do congratulate you!"

She hesitated. "You've given me . . ." She skipped, then alighted--"Ever since I was a child I've felt . . ." A film fell over her eyes, shutting off the present. She tried to recall her childhood; then gave it up; and, with a little wave of her hand, as if asking Miss La Trobe to help her out, continued: "This daily round; this going up and down stairs; this saying 'What am I going for? My specs? I have 'em on my nose.' . . ."

She gazed at Miss La Trobe with a cloudless old-aged stare. Their eyes met in a common effort to bring a common meaning to birth. They failed; and Mrs. Swithin, laying hold desperately of a fraction of her meaning, said: "What a small part I've had to play! But you've made me feel I could have played . . . Cleopatra!"

She nodded between the trembling bushes and ambled off.

The villagers winked. "Batty" was the word for old Flimsy, breaking through the bushes.

"I might have been--Cleopatra," Miss La Trobe repeated. "You've stirred in me my unacted part," she meant.

"Now for the skirt, Mrs. Rogers," she said.

Mrs. Rogers stood grotesque in her black stockings. Miss La Trobe pulled the voluminous flounces of the Victorian age over her head. She tied the tapes. "You've twitched the invisible strings," was what the old lady meant; and revealed--of all people--Cleopatra! Glory possessed her. Ah, but she was not merely a twitcher of individual strings; she was one who seethes wandering bodies and floating voices in a cauldron, and makes rise up from its amorphous mass a recreated world. Her moment was on her--her glory.

"There!" she said, tying the black ribbons under Mrs. Rogers' chin. "That's done it! Now for the gentleman. Hammond!"

She beckoned Hammond. Sheepishly he came forward, and submitted to the application of black side whiskers. With his eyes half shut, his head leant back, he looked, Miss La Trobe thought, like King Arthur--noble, knightly, thin.

"Where's the Major's old frock coat?" she asked, trusting to the effect of that to transform him.

Tick, tick, tick, the machine continued. Time was passing. The audience was wandering, dispersing. Only the tick tick of the gramophone held them together. There, sauntering solitary far away by the flower beds was Mrs. Giles escaping.

"The tune!" Miss La Trobe commanded. "Hurry up! The tune! The next tune! Number Ten!"

"Now may I pluck," Isa murmured, picking a rose, "my single flower. The white or the pink? And press it so, twixt thumb and finger. . . ."

She looked among the passing faces for the face of the man in grey. There he was for one second; but surrounded, inaccessible. And now vanished.

She dropped her flower. What single, separate leaf could she press? None. Nor stray by the beds alone. She must go on; and she turned in the direction of the stable.

"Where do I wander?" she mused. "Down what draughty tunnels? Where the eyeless wind blows? And there grows nothing for the eye. No rose. To issue where? In some harvestless dim field where no evening lets fall her mantle; nor sun rises. All's equal there. Unblowing, ungrowing are the roses there. Change is not; nor the mutable and lovable; nor greetings nor partings; nor furtive findings and feelings, where hand seeks hand and eye seeks shelter from the eye."

She had come into the stable yard where the dogs were chained; where the buckets stood; where the great pear tree spread its ladder of branches against the wall. The tree whose roots went beneath the flags, was weighted with hard green pears. Fingering one of them she murmured: "How am I burdened with what they drew from the earth; memories; possessions. This is the burden that the past laid on me, last little donkey in the long caravanserai crossing the desert. 'Kneel down,' said the past. 'Fill your pannier from our tree. Rise up, donkey. Go your way till your heels blister and your hoofs crack.'"

The pear was hard as stone. She looked down at the cracked flags beneath which the roots spread. "That was the burden," she mused, "laid on me in the cradle; murmured by waves; breathed by restless elm trees; crooned by singing women; what we must remember; what we would forget."

She looked up. The gilt hands of the stable clock pointed inflexibly at two minutes to the hour. The clock was about to strike.

"Now comes the lightning," she muttered, "from the stone blue sky. The thongs are burst that the dead tied. Loosed are our possessions."

Voices interrupted. People passed the stable yard, talking.

"It's a good day, some say, the day we are stripped naked. Others, it's the end of the day. They see the Inn and the Inn's keeper. But none speaks with a single voice. None with a voice free from the old vibrations. Always I hear corrupt murmurs; the chink of gold and metal. Mad music. . . ."

More voices sounded. The audience was streaming back to the terrace. She roused herself. She encouraged herself. "On little donkey, patiently stumble. Hear not the frantic cries of the leaders who in that they seek to lead desert us. Nor the chatter of china faces glazed and hard. Hear rather the shepherd, coughing by the farmyard wall; the withered tree that sighs when the Rider gallops; the brawl in the barrack room when they stripped her naked; or the cry which in London when I thrust the window open someone cries . . ." She had come out on to the path that led past the greenhouse. The door was kicked open. Out came Mrs. Manresa and Giles. Unseen, Isa followed them across the lawns to the front row of seats.

The chuff, chuff, chuff of the machine in the bushes had stopped. In obedience to Miss La Trobe's command, another tune had been put on the gramophone. Number Ten. London street cries it was called. "A Pot Pourri."

"Lavender, sweet lavender, who'll buy my sweet lavender" the tune trilled and tinkled, ineffectively shepherding the audience. Some ignored it. Some still wandered. Others stopped, but stood upright. Some, like Colonel and Mrs. Mayhew, who had never left their seats, brooded over the blurred carbon sheet which had been issued for their information.

"The Nineteenth Century." Colonel Mayhew did not dispute the producer's right to skip two hundred years in less than fifteen minutes. But the choice of scenes baffled him.

"Why leave out the British Army? What's history without the Army, eh?" he mused. Inclining her head, Mrs. Mayhew protested after all one mustn't ask too much. Besides, very likely there would be a Grand Ensemble, round the Union Jack, to end with. Meanwhile, there was the view. They looked at the view.

"Sweet lavender . . . sweet lavender. . . ." Humming the tune old Mrs. Lynn Jones (of the Mount) pushed a chair forward. "Here Etty," she said, and plumped down, with Etty Springett, with whom, since both were widows now, she shared a house.

"I remember . . ." she nodded in time to the tune, "You remember too--how they used to cry it down the streets." They remembered--the curtains blowing, and the men crying: "All a blowing, all a growing," as they came with geraniums, sweet william, in pots, down the street.

"A harp, I remember, and a hansom and a growler. So quiet the street was then. Two for a hansom, was it? One for a growler? And Ellen, in cap and apron, whistling in the street? D'you remember? And the runners, my dear, who followed, all the way from the station, if one had a box."

The tune changed. "Any old iron, any old iron to sell?" "D'you remember? That was what the men shouted in the fog. Seven Dials they came from. Men with red handkerchiefs. Garotters, did they call them? You couldn't walk--O, dear me, no-- home from the play. Regent Street. Piccadilly. Hyde Park Corner. The loose women . . . And everywhere loaves of bread in the gutter. The Irish you know round Covent Garden . . . Coming back from a Ball, past the clock at Hyde Park Corner, d'you remember the feel of white gloves? . . . My father remembered the old Duke in the Park. Two fingers like that--he'd touch his hat . . . I've got my mother's album. A lake and two lovers. She'd copied out Byron, I suppose, in what was called then the Italian hand. . . ."

"What's that? 'Knocked 'em in the Old Kent Road.' I remember the bootboy whistled it. O, my dear, the servants . . . Old Ellen . . . Sixteen pound a year wages . . . And the cans of hot water! And the crinolines! And the stays! D'you remember the Crystal Palace, and the fireworks, and how Mira's slipper got lost in the mud?"

"That's young Mrs. Giles . . . I remember her mother. She died in India . . . We wore, I suppose, a great many petticoats then. Unhygienic? I dare say . . . Well, look at my daughter. To the right, just behind you. Forty, but slim as a wand. Each flat has its refrigerator . . . It took my mother half the morning to order dinner. . . . We were eleven. Counting servants, eighteen in family. . . . Now they simply ring up the Stores . . . That's Giles coming, with Mrs. Manresa. She's a type I don't myself fancy. I may be wrong . . . And Colonel Mayhew, as spruce as ever . . . And Mr. Cobbet of Cobbs Corner, there, under the Monkey Puzzle Tree. One don't see him often . . . That's what's so nice--it brings people together. These days, when we're all so busy, that's what one wants . . . The programme? Have you got it? Let's see what comes next . . . The Nineteenth Century . . . Look, there's the chorus, the villagers, coming on now, between the trees. First, there's a prologue. . . ."

A great box, draped in red baize festooned with heavy gold tassels had been moved into the middle of the stage. There was a swish of dresses, a stir of chairs. The audience seated themselves, hastily, guiltily. Miss La Trobe's eye was on them. She gave them ten seconds to settle their faces. Then she flicked her hand. A pompous march tune brayed. "Firm, elatant, bold and blatant," etc. . . . And once more a huge symbolical figure emerged from the bushes. It was Budge the publican; but so disguised that even cronies who drank with him nightly failed to recognize him; and a little titter of enquiry as to his identity ran about among the villagers. He wore a long black many-caped cloak; waterproof; shiny; of the substance of a statue in Parliament Square; a helmet which suggested a policeman; a row of medals crossed his breast; and in his right hand he held extended a special constable's baton (loaned by Mr. Willert of the Hall). It was his voice, husky and rusty, issuing from a thick black cotton-wool beard that gave him away.

"Budge, Budge. That's Mr. Budge," the audience whispered.

Budge extended his truncheon and spoke:

It ain't an easy job, directing the traffic at 'Yde Park Corner. Buses and 'ansom cabs. All a-clatter on the cobbles. Keep to the right, can't you? Hi there, Stop!

(He waved his truncheon)

There she goes, the old party with the umbrella right under the 'orse's nose.

(The truncheon pointed markedly at Mrs. Swithin)

She raised her skinny hand as if in truth she had fluttered off the pavement on the impulse of the moment to the just rage of authority. Got her, Giles thought, taking sides with authority against his aunt.

Fog or fine weather, I does my duty (Budge continued). *At Piccadilly Circus; at 'Yde Park Corner, directing the traffic of 'Er Majesty's Empire. The Shah of Persia; Sultan of Morocco; or it may be 'Er Majesty in person; or Cook's tourists; black men; white men; sailors, soldiers; crossing the ocean; to proclaim her Empire; all of 'em Obey the Rule of my truncheon.*

(He flourished it magnificently from right to left)

But my job don't end there. I take under my protection and direction the purity and security of all Her Majesty's minions; in all parts of her dominions; insist that they obey the laws of God and Man.

The laws of God and Man (he repeated and made as if to consult a Statute; engrossed on a sheet of parchment which with great deliberation he now produced from his trouser pocket)

Go to Church on Sunday; on Monday, nine sharp, catch the City Bus. On Tuesday it may be, attend a meeting at the Mansion House for the redemption of the sinner; at dinner on Wednesday attend another--turtle soup. Some bother it may be in Ireland; Famine. Fenians. What not. On Thursday it's the natives of Peru require protection and correction; we give 'em what's due. But mark you, our rule don't end there. It's a Christian country, our Empire; under the White Queen Victoria. Over thought and religion; drink; dress; manners; marriage too, I wield my truncheon. Prosperity and respectability always go, as we know, 'and in 'and. The ruler of an Empire must keep his eye on the cot; spy too in the kitchen; drawing-room; library; wherever one or two, me and you, come together. Purity our watchword; prosperity and respectability. If not, why, let 'em fester in . . .

(He paused--no, he had not forgotten his words)

Cripplegate; St. Giles's; Whitechapel; the Minories. Let 'em sweat at the mines; cough at the looms; rightly endure their lot. That's the price of Empire; that's the white man's burden. And, I can tell you, to direct the traffic orderly, at 'Yde Park Corner, Piccadilly Circus, is a whole-time, white man's job.

He paused, eminent, dominant, glaring from his pedestal. A very fine figure of a man he was, everyone agreed, his truncheon extended; his waterproof pendant. It only wanted a shower of rain, a flight of pigeons round his head, and the pealing bells of St. Paul's and the Abbey to transform him into the very spit and image of a Victorian constable; and to transport them to a foggy London afternoon, with the muffin bells ringing and the church bells pealing at the very height of Victorian prosperity.

There was a pause. The voices of the pilgrims singing, as they wound in and out between the trees, could be heard; but the words were inaudible. The audience sat waiting.

"Tut-tut-tut," Mrs. Lynn-Jones expostulated. "There were grand men among them . . ." Why she did not know, yet somehow she felt that a sneer had been aimed at her father; therefore at herself.

Etty Springett tutted too. Yet, children did draw trucks in mines; there was the basement; yet Papa read Walter Scott aloud after dinner; and divorced ladies were not received at Court. How difficult to come to any conclusion! She wished they would hurry on with the next scene. She liked to leave a theatre knowing exactly what was meant. Of course this was only a village play. . . . They were setting another scene, round the red baize box. She read out from her programme:

"The Picnic Party. About 1860. Scene: A Lake. Characters--"

She stopped. A sheet had been spread on the Terrace. It was a lake apparently. Roughly painted ripples represented water. Those green stakes were bulrushes. Rather prettily, real swallows darted across the sheet.

"Look, Minnie!" she exclaimed. "Those are real swallows!"

"Hush, hush," she was admonished. For the scene had begun. A young man in peg-top trousers and side whiskers carrying a spiked stick appeared by the lake.

EDGAR T. . . . *Let me help you, Miss Hardcastle! There!*

(he helps Miss Eleanor Hardcastle, a young lady in crinoline and mushroom hat to the top. They stand for a moment panting slightly, looking at the view.)

ELEANOR. *How small the Church looks down among the trees!*

EDGAR. . . . *So this is Wanderer's Well, the trysting-place.*

ELEANOR. . . . *Please Mr. Thorold, finish what you were saying before the others come. You were saying, "Our aim in life . . ."*

EDGAR. . . . *Should be to help our fellow men.*

ELEANOR (sighing deeply) *How true--how profoundly true!*

EDGAR. . . . *Why sigh, Miss Hardcastle?--You have nothing to reproach yourself with-- you whose whole life is spent in the service of others. It was of myself that I was thinking. I am no longer young. At twenty-four the best days of life are over. My life has passed* (he throws a pebble on to the lake) *like a ripple in water.*

ELEANOR. *Oh Mr, Thorold, you do not know me. I am not what I seem. I too--*

EDGAR. . . . *Do not tell me, Miss Hardcastle--no, I cannot believe it--You have doubted?*

ELEANOR. *Thank Heaven not that, not that . . . But safe and sheltered as I am, always at home, protected as you see me, as you think me. O what am I saying? But yes, I will speak the truth, before Mama comes. I too have longed to convert the heathen!*

EDGAR. . . . *Miss Hardcastle . . . Eleanor . . . You tempt me! Dare I ask you? No--so young, so fair, so innocent. Think, I implore you, before you answer.*

ELEANOR. . . . *I have thought--on my knees!*

EDGAR (taking a ring from his pocket) *Then. . . . My mother with her last breath charged me to give this ring only to one to whom a lifetime in the African desert among the heathens would be--*

ELEANOR (taking the ring) *Perfect happiness! But hist!* (She slips the ring into her pocket) *Here's Mama!* (They start asunder)

(Enter Mrs. Hardcastle, a stout lady in black bombazine, upon a donkey, escorted by an elderly gentleman in a deer-stalker's cap)

MRS. H. . . . *So you stole a march upon us, young people. There was a time, Sir John, when you and I were always first on top. Now . . .*

(He helps her to alight. Children, young men, young women, some carrying hampers, others butterfly nets, others spy-glasses, others tin botanical cases arrive. A rug is thrown by the lake and Mrs. H. and Sir John seat themselves on camp stools.)

MRS. H. . . . *Now who'll fill the kettles? Who'll gather the sticks? Alfred* (to a small boy), *don't run about chasing butterflies or you'll make yourself sick . . . Sir John and I will unpack the hampers, here where the grass is burnt, where we had the picnic last year.*

(The young people scatter off in different directions. Mrs. H. and Sir John begin to unpack the hamper)

MRS. H. . . . *Last year poor dear Mr. Beach was with us. It was a blessed release.* (She takes out a black-bordered handkerchief and wipes her eyes). *Every year one of us is missing. That's the ham . . . That's the grouse . . . There in that packet are the game pasties . . .* (She spreads the eatables on the grass) *As I was saying poor dear Mr. Beach . . . I do hope the cream hasn't curdled. Mr. Hardcastle is bringing the claret. I always leave that to him. Only when Mr. Hardcastle gets talking with Mr. Pigott about the Romans . . . last year they quite came to words. . . . But it's nice for gentlemen to have a hobby, though they do gather the dust--those skulls and things. . . . But I was saying--poor dear Mr. Beach. . . . I wanted to ask you* (she drops her voice) *as a friend of the family, about the new clergyman--they can't hear us, can they? No, they're picking up sticks. . . . Last year, such a disappointment. Just got the things out . . . down came the rain. But I wanted to ask you, about the new clergyman, the one who's come in place of dear Mr. Beach. I'm told the name's Sibthorp. To be sure, I hope I'm right, for I had a cousin who married a girl of that name, and as a friend of the family, we don't stand on ceremony . . . And when one has daughters--I'm sure I quite envy you, with only one daughter, Sir John, and I have four! So I was asking you to tell me in confidence, about this young--if that's-his-name--Sibthorp, for I must tell you the day before yesterday our Mrs. Potts happened to say, as she passed the Rectory, bringing our laundry, they were unpacking the furniture; and what did she see on top of the wardrobe? A tea cosy! But of course she might be mistaken . . . But it occurred to me to ask you, as a friend of the family, in confidence,* has Mr. Sibthorp a wife?

Here a chorus composed of villagers in Victorian mantles, side whiskers and top hats sang in concert:

O has Mr. Sibthorp a wife? O has Mr. Sibthorp a wife? That is the hornet, the bee in the bonnet, the screw in the cork and the drill; that whirling and twirling are for ever unfurling the folds of the motherly heart; for a mother must ask, if daughters she has, begot in the feathery billowy fourposter family bed, O did he unpack, with his prayer book and bands; his gown and his cane; his rod and his line; and the family album and gun; did he also display the connubial respectable tea-table token, a cosy with honeysuckle embossed. Has Mr. Sibthorp a wife? O has Mr. Sibthorp a wife?

While the chorus was sung, the picnickers assembled. Corks popped. Grouse, ham, chickens were sliced. Lips munched. Glasses were drained. Nothing was heard but the chump of jaws and the chink of glasses.

"They did eat," Mrs. Lynn Jones whispered to Mrs. Springett. "That's true. More than was good for them, I dare say."

MR. HARDCASTLE . . . (brushing flakes of meat from his whiskers) *Now . . .*

"Now what?" whispered Mrs. Springett, anticipating further travesty.

Now that we have gratified the inner man, let us gratify the desire of the spirit. I call upon one of the young ladies for a song.

CHORUS OF YOUNG LADIES . . . *O not me . . . not me . . . I really couldn't . . . No, you cruel thing, you know I've lost my voice . . . I can't sing without the instrument . . . etc., etc.*

CHORUS OF YOUNG MEN. *O bosh! Let's have "The Last Rose of Summer." Let's have "I never loved a Dear Gazelle."*

MRS. H. (authoritatively) *Eleanor and Mildred will now sing "I'd be a Butterfly."*

(Eleanor and Mildred rise obediently and sing a duet: "I'd be a Butterfly.")

MRS. H. *Thank you very much, my dears. And now gentlemen, Our Country!*

(Arthur and Edgar sing "Rule Britannia.")

MRS. H. . . . *Thank you very much. Mr. Hardcastle--*

MR. HARDCASTLE (rising to his feet, clasping his fossil) *Let us pray.*

(the whole company rise to their feet)

"This is too much, too much," Mrs. Springett protested.

MR. H. . . . *Almighty God, giver of all good things, we thank Thee; for our food and drink; for the beauties of Nature; for the understanding with which Thou hast enlightened us* (he fumbled with his fossil) *And for thy great gift of Peace. Grant us to be thy servants on earth; grant us to spread the light of thy . . .*

Here the hindquarters of the donkey, represented by Albert the idiot, became active. Intentional was it, or accidental? "Look at the donkey! Look at the donkey!" A titter drowned Mr. Hardcastle's prayer; and then he was heard saying:

. . . a happy homecoming with bodies refreshed by thy bounty, and minds inspired by thy wisdom. Amen.

Holding his fossil in front of him, Mr. Hardcastle marched off. The donkey was captured; hampers were loaded; and forming into a procession, the picnickers began to disappear over the hill.

EDGAR (winding up the procession with Eleanor) *To convert the heathen!*

ELEANOR. *To help our fellow men!*

(The actors disappeared into the bushes.)

BUDGE. . . . *It's time, gentlemen, time ladies, time to pack up and be gone. From where I stand, truncheon in hand, guarding respectability, and prosperity, and the purity of Victoria's land, I see before me--*(he pointed: there was Pointz Hall; the rooks cawing; the smoke rising)

'Ome, Sweet 'Ome.

The gramophone took up the strain: *Through pleasures and palaces, etc. There's no place like Home.*

BUDGE. . . . *Home, gentlemen; home, ladies, it's time to pack up and go home. Don't I see the fire* (he pointed: one window blazed red) *blazing ever higher? In kitchen; and nursery; drawing-room and library? That's the fire of 'Ome. And see! Our Jane has brought the tea. Now children where's the toys? Mama, your knitting, quick. For here* (he swept his truncheon at Cobbet of Cobbs Corner) *comes the bread-winner, home from the city, home from the counter, home from the shop. "Mama, a cup o' tea." "Children, gather round my knee. I will read aloud. Which shall it be? Sindbad the sailor? Or some simple tale from the Scriptures? And show you the pictures? What none of 'em? Then out with the bricks. Let's build: A conservatory. A laboratory? A mechanics' institute? Or shall it be a tower; with our flag on top; where our widowed Queen, after tea, calls the Royal orphans round her knee? For it's 'Ome, ladies, 'Ome, gentlemen. Be it never so humble, there's no place like 'Ome."*

The gramophone warbled Home, Sweet Home, and Budge, swaying slightly, descended from his box and followed the procession off the stage.

There was an interval.

"Oh but it was beautiful," Mrs. Lynn Jones protested. Home she meant; the lamplit room; the ruby curtains; and Papa reading aloud.

They were rolling up the lake and uprooting the bulrushes. Real swallows were skimming over real grass. But she still saw the home.

"It was . . ." she repeated, referring to the home.

"Cheap and nasty, I call it," snapped Etty Springett, referring to the play, and shot a vicious glance at Dodge's green trousers, yellow spotted tie, and unbuttoned waistcoat.

But Mrs. Lynn Jones still saw the home. Was there, she mused, as Budge's red baize pediment was rolled off, something--not impure, that wasn't the word--but perhaps "unhygienic" about the home? Like a bit of meat gone sour, with whiskers, as the servants called it? Or why had it perished? Time went on and on like the hands of the kitchen clock. (The machine chuffed in the bushes.) If they had met with no resistance, she mused, nothing wrong, they'd still be going round and round and round. The Home would have remained; and Papa's beard, she thought, would have grown and grown; and Mama's knitting--what did she do with all her knitting?-- Change had to come, she said to herself, or there'd have been yards and yards of Papa's beard, of Mama's knitting. Nowadays her son-in-law was clean shaven. Her daughter had a refrigerator. . . . Dear, how my mind wanders, she checked herself. What she meant was, change had to come, unless things were perfect; in which case she supposed they resisted Time. Heaven was changeless.

"Were they like that?" Isa asked abruptly. She looked at Mrs. Swithin as if she had been a dinosaur or a very diminutive mammoth. Extinct she must be, since she had lived in the reign of Queen Victoria.

Tick, tick, tick, went the machine in the bushes.

"The Victorians," Mrs. Swithin mused. "I don't believe" she said with her odd little smile, "that there ever were such people. Only you and me and William dressed differently."

"You don't believe in history," said William.

The stage remained empty. The cows moved in the field. The shadows were deeper under the trees.

Mrs. Swithin caressed her cross. She gazed vaguely at the view. She was off, they guessed, on a circular tour of the imagination--one-making. Sheep, cows, grass, trees, ourselves--all are one. If discordant, producing harmony--if not to us, to a gigantic ear attached to a gigantic head. And thus--she was smiling benignly--the agony of the particular sheep, cow, or human being is necessary; and so--she was beaming seraphically at the gilt vane in the distance--we reach the conclusion that *all* is harmony, could we hear it. And we shall. Her eyes now rested on the white summit of a cloud. Well, if the thought gave her comfort, William and Isa smiled across her, let her think it.

Tick tick tick the machine reiterated.

"D'you get her meaning?" said Mrs. Swithin alighting suddenly. "Miss La Trobe's?"

Isa, whose eyes had been wandering, shook her head.

"But you might say the same of Shakespeare," said Mrs. Swithin.

"Shakespeare and the musical glasses!" Mrs. Manresa intervened. "Dear, what a barbarian you all make me feel!"

She turned to Giles. She invoked his help against this attack upon the jolly human heart.

"Tosh," Giles muttered.

Nothing whatever appeared on the stage.

Darts of red and green light flashed from the rings on Mrs. Manresa's fingers. He looked from them at Aunt Lucy. From her to William Dodge. From him to Isa. She refused to meet his eyes. And he looked down at his blood-stained tennis shoes.

He said (without words) "I'm damnably unhappy."

"So am I," Dodge echoed.

"And I too," Isa thought.

They were all caught and caged; prisoners; watching a spectacle. Nothing happened. The tick of the machine was maddening.

"On, little donkey" Isa murmured, "crossing the desert . . . bearing your burden . . ."

She felt Dodge's eye upon her as her lips moved. Always some cold eye crawled over the surface like a winter blue-bottle! She flicked him off.

"What a time they take!" she exclaimed irritably.

"Another interval," Dodge read out, looking at the programme.

"And after that, what?" asked Lucy.

"Present time. Ourselves," he read.

"Let's hope to God that's the end," said Giles gruffly.

"Now you're being naughty," Mrs. Manresa reproved her little boy, her surly hero.

No one moved. There they sat, facing the empty stage, the cows, the meadows and the view, while the machine ticked in the bushes.

"What's the object," said Bartholomew, suddenly rousing himself, "of this entertainment?"

"The profits," Isa read out from her blurred carbon copy, "are to go to a fund for installing electric light in the Church."

"All our village festivals," Mr. Oliver snorted turning to Mrs. Manresa, "end with a demand for money."

"Of course, of course," she murmured, deprecating his severity, and the coins in her bead bag jingled.

"Nothing's done for nothing in England," the old man continued. Mrs. Manresa protested. It might be true, perhaps, of the Victorians; but surely not of ourselves? Did she really believe that we were disinterested? Mr. Oliver demanded.

"Oh you don't know my husband!" the wild child exclaimed, striking an attitude.

Admirable woman! You could trust her to crow when the hour struck like an alarm clock; to stop like an old bus horse when the bell rang. Oliver said nothing. Mrs. Manresa had out her mirror and attended to her face.

All their nerves were on edge. They sat exposed. The machine ticked. There was no music. The horns of cars on the high road were heard. And the swish of trees. They were neither one thing nor the other; neither Victorians nor themselves. They were suspended, without being, in limbo. Tick, tick, tick went the machine.

Isa fidgeted; glancing to right and to left over her shoulder.

"Four and twenty blackbirds, strung upon a string," she muttered.

"Down came an Ostrich, an eagle, an executioner,

'Which of you is ripe,' he said, 'to bake in my pie?

Which of you is ripe, which of you is ready,

Come my pretty gentleman,

Come my pretty lady.' . . ."

How long was she going to keep them waiting? "The present time. Ourselves." They read it on the programme. Then they read what came next: "The profits are to go to a fund for installing electric light in the Church." Where was the Church? Over there. You could see the spire among the trees.

"Ourselves. . . ." They returned to the programme. But what could she know about ourselves? The Elizabethans yes; the Victorians, perhaps; but ourselves; sitting here on a June day in 1939--it was ridiculous. "Myself"--it was impossible. Other people, perhaps . . . Cobbet of Cobbs Corner; the Major; old Bartholomew; Mrs. Swithin--them, perhaps. But she won't get me--no, not me. The audience fidgeted. Sounds of laughter came from the bushes. But nothing whatsoever appeared on the stage.

"What's she keeping us waiting for?" Colonel Mayhew asked irritably. "They don't need to dress up if it's present time."

Mrs. Mayhew agreed. Unless of course she was going to end with a Grand Ensemble. Army; Navy; Union Jack; and behind them perhaps--Mrs. Mayhew sketched what she would have done had it been her pageant--the Church. In cardboard. One window, looking east, brilliantly illuminated to symbolize--she could work that out when the time came.

"There she is, behind the tree," she whispered, pointing at Miss La Trobe.

Miss La Trobe stood there with her eye on her script. "After Vic." she had written, "try ten mins. of present time. Swallows, cows etc." She wanted to expose them, as it were, to douche them, with present-time reality. But something was going wrong with the experiment. "Reality too strong," she muttered. "Curse 'em!" She felt everything they felt. Audiences were the devil. O to write a play without an audience--*the* play. But here she was fronting her audience. Every second they were slipping the noose. Her little game had gone wrong. If only she'd a back-cloth to hang between the trees--to shut out cows, swallows, present time! But she had nothing. She had forbidden music. Grating her fingers in the bark, she damned the audience. Panic seized her. Blood seemed to pour from her shoes. This is death, death, death, she noted in the margin of her mind; when illusion fails. Unable to lift her hand, she stood facing the audience.

And then the shower fell, sudden, profuse.

No one had seen the cloud coming. There it was, black, swollen, on top of them. Down it poured like all the people in the world weeping. Tears, Tears. Tears.

"O that our human pain could here have ending!" Isa murmured. Looking up she received two great blots of rain full in her face. They trickled down her cheeks as if they were her own tears. But they were all people's tears, weeping for all people. Hands were raised. Here and there a parasol opened. The rain was sudden and universal. Then it stopped. From the grass rose a fresh earthy smell.

"That's done it," sighed Miss La Trobe, wiping away the drops on her cheeks. Nature once more had taken her part. The risk she had run acting in the open air was justified. She brandished her script. Music began--A.B.C.--A.B.C. The tune was as simple as could be. But now that the shower had fallen, it was the other voice speaking, the voice that was no one's voice. And the voice that wept for human pain unending said:

> *The King is in his counting house,*
> *Counting out his money,*
> *The Queen is in her parlour . . .*

"O that my life could here have ending," Isa murmured (taking care not to move her lips). Readily would she endow this voice with all her treasure if so be tears could be ended. The little twist of sound could have the whole of her. On the altar of the rain-soaked earth she laid down her sacrifice. . . .

"O look!" she cried aloud.

That was a ladder. And that (a cloth roughly painted) was a wall. And that a man with a hod on his back. Mr. Page the reporter, licking his pencil, noted: "With the very limited means at her disposal, Miss La Trobe conveyed to the audience Civilization (the wall) in ruins; rebuilt (witness man with hod) by human effort; witness also woman handing bricks. Any fool could grasp that. Now issued black man in fuzzy wig; coffee-coloured ditto in silver turban; they signify presumably the League of . . ."

A burst of applause greeted this flattering tribute to ourselves. Crude of course. But then she had to keep expenses down. A painted cloth must convey--what the *Times*and *Telegraph* both said in their leaders that very morning.

The tune hummed:

> *The King is in his counting house,*
> *Counting out his money,*
> *The Queen is in her parlour*
> *Eating . . .*

Suddenly the tune stopped. The tune changed. A waltz, was it? Something half known, half not. The swallows danced it. Round and round, in and out they skimmed. Real swallows. Retreating and advancing. And the trees, O the trees, how gravely and sedately like senators in council, or the spaced pillars of some cathedral church. . . . Yes, they barred the music, and massed and hoarded; and prevented what was fluid from overflowing. The swallows--or martins were they?--The temple-haunting martins who come, have always come . . . Yes, perched on the wall, they seemed to foretell what after all the *Times* was saying yesterday. Homes will be built. Each flat with its refrigerator, in the crannied wall. Each of us a free man; plates washed by machinery; not an aeroplane to vex us; all liberated; made whole. . . .

The tune changed; snapped; broke; jagged. Fox-trot was it? Jazz? Anyhow the rhythm kicked, reared, snapped short. What a jangle and a jingle! Well, with the means at her disposal, you can't ask too much. What a cackle, a cacophony! Nothing ended. So abrupt. And corrupt. Such an outrage; such an insult. And not plain. Very up to date, all the same. What is her game? To disrupt? Jog and trot? Jerk and smirk? Put the finger to the nose? Squint and pry? Peak and spy? O the irreverence of the generation which is only momentarily--thanks be--"the young." The young, who can't make, but only break; shiver into splinters the old vision; smash to atoms what was whole. What a cackle, what a rattle, what a yaffle--as they call the woodpecker, the laughing bird that flits from tree to tree.

Look! Out they come, from the bushes--the riff-raff. Children? Imps--elves--demons. Holding what? Tin cans? Bedroom candlesticks? Old jars? My dear, that's the cheval glass from the Rectory! And the mirror--that I lent her. My mother's. Cracked. What's the notion? Anything that's bright enough to reflect, presumably, ourselves?

Ourselves! Ourselves!

Out they leapt, jerked, skipped. Flashing, dazzling, dancing, jumping. Now old Bart . . . he was caught. Now Manresa. Here a nose . . . There a skirt . . . Then trousers only . . . Now perhaps a face. . . . Ourselves? But that's cruel. To snap us as we are, before we've had time to assume . . . And only, too, in parts. . . . That's what's so distorting and upsetting and utterly unfair.

Mopping, mowing, whisking, frisking, the looking glasses darted, flashed, exposed. People in the back rows stood up to see the fun. Down they sat, caught themselves . . . What an awful show-up! Even for the old who, one might suppose, hadn't any longer any care about their faces. . . . And Lord! the jangle and the din! The very cows joined in. Walloping, tail lashing, the reticence of nature was undone, and the barriers which should divide Man the Master from the Brute were dissolved. Then the dogs joined in. Excited by the uproar, scurrying and worrying, here they came! Look at them! And the hound, the Afghan hound . . . look at him!

Then once more, in the uproar which by this time has passed quite beyond control, behold Miss Whatshername behind the tree summoned from the bushes--or was it*they* who broke away--Queen Bess; Queen Anne; and the girl in the Mall; and the Age of Reason; and Budge the policeman. Here they came. And the Pilgrims. And the lovers. And the grandfather's clock. And the old man with a beard. They all appeared. What's more, each declaimed some phrase or fragment from their parts . . . . *I am not (said one) in my perfect mind . . . Another, Reason am I . . . And I? I'm the old top hat. . . . Home is the hunter, home from the hill . . . Home? Where the miner sweats, and the maiden faith is rudely strumpeted. . . . Sweet and low; sweet and low, wind of the western sea . . . Is* *that a dagger that I see before me? . . . The owl hoots and the ivy mocks tap-tap-tapping on the pane. . . . Lady I love till I die, leave thy chamber and come . . . Where the worm weaves its winding sheet . . . I'd be a butterfly. I'd be a butterfly. . . . In thy will is our peace. . . . Here, Papa, take your book and read aloud. . . . Hark, hark, the dogs do bark and the beggars . . .*

It was the cheval glass that proved too heavy. Young Bonthorp for all his muscle couldn't lug the damned thing about any longer. He stopped. So did they all-- hand glasses, tin cans, scraps of scullery glass, harness room glass, and heavily embossed silver mirrors--all stopped. And the audience saw themselves, not whole by any means, but at any rate sitting still.

The hands of the clock had stopped at the present moment. It was now. Ourselves.

So that was her little game! To show us up, as we are, here and how. All shifted, preened, minced; hands were raised, legs shifted. Even Bart, even Lucy, turned away. All evaded or shaded themselves--save Mrs. Manresa who, facing herself in the glass, used it as a glass; had out her mirror; powdered her nose; and moved one curl, disturbed by the breeze, to its place.

"Magnificent!" cried old Bartholomew. Alone she preserved unashamed her identity, and faced without blinking herself. Calmly she reddened her lips.

The mirror bearers squatted; malicious; observant; expectant; expository.

"That's them," the back rows were tittering. "Must we submit passively to this malignant indignity?" the front row demanded. Each turned ostensibly to say--O whatever came handy--to his neighbour. Each tried to shift an inch or two beyond the inquisitive insulting eye. Some made as if to go.

"The play's over, I take it," muttered Colonel Mayhew, retrieving his hat. "It's time . . ."

But before they had come to any common conclusion, a voice asserted itself. Whose voice it was no one knew. It came from the bushes--a megaphontic, anonymous, loud-speaking affirmation. The voice said:

Before we part, ladies and gentlemen, before we go . . . (Those who had risen sat down) . . . let's talk in words of one syllable, without larding, stuffing or cant. Let's break the rhythm and forget the rhyme. And calmly consider ourselves. Ourselves. Some bony. Some fat. (The glasses confirmed this.) Liars most of us. Thieves too.(The glasses made no comment on that.) The poor are as bad as the rich are. Perhaps worse. Don't hide among rags. Or let our cloth protect us. Or for the matter of that book learning; or skilful practice on pianos; or laying on of paint. Or presume there's innocency in childhood. Consider the sheep. Or faith in love. Consider the dogs. Or virtue in those that have grown white hairs. Consider the gun slayers, bomb droppers here or there. They do openly what we do shyly. Take for example (here the megaphone adopted a colloquial, conversational tone) Mr. M's bungalow. A view spoilt for ever. That's murder . . . Or Mrs. E's lipstick and blood-red nails. . . . A tyrant, remember, is half a slave. Item the vanity of Mr. H. the writer, scraping in the dunghill for sixpenny fame . . . Then there's the amiable condescension of the lady of the manor--the upper class manner. And buying shares in the market to sell 'em. . . . O we're all the same. Take myself now. Do I escape my own reprobation, simulating indignation, in the bush, among the leaves? There's a rhyme, to suggest, in spite of protestation and the desire for immolation, I too have had some, what's called, education . . . Look at ourselves, ladies and gentlemen! Then at the wall; and ask how's this wall, the great wall, which we call, perhaps miscall, civilization, to be built by (here the mirrors flicked and flashed) orts, scraps and fragments like ourselves?

All the same here I change (by way of the rhyme mark ye) to a loftier strain--there's something to be said: for our kindness to the cat; note too in to-day's paper "Dearly loved by his wife"; and the impulse which leads us--mark you, when no one's looking--to the window at midnight to smell the bean. Or the resolute refusal of some pimpled dirty little scrub in sandals to sell his soul. There is such a thing--you can't deny it. What? You can't descry it? All you can see of yourselves is scraps, orts and fragments? Well then listen to the gramophone affirming. . . .

A hitch occurred here. The records had been mixed. Fox trot, Sweet lavender, Home Sweet Home, Rule Britannia--sweating profusely, Jimmy, who had charge of the music, threw them aside and fitted the right one--was it Bach, Handel, Beethoven, Mozart or nobody famous, but merely a traditional tune? Anyhow, thank heaven, it was somebody speaking after the anonymous bray of the infernal megaphone.

Like quicksilver sliding, filings magnetized, the distracted united. The tune began; the first note meant a second; the second a third. Then down beneath a force was born in opposition; then another. On different levels they diverged. On different levels ourselves went forward; flower gathering some on the surface; others descending to wrestle with the meaning; but all comprehending; all enlisted. The whole population of the mind's immeasurable profundity came flocking; from the unprotected, the unskinned; and dawn rose; and azure; from chaos and cacophony measure; but not the melody of surface sound alone controlled it; but also the warring battle-plumed warriors straining asunder: To part? No. Compelled from the ends of the horizon; recalled from the edge of appalling crevasses; they crashed; solved; united. And some relaxed their fingers; and others uncrossed their legs.

Was that voice ourselves? Scraps, orts and fragments, are we, also, that? The voice died away.

As waves withdrawing uncover; as mist uplifting reveals; so, raising their eyes (Mrs. Manresa's were wet; for an instant tears ravaged her powder) they saw, as waters withdrawing leave visible a tramp's old boot, a man in a clergyman's collar surreptitiously mounting a soap-box.

"The Rev. G. W. Streatfield," the reporter licked his pencil and noted "then spoke . . ."

All gazed. What an intolerable constriction, contraction, and reduction to simplified absurdity he was to be sure! Of all incongruous sights a clergyman in the livery of his servitude to the summing up was the most grotesque and entire. He opened his mouth. O Lord, protect and preserve us from words the defilers, from words the impure! What need have we of words to remind us? Must I be Thomas, you Jane?

As if a rook had hopped unseen to a prominent bald branch, he touched his collar and hemmed his preliminary croak. One fact mitigated the horror; his forefinger, raised in the customary manner, was stained with tobacco juice. He wasn't such a bad fellow; the Rev. G. W. Streatfield; a piece of traditional church furniture;

a corner cupboard; or the top beam of a gate, fashioned by generations of village carpenters after some lost-in-the-mists-of-antiquity model.

He looked at the audience; then up at the sky. The whole lot of them, gentles and simples, felt embarrassed, for him, for themselves. There he stood their representative spokesman; their symbol; themselves; a butt, a clod, laughed at by looking-glasses; ignored by the cows, condemned by the clouds which continued their majestic rearrangement of the celestial landscape; an irrelevant forked stake in the flow and majesty of the summer silent world.

His first words (the breeze had risen; the leaves were rustling) were lost. Then he was heard saying: "What." To that word he added another "Message"; and at last a whole sentence emerged; not comprehensible; say rather audible. "What message," it seemed he was asking, "was our pageant meant to convey?"

They folded their hands in the traditional manner as if they were seated in church.

"I have been asking myself"--the words were repeated--"what meaning, or message, this pageant was meant to convey?"

If he didn't know, calling himself Reverend, also M.A., who after all could?

"As one of the audience," he continued (words now put on meaning) "I will offer, very humbly, for I am not a critic"--and he touched the white gate that enclosed his neck with a yellow forefinger--"my interpretation. No, that is too bold a word. The gifted lady . . ." He looked round. La Trobe was invisible. He continued: "Speaking merely as one of the audience, I confess I was puzzled. For what reason, I asked, were we shown these scenes? Briefly, it is true. The means at our disposal this afternoon were limited. Still we were shown different groups. We were shown, unless I mistake, the effort renewed. A few were chosen; the many passed in the background. That surely we were shown. But again, were we not given to understand--am I too presumptuous? Am I treading, like angels, where as a fool I should absent myself? To me at least it was indicated that we are members one of another. Each is part of the whole. Yes, that occurred to me, sitting among you in the audience. Did I not perceive Mr. Hardcastle here" (he pointed) "at one time a Viking? And in Lady Harridan--excuse me, if I get the names wrong--a Canterbury pilgrim? We act different parts; but are the same. That I leave to you. Then again, as the play or pageant proceeded, my attention was distracted. Perhaps that too was part of the producer's intention? I thought I perceived that nature takes her part. Dare we, I asked myself, limit life to ourselves? May we not hold that there is a spirit that inspires, pervades . . ." (the swallows were sweeping round him. They seemed cognizant of his meaning. Then they swept out of sight.) "I leave that to you. I am not here to explain. That role has not been assigned me. I speak only as one of the audience, one of ourselves. I caught myself too reflected, as it happened in my own mirror . . ." (Laughter) "Scraps, orts and fragments! Surely, we should unite?"

"But" ("but" marked a new paragraph) "I speak also in another capacity. As Treasurer of the Fund. In which capacity" (he consulted a sheet of paper) "I am glad to be able to tell you that a sum of thirty-six pounds ten shillings and eightpence has been raised by this afternoon's entertainment towards our object: the illumination of our dear old church."

"Applause," the reporter reported.

Mr. Streatfield paused. He listened. Did he hear some distant music?

He continued: "But there is still a deficit" (he consulted his paper) "of one hundred and seventy-five pounds odd. So that each of us who has enjoyed this pageant has still an opp . . ." The word was cut in two. A zoom severed it. Twelve aeroplanes in perfect formation like a flight of wild duck came overhead. *That* was the music. The audience gaped; the audience gazed. Then zoom became drone. The planes had passed.

". . . portunity," Mr. Streatfield continued, "to make a contribution." He signalled. Instantly collecting boxes were in operation. Hidden behind glasses they emerged. Coppers rattled. Silver jingled. But O what a pity--how creepy it made one feel! Here came Albert, the idiot, jingling his collecting box--an aluminium saucepan without a lid. You couldn't very well deny him, poor fellow. Shillings were dropped. He rattled and sniggered; chattered and jibbered. As Mrs. Parker made her contribution--half a crown as it happened--she appealed to Mr. Streatfield to exorcize this evil, to extend the protection of his cloth.

The good man contemplated the idiot benignly. His faith had room, he indicated, for him too. He too, Mr. Streatfield appeared to be saying, is part of ourselves. But not a part we like to recognize, Mrs. Springett added silently, dropping her sixpence.

Contemplating the idiot, Mr. Streatfield had lost the thread of his discourse. His command over words seemed gone. He twiddled the cross on his watchchain. Then his hand sought his trouser pocket. Surreptitiously he extracted a small silver box. It was plain to all that the natural desire of the natural man was overcoming him. He had no further use for words.

"And now," he resumed, cuddling the pipe lighter in the palm of his hand, "for the pleasantest part of my duty. To propose a vote of thanks to the gifted lady . . ." He looked round for an object corresponding to this description. None such was visible. ". . . who wishes it seems to remain anonymous." He paused. "And so . . ." He paused again.

It was an awkward moment. How to make an end? Whom to thank? Every sound in nature was painfully audible; the swish of the trees; the gulp of a cow; even the skim of the swallows over the grass could be heard. But no one spoke. Whom could they make responsible? Whom could they thank for their entertainment? Was there no one?

Then there was a scuffle behind the bush; a preliminary premonitory scratching. A needle scraped a disc; chuff, chuff chuff; then having found the rut, there was a roll and a flutter which portended *God* . . . (they all rose to their feet) *Save the King.*

Standing the audience faced the actors; who also stood with their collecting boxes quiescent, their looking-glasses hidden, and the robes of their various parts hanging stiff.

Happy and glorious,
Long to reign over us
God save the King

The notes died away.

Was that the end? The actors were reluctant to go. They lingered; they mingled. There was Budge the policeman talking to old Queen Bess. And the Age of Reason hobnobbed with the foreparts of the donkey. And Mrs. Hardcastle patted out the folds of her crinoline. And little England, still a child, sucked a peppermint drop out of a bag. Each still acted the unacted part conferred on them by their clothes. Beauty was on them. Beauty revealed them. Was it the light that did it?--the tender, the fading, the uninquisitive but searching light of evening that reveals depths in water and makes even the red brick bungalow radiant?

"Look," the audience whispered, "O look, look, look.--" And once more they applauded; and the actors joined hands and bowed.

Old Mrs. Lynn Jones, fumbling for her bag, sighed, "What a pity--must they change?"

But it was time to pack up and be off.

"Home, gentlemen; home ladies; it's time to pack up and be off," the reporter whistled, snapping the band round his notebook. And Mrs. Parker was stooping.

"I'm afraid I've dropped my glove. I'm so sorry to trouble you. Down there, between the seats. . . ."

The gramophone was affirming in tones there was no denying, triumphant yet valedictory: *Dispersed are we; who have come together. But*, the gramophone asserted, *let us retain whatever made that harmony.*

O let us, the audience echoed (stooping, peering, fumbling), keep together. For there is joy, sweet joy, in company.

Dispersed are we, the gramophone repeated.

And the audience turning saw the flaming windows, each daubed with golden sun; and murmured: "Home, gentlemen; sweet. . ." yet delayed a moment, seeing through the golden glory perhaps a crack in the boiler; perhaps a hole in the carpet; and hearing, perhaps, the daily drop of the daily bill.

Dispersed are we, the gramophone informed them. And dismissed them. So, straightening themselves for the last time, each grasping, it might be a hat, or a stick or a pair of suede gloves, for the last time they applauded Budge and Queen Bess; the trees; the white road; Bolney Minster; and the Folly. One hailed another, and they dispersed, across lawns, down paths, past the house to the gravel-strewn crescent, where cars, push bikes and cycles were crowded together.

Friends hailed each other in passing.

"I do think," someone was saying, "Miss Whatshername should have come forward and not left it to the rector . . . After all, she wrote it. . . . I thought it brilliantly clever . . . O my dear, I thought it utter bosh. Did *you* understand the meaning? Well, he said she meant we all act all parts. . . . He said, too, if I caught his meaning, Nature takes part. . . . Then there was the idiot. . . . Also, why leave out the Army, as my husband was saying, if it's history? And if one spirit animates the whole, what about the aeroplanes? . . . Ah, but you're being too exacting. After all, remember, it was only a village play. . . . For my part, I think they should have passed a vote of thanks to the owners. When we had our pageant, the grass didn't recover till autumn . . . Then we had tents. . . . That's the man, Cobbet of Cobbs Corner, who wins all the prizes at all the shows. I don't myself admire prize flowers, nor yet prize dogs . . ."

Dispersed are we, the gramophone triumphed, yet lamented, *Dispersed are we*. . . .

"But you must remember," the old cronies chatted, "they had to do it on the cheap. You can't get people, at this time o' year, to rehearse. There's the hay, let alone the movies. . . . What we need is a centre. Something to bring us all together . . . The Brookes have gone to Italy, in spite of everything. Rather rash? . . . If the worst should come--let's hope it won't--they'd hire an aeroplane, so they said. . . . What amused me was old Streatfield, feeling for his pouch. I like a man to be natural, not always on a perch . . . Then those voices from the bushes. . . . Oracles? You're referring to the Greeks? Were the oracles, if I'm not being irreverent, a foretaste of our own religion? Which is what? . . . Crepe soles? That's so sensible . . . They last much longer and protect the feet. . . . But I was saying: can the Christian faith adapt itself? In times like these . . . At Larting no one goes to church . . . There's the dogs, there's the pictures. . . . It's odd that science, so they tell me, is making things (so to speak) more spiritual . . . The very latest notion, so I'm told is, nothing's solid . . . There, you can get a glimpse of the church through the trees. . . .

"Mr. Umphelby! How nice to see you! Do come and dine . . . No, alas, we're going back to town. The House is sitting . . . I was telling them, the Brookes have gone to Italy. They've seen the volcano. Most impressive, so they say--they were lucky--in eruption. I agree--things look worse than ever on the continent. And what's the channel, come to think of it, if they mean to invade us? The aeroplanes, I didn't like to say it, made one think. . . . No, I thought it much too scrappy. Take the idiot. Did she mean, so to speak, something hidden, the unconscious as they call it? But why always drag in sex. . . . It's true, there's a sense in which we all, I admit, are savages still. Those women with red nails. And dressing up--what's that? The old savage, I suppose. . . . That's the bell. Ding dong. Ding . . . Rather a cracked old bell . . . And the mirrors! Reflecting us . . . I called that cruel. One feels such a fool, caught unprotected . . . There's Mr. Streatfield, going, I suppose to take the evening service. He'll have to hurry, or he won't have time to change. . . . He said she meant we all act. Yes, but whose play? Ah, that's the question! And if we're left asking questions, isn't it a failure, as a play? I must say I like to feel sure if I go to the theatre, that I've grasped the meaning . . . Or was that, perhaps, what she meant? . . . Ding dong. Ding . . . that if we don't jump to conclusions, if you think, and I think, perhaps one day, thinking differently, we shall think the same?

"There's dear old Mr. Carfax . . . Can't we give you a lift, if you don't mind playing bodkin? We were asking questions, Mr. Carfax, about the play. The looking-glasses now--did they mean the reflection is the dream; and the tune--was it Bach, Handel, or no one in particular--is the truth? Or was it t'other way about?

"Bless my soul, what a dither! Nobody seems to know one car from another. That's why I have a mascot, a monkey . . . But I can't see it . . . While we're waiting, tell me, did you feel when the shower fell, someone wept for us all? There's a poem, *Tears tears tears*, it begins. And goes on *O then the unloosened ocean* . . . but I can't remember the rest.

"Then when Mr. Streatfield said: One spirit animates the whole--the aeroplanes interrupted. That's the worst of playing out of doors. . . . Unless of course she meant that very thing . . . Dear me, the parking arrangements are not what you might call adequate . . . I shouldn't have expected either so many Hispano-Suizas . . . That's a Rolls . . . That's a Bentley . . . That's the new type of Ford. . . . To return to the meaning--Are machines the devil, or do they introduce a discord . . . Ding dong, ding . . . by means of which we reach the final . . . Ding dong. . . . Here's the car with the monkey . . . Hop in . . . And good-bye, Mrs. Parker . . . Ring us up. Next time we're down don't forget . . . Next time . . . Next time . . ."

The wheels scrurred on the gravel. The cars drove off.

The gramophone gurgled *Unity--Dispersity*. It gurgled *Un . . dis* . . . And ceased.

The little company who had come together at luncheon were left standing on the terrace. The pilgrims had bruised a lane on the grass. Also, the lawn would need a deal of clearing up. Tomorrow the telephone would ring: "Did I leave my handbag? . . . A pair of spectacles in a red leather case? . . . A little old brooch of no value to anyone but me?" Tomorrow the telephone would ring. Now Mr. Oliver said: "Dear lady," and, taking Mrs. Manresa's gloved hand in his, pressed it, as if to say: "You have given me what you now take from me." He would have liked to hold on for a moment longer to the emeralds and rubies dug up, so people said, by thin Ralph Manresa in his ragamuffin days. But alas, sunset light was unsympathetic to her make-up; plated it looked, not deeply interfused. And he dropped her hand; and she gave him an arch roguish twinkle, as if to say--but the end of that sentence was cut short. For she turned, and Giles stepped forward; and the light breeze which the meteorologist had foretold fluttered her skirts; and she went, like a goddess, buoyant, abundant, with flower-chained captives following in her wake.

All were retreating, withdrawing and dispersing; and he was left with the ash grown cold and no glow, no glow on the log. What word expressed the sag at his heart, the effusion in his veins, as the retreating Manresa, with Giles attendant, admirable woman, all sensation, ripped the rag doll and let the sawdust stream from his heart?

The old man made a guttural sound, and turned to the right. On with the hobble, on with the limp, since the dance was over. He strolled alone past the trees. It was here, early that very morning, that he had destroyed the little boy's world. He had popped out with his newspaper; the child had cried.

Down in the dell, past the lily pool, the actors were undressing. He could see them among the brambles. In vests and trousers; unhooking; buttoning up: on all fours; stuffing clothes into cheap attaché cases; with silver swords, beards and emeralds on the grass. Miss La Trobe in coat and skirt--too short, for her legs were stout--battled with the billows of a crinoline. He must respect the conventions. So he stopped, by the pool. The water was opaque over the mud.

Then, coming up behind him, "Oughtn't we to thank her?" Lucy asked him. She gave him a light pat on the arm.

How imperceptive her religion made her! The fumes of that incense obscured the human heart. Skimming the surface, she ignored the battle in the mud. After La Trobe had been excruciated by the Rector's interpretation, by the maulings and the manglings of the actors . . . "She don't want our thanks, Lucy," he said gruffly. What she wanted, like that carp (something moved in the water) was darkness in the mud; a whisky and soda at the pub; and coarse words descending like maggots through the waters.

"Thank the actors, not the author," he said. "Or ourselves, the audience."

He looked over his shoulder. The old lady, the indigenous, the prehistoric, was being wheeled away by a footman. He rolled her through the arch. Now the lawn was empty. The line of the roof, the upright chimneys, rose hard and red against the blue of the evening. The house emerged; the house that had been obliterated. He was damned glad it was over--the scurry and the scuffle, the rouge and the rings. He stooped and raised a peony that had shed its petals. Solitude had come again. And reason and the lamplit paper. . . . But where was his dog? Chained in a kennel? The little veins swelled with rage on his temples. He whistled. And here, released by Candish, racing across the lawn with a fleck of foam on the nostril, came his dog.

Lucy still gazed at the lily pool. "All gone," she murmured, "under the leaves." Scared by shadows passing, the fish had withdrawn. She gazed at the water. Perfunctorily she caressed her cross. But her eyes went water searching, looking for fish. The lilies were shutting; the red lily, the white lily, each on its plate of leaf. Above, the air rushed; beneath was water. She stood between two fluidities, caressing her cross. Faith required hours of kneeling in the early morning. Often the delight of the roaming eye seduced her--a sunbeam, a shadow. Now the jagged leaf at the corner suggested, by its contours, Europe. There were other leaves. She fluttered her eye over the surface, naming leaves India, Africa, America. Islands of security, glossy and thick.

"Bart . . ." She spoke to him. She had meant to ask him about the dragon-fly-- couldn't the blue thread settle, if we destroyed it here, then there? But he had gone into the house.

Then something moved in the water; her favourite fantail. The golden orfe followed. Then she had a glimpse of silver--the great carp himself, who came to the surface so very seldom. They slid on, in and out between the stalks, silver; pink; gold; splashed; streaked; pied.

"Ourselves," she murmured. And retrieving some glint of faith from the grey waters, hopefully, without much help from reason, she followed the fish; the speckled, streaked, and blotched; seeing in that vision beauty, power, and glory in ourselves.

Fish had faith, she reasoned. They trust us because we've never caught 'em. But her brother would reply: "That's greed." "Their beauty!" she protested. "Sex," he would say. "Who makes sex susceptible to beauty?" she would argue. He shrugged who? Why? Silenced, she returned to her private vision; of beauty which is goodness; the sea on which we float. Mostly impervious, but surely every boat sometimes leaks?

He would carry the torch of reason till it went out in the darkness of the cave. For herself, every morning, kneeling, she protected her vision. Every night she opened the window and looked at leaves against the sky. Then slept. Then the random ribbons of birds' voices woke her.

The fish had come to the surface. She had nothing to give them--not a crumb of bread. "Wait, my darlings," she addressed them. She would trot into the house and ask Mrs. Sands for a biscuit. Then a shadow fell. Off they flashed. How vexatious! Who was it? Dear me, the young man whose name she had forgotten; not Jones; nor Hodge . . .

Dodge had left Mrs. Manresa abruptly. All over the garden he had been searching for Mrs. Swithin. Now he found her; and she had forgotten his name.

"I'm William," he said. At that she revived, like a girl in a garden in white, among roses, who came running to meet him--an unacted part.

"I was going to get a biscuit--no, to thank the actors," she stumbled, virginal, blushing. Then she remembered her brother. "My brother," she added "says one mustn't thank the author, Miss La Trobe."

It was always "my brother . . . my brother" who rose from the depths of her lily pool.

As for the actors, Hammond had detached his whiskers and was now buttoning up his coat. When the chain was inserted between the buttons he was off.

Only Miss La Trobe remained, bending over something in the grass.

"The play's over," he said. "The actors have departed."

"And we mustn't, my brother says, thank the author," Mrs. Swithin repeated, looking in the direction of Miss La Trobe.

"So I thank you," he said. He took her hand and pressed it. Putting one thing with another, it was unlikely that they would ever meet again.

The church bells always stopped, leaving you to ask: Won't there be another note? Isa, half-way across the lawn, listened. . . . Ding, dong, ding . . . There was not going to be another note. The congregation was assembled, on their knees, in the church. The service was beginning. The play was over; swallows skimmed the grass that had been the stage.

There was Dodge, the lip reader, her semblable, her conspirator, a seeker like her after hidden faces. He was hurrying to rejoin Mrs. Manresa who had gone in front with Giles--"the father of my children," she muttered. The flesh poured over her, the hot, nerve wired, now lit up, now dark as the grave physical body. By way of healing the rusty fester of the poisoned dart she sought the face that all day long she had been seeking. Preening and peering, between backs, over shoulders, she had sought the man in grey. He had given her a cup of tea at a tennis party; handed her, once, a racquet. That was all. But, she was crying, had we met before the salmon leapt like a bar of silver . . . had we met, she was crying. And when her little boy came battling through the bodies in the Barn "Had he been his son," she had muttered . . . In passing she stripped the bitter leaf that grew, as it happened, outside the nursery window. Old Man's Beard. Shrivelling the shreds in lieu of words, for no words grow there, nor roses either, she swept past her conspirator, her semblable, the seeker after vanished faces "like Venus" he thought, making a rough translation, "to her prey . . ." and followed after.

Turning the corner, there was Giles attached to Mrs. Manresa. She was standing at the door of her car. Giles had his foot on the edge of the running board. Did they perceive the arrows about to strike them?

"Jump in, Bill," Mrs. Manresa chaffed him.

And the wheels scurred on the gravel, and the car drove off.

At last, Miss La Trobe could raise herself from her stooping position. It had been prolonged to avoid attention. The bells had stopped; the audience had gone; also the actors. She could straighten her back. She could open her arms. She could say to the world, You have taken my gift! Glory possessed her--for one moment. But what had she given? A cloud that melted into the other clouds on the horizon. It was in the giving that the triumph was. And the triumph faded. Her gift meant nothing. If they had understood her meaning; if they had known their parts; if the pearls had been real and the funds illimitable--it would have been a better gift. Now it had gone to join the others.

"A failure," she groaned, and stooped to put away the records.

Then suddenly the starlings attacked the tree behind which she had hidden. In one flock they pelted it like so many winged stones. The whole tree hummed with the whizz they made, as if each bird plucked a wire. A whizz, a buzz rose from the bird-buzzing, bird-vibrant, bird-blackened tree. The tree became a rhapsody, a quivering cacophony, a whizz and vibrant rapture, branches, leaves, birds syllabling discordantly life, life, life, without measure, without stop devouring the tree. Then up! Then off!

What interrupted? It was old Mrs. Chalmers, creeping through the grass with a bunch of flowers--pinks apparently--to fill the vase that stood on her husband's grave. In winter it was holly, or ivy. In summer, a flower. It was she who had scared the starlings. Now she passed.

Miss La Trobe nicked the lock and hoisted the heavy case of gramophone records to her shoulder. She crossed the terrace and stopped by the tree where the starlings had gathered. It was here that she had suffered triumph, humiliation, ecstasy, despair--for nothing. Her heels had ground a hole in the grass.

It was growing dark. Since there were no clouds to trouble the sky, the blue was bluer, the green greener. There was no longer a view--no Folly, no spire of Bolney Minster. It was land merely, no land in particular. She put down her case and stood looking at the land. Then something rose to the surface.

"I should group them," she murmured, "here." It would be midnight; there would be two figures, half concealed by a rock. The curtain would rise. What would the first words be? The words escaped her.

Again she lifted the heavy suit case to her shoulder. She strode off across the lawn. The house was dormant; one thread of smoke thickened against the trees. It was strange that the earth, with all those flowers incandescent--the lilies, the roses, and clumps of white flowers and bushes of burning green--should still be hard. From the earth green waters seemed to rise over her. She took her voyage away from the shore, and, raising her hand, fumbled for the latch of the iron entrance gate.

She would drop her suit case in at the kitchen window, and then go on up to the Inn. Since the row with the actress who had shared her bed and her purse the need of drink had grown on her. And the horror and the terror of being alone. One of these days she would break--which of the village laws? Sobriety? Chastity? Or take something that did not properly belong to her?

At the corner she ran into old Mrs. Chalmers returning from the grave. The old woman looked down at the dead flowers she was carrying and cut her. The women in the cottages with the red geraniums always did that. She was an outcast. Nature had somehow set her apart from her kind. Yet she had scribbled in the margin of her manuscript: "I am the slave of my audience."

She thrust her suit case in at the scullery window and walked on, till at the corner she saw the red curtain at the bar window. There would be shelter; voices; oblivion. She turned the handle of the public house door. The acrid smell of stale beer saluted her; and voices talking. They stopped. They had been talking about Bossy as they called her--it didn't matter. She took her chair and looked through the smoke at a crude glass painting of a cow in a stable; also at a cock and a hen. She raised her glass to her lips. And drank. And listened. Words of one syllable sank down into the mud. She drowsed; she nodded. The mud became fertile. Words rose above the intolerably laden dumb oxen plodding through the mud. Words without meaning--wonderful words.

The cheap clock ticked; smoke obscured the pictures. Smoke became tart on the roof of her mouth. Smoke obscured the earth-coloured jackets. She no longer saw them, yet they upheld her, sitting arms akimbo with her glass before her. There was the high ground at midnight; there the rock; and two scarcely perceptible figures. Suddenly the tree was pelted with starlings. She set down her glass. She heard the first words.

Down in the hollow, at Pointz Hall, beneath the trees, the table was cleared in the dining room. Candish, with his curved brush had swept the crumbs; had spared the petals and finally left the family to dessert. The play was over, the strangers gone, and they were alone--the family.

Still the play hung in the sky of the mind--moving, diminishing, but still there. Dipping her raspberry in sugar, Mrs. Swithin looked at the play. She said, popping the berry into her mouth, "What did it mean?" and added: "The peasants; the kings; the fool and" (she swallowed) "ourselves?"

They all looked at the play; Isa, Giles and Mr. Oliver. Each of course saw something different. In another moment it would be beneath the horizon, gone to join the other plays. Mr. Oliver, holding out his cheroot said: "Too ambitious." And, lighting his cheroot he added: "Considering her means."

It was drifting away to join the other clouds: becoming invisible. Through the smoke Isa saw not the play but the audience dispersing. Some drove; others cycled. A gate swung open. A car swept up the drive to the red villa in the cornfields. Low hanging boughs of acacia brushed the roof. Acacia petalled the car arrived.

"The looking-glasses and the voices in the bushes," she murmured. "What did she mean?"

"When Mr. Streatfield asked her to explain, she wouldn't," said Mrs. Swithin.

Here, with its sheaf sliced in four, exposing a white cone, Giles offered his wife a banana. She refused it. He stubbed his match on the plate. Out it went with a little fizz in the raspberry juice.

"We should be thankful," said Mrs. Swithin, folding her napkin, "for the weather, which was perfect, save for one shower."

Here she rose, Isa followed her across the hall to the big room.

They never pulled the curtains till it was too dark to see, nor shut the windows till it was too cold. Why shut out the day before it was over? The flowers were still bright; the birds chirped. You could see more in the evening often when nothing interrupted, when there was no fish to order, no telephone to answer. Mrs. Swithin stopped by the great picture of Venice--school of Canaletto. Possibly in the hood of the gondola there was a little figure--a woman, veiled; or a man?

Isa, sweeping her sewing from the table, sank, her knee doubled, into the chair by the window. Within the shell of the room she overlooked the summer night. Lucy returned from her voyage into the picture and stood silent. The sun made each pane of her glasses shine red. Silver sparkled on her black shawl. For a moment she looked like a tragic figure from another play.

Then she spoke in her usual voice. "We made more this year than last, he said. But then last year it rained."

"This year, last year, next year, never . . ." Isa murmured. Her hand burnt in the sun on the window sill. Mrs. Swithin took her knitting from the table.

"Did you feel," she asked "what he said: we act different parts but are the same?"

"Yes," Isa answered. "No," she added. It was Yes, No. Yes, yes, yes, the tide rushed out embracing. No, no no, it contracted. The old boot appeared on the shingle.

"Orts, scraps and fragments," she quoted what she remembered of the vanishing play.

Lucy had just opened her lips to reply, and had laid her hand on her cross caressingly, when the gentlemen came in. She made her little chirruping sound of welcome. She shuffled her feet to clear a space. But in fact there was more space than was needed, and great hooded chairs.

They sat down, ennobled both of them by the setting sun. Both had changed. Giles now wore the black coat and white tie of the professional classes, which needed--Isa looked down at his feet--patent leather pumps. "Our representative, our spokesman," she sneered. Yet he was extraordinarily handsome. "The father of my children, whom I love and hate." Love and hate--how they tore her asunder! Surely it was time someone invented a new plot, or that the author came out from the bushes . . .

Here Candish came in. He brought the second post on a silver salver. There were letters; bills; and the morning paper--the paper that obliterated the day before. Like a fish rising to a crumb of biscuit, Bartholomew snapped at the paper. Giles slit the flap of an apparently business document. Lucy read a criss-cross from an old friend at Scarborough. Isa had only bills.

The usual sounds reverberated through the shell; Sands making up the fire; Candish stoking the boiler. Isa had done with her bills. Sitting in the shell of the room she watched the pageant fade. The flowers flashed before they faded. She watched them flash.

The paper crackled. The second hand jerked on. M. Daladier had pegged down the franc. The girl had gone skylarking with the troopers. She had screamed. She had hit him. . . . What then?

When Isa looked at the flowers again, the flowers had faded.

Bartholomew flicked on the reading lamp. The circle of the readers, attached to white papers, was lit up. There in that hollow of the sun-baked field were congregated the grasshopper, the ant, and the beetle, rolling pebbles of sun-baked earth through the glistening stubble. In that rosy corner of the sun-baked field Bartholomew, Giles and Lucy polished and nibbled and broke off crumbs. Isa watched them.

Then the newspaper dropped.

"Finished?" said Giles, taking it from his father.

The old man relinquished his paper. He basked. One hand caressing the dog rippled folds of skin towards the collar.

The clock ticked. The house gave little cracks as if it were very brittle, very dry. Isa's hand on the window felt suddenly cold. Shadow had obliterated the garden. Roses had withdrawn for the night.

Mrs. Swithin folding her letter murmured to Isa: "I looked in and saw the babies, sound asleep, under the paper roses."

"Left over from the coronation," Bartholomew muttered, half asleep.

"But we needn't have been to all that trouble with the decorations," Lucy added, "for it didn't rain this year."

"This year, last year, next year, never," Isa murmured.

"Tinker, tailor, soldier, sailor," Bartholomew echoed. He was talking in his sleep.

Lucy slipped her letter into its envelope. It was time to read now, her Outline of History. But she had lost her place. She turned the pages looking at pictures-- mammoths, mastodons, prehistoric birds. Then she found the page where she had stopped.

The darkness increased. The breeze swept round the room. With a little shiver Mrs. Swithin drew her sequin shawl about her shoulders. She was too deep in the story to ask for the window to be shut. "England," she was reading, "was then a swamp. Thick forests covered the land. On the top of their matted branches birds sang . . ."

The great square of the open window showed only sky now. It was drained of light, severe, stone cold. Shadows fell. Shadows crept over Bartholomew's high forehead; over his great nose. He looked leafless, spectral, and his chair monumental. As a dog shudders its skin, his skin shuddered. He rose, shook himself, glared at nothing, and stalked from the room. They heard the dog's paws padding on the carpet behind him.

Lucy turned the page, quickly, guiltily, like a child who will be told to go to bed before the end of the chapter.

"Prehistoric man," she read, "half-human, half-ape, roused himself from his semi-crouching position and raised great stones."

She slipped the letter from Scarborough between the pages to mark the end of the chapter, rose, smiled, and tiptoed silently out of the room.

The old people had gone up to bed. Giles crumpled the newspaper and turned out the light. Left alone together for the first time that day, they were silent. Alone, enmity was bared; also love. Before they slept, they must fight; after they had fought, they would embrace. From that embrace another life might be born. But first they must fight, as the dog fox fights with the vixen, in the heart of darkness, in the fields of night.

Isa let her sewing drop. The great hooded chairs had become enormous. And Giles too. And Isa too against the window. The window was all sky without colour. The house had lost its shelter. It was night before roads were made, or houses. It was the night that dwellers in caves had watched from some high place among rocks.

Then the curtain rose. They spoke.

THE END.

A Room
of One's Own

f

ONE

But, you may say, we asked you to speak about women and fiction--what, has that got to do with a room of one's own? I will try to explain. When you asked me to speak about women and fiction I sat down on the banks of a river and began to wonder what the words meant. They might mean simply a few remarks about Fanny Burney; a few more about Jane Austen; a tribute to the Brontës and a sketch of Haworth Parsonage under snow; some witticisms if possible about Miss Mitford; a respectful allusion to George Eliot; a reference to Mrs Gaskell and one would have done. But at second sight the words seemed not so simple. The title women and fiction might mean, and you may have meant it to mean, women and what they are like, or it might mean women and the fiction that they write; or it might mean women and the fiction that is written about them, or it might mean that somehow all three are inextricably mixed together and you want me to consider them in that light. But when I began to consider the subject in this last way, which seemed the most interesting, I soon saw that it had one fatal drawback. I should never be able to come to a conclusion. I should never be able to fulfil what is, I understand, the first duty of a lecturer to hand you after an hour's discourse a nugget of pure truth to wrap up between the pages of your notebooks and keep on the mantelpiece for ever. All I could do was to offer you an opinion upon one minor point--a woman must have money and a room of her own if she is to write fiction; and that, as you will see, leaves the great problem of the true nature of woman and the true nature of fiction unsolved. I have shirked the duty of coming to a conclusion upon these two questions--women and fiction remain, so far as I am concerned, unsolved problems. But in order to make some amends I am going to do what I can to show you how I arrived at this opinion about the room and the money. I am going to develop in your presence as fully and freely as I can the train of thought which led me to think this. Perhaps if I lay bare the ideas, the prejudices, that lie behind this statement you will find that they have some bearing upon women and some upon fiction. At any rate, when a subject is highly controversial--and any question about sex is that--one cannot hope to tell the truth. One can only show how one came to hold whatever opinion one does hold. One can only give one's audience the chance of drawing their own conclusions as they observe the limitations, the prejudices, the idiosyncrasies of the speaker. Fiction here is likely to contain more truth than fact. Therefore I propose, making use of all the liberties and licences of a novelist, to tell you the story of the two days that preceded my coming here--how, bowed down by the weight of the subject which you have laid upon my shoulders, I pondered it, and made it work in and out of my daily life. I need not say that what I am about to describe has no existence; Oxbridge is an invention; so is Fernham; 'I' is only a convenient term for somebody who has no real being. Lies will flow from my lips, but there may perhaps be some truth mixed up with them; it is for you to seek out this truth and to decide whether any part of it is worth keeping. If not, you will of course throw the whole of it into the waste-paper basket and forget all about it.

Here then was I (call me Mary Beton, Mary Seton, Mary Carmichael or by any name you please--it is not a matter of any importance) sitting on the banks of a river a week or two ago in fine October weather, lost in thought. That collar I have spoken of, women and fiction, the need of coming to some conclusion on a subject that raises all sorts of prejudices and passions, bowed my head to the ground. To the right and left bushes of some sort, golden and crimson, glowed with the colour, even it seemed burnt with the heat, of fire. On the further bank the willows wept in perpetual lamentation, their hair about their shoulders. The river reflected whatever it chose of sky and bridge and burning tree, and when the undergraduate had oared his boat through the reflections they closed again, completely, as if he had never been. There one might have sat the clock round lost in thought. Thought--to call it by a prouder name than it deserved--had let its line down into the stream. It swayed, minute after minute, hither and thither among the reflections and the weeds, letting the water lift it and sink it until--you know the little tug--the sudden conglomeration of an idea at the end of one's line: and then the cautious hauling of it in, and the careful laying of it out? Alas, laid on the grass how small, how insignificant this thought of mine looked; the sort of fish that a good fisherman puts back into the water so that it may grow fatter and be one day worth cooking and eating. I will not trouble you with that thought now, though if you look carefully you may find it for yourselves in the course of what I am going to say.

But however small it was, it had, nevertheless, the mysterious property of its kind--put back into the mind, it became at once very exciting, and important; and as it darted and sank, and flashed hither and thither, set up such a wash and tumult of ideas that it was impossible to sit still. It was thus that I found myself walking with extreme rapidity across a grass plot. Instantly a man's figure rose to intercept me. Nor did I at first understand that the gesticulations of a curious-looking object, in a cut-away coat and evening shirt, were aimed at me. His face expressed horror and indignation. Instinct rather than reason came to my help, he was a Beadle; I was a woman. This was the turf; there was the path. Only the Fellows and Scholars are allowed here; the gravel is the place for me. Such thoughts were the work of a moment. As I regained the path the arms of the Beadle sank, his face assumed its usual repose, and though turf is better walking than gravel, no very great harm was done. The only charge I could bring against the Fellows and Scholars of whatever the college might happen to be was that in protection of their turf, which has been rolled for 300 years in succession they had sent my little fish into hiding.

What idea it had been that had sent me so audaciously trespassing I could not now remember. The spirit of peace descended like a cloud from heaven, for if the spirit of peace dwells anywhere, it is in the courts and quadrangles of Oxbridge on a fine October morning. Strolling through those colleges past those ancient halls the roughness of the present seemed smoothed away; the body seemed contained in a miraculous glass cabinet through which no sound could penetrate, and the mind, freed from any contact with facts (unless one trespassed on the turf again), was at liberty to settle down upon whatever meditation was in harmony with the moment. As chance would have it, some stray memory of some old essay about revisiting Oxbridge in the long vacation brought Charles Lamb to mind--Saint Charles, said Thackeray, putting a letter of Lamb's to his forehead. Indeed, among all the dead (I give you my thoughts as they came to me), Lamb is one of the most congenial; one to whom one would have liked to say, Tell me then how you wrote your essays? For his essays are superior even to Max Beerbohm's, I thought, with all their perfection, because of that wild flash of imagination, that lightning crack of genius in the middle of them which leaves them flawed and imperfect, but starred with poetry. Lamb then came to Oxbridge perhaps a hundred years ago. Certainly he wrote an essay--the name escapes me--about the manuscript of one of Milton's poems which he saw here. It was LYCIDAS perhaps, and Lamb wrote how it shocked him to think it possible that any word in LYCIDAS could have been different from what it is. To think of Milton changing the words in that poem seemed to him a sort of sacrilege. This led me to remember what I could of LYCIDAS and to amuse myself with guessing which word it could have been that Milton had altered, and why. It then occurred to me that the very manuscript itself which Lamb had looked at was only a few hundred yards away, so that one could follow Lamb's footsteps across the quadrangle to that famous library where the treasure is kept. Moreover, I recollected, as I put this plan into execution, it is in this famous library that the manuscript of Thackeray's ESMOND is also preserved. The critics often say that ESMOND is Thackeray's most perfect novel. But the affectation of the style, with its imitation of the eighteenth century, hampers one, so far as I can remember; unless indeed the eighteenth-century style was natural to Thackeray--a fact that one might prove by looking at the manuscript and seeing whether the alterations were for the benefit of the style or of the sense. But then one would have to decide what is style and what is meaning, a question which--but here I was actually at the door which leads into the library itself. I must have opened it, for instantly there issued, like a guardian angel barring the way with a flutter of black gown instead of white wings, a deprecating, silvery, kindly gentleman, who regretted in a low voice as he waved me back that ladies are only admitted to the library if accompanied by a Fellow of the College or furnished with a letter of introduction.

That a famous library has been cursed by a woman is a matter of complete indifference to a famous library. Venerable and calm, with all its treasures safe locked within its breast, it sleeps complacently and will, so far as I am concerned, so sleep for ever. Never will I wake those echoes, never will I ask for that hospitality again, I vowed as I descended the steps in anger. Still an hour remained before luncheon, and what was one to do? Stroll on the meadows? sit by the river? Certainly it was a lovely autumn morning; the leaves were fluttering red to the ground; there was no great hardship in doing either. But the sound of music reached my ear. Some service or celebration was going forward. The organ complained magnificently as I passed the chapel door. Even the sorrow of Christianity sounded in that serene air more like the recollection of sorrow than sorrow itself; even the groanings of the ancient organ seemed lapped in peace. I had no wish to enter had I the right, and this time the verger might have stopped me, demanding perhaps my baptismal certificate, or a letter of introduction from the Dean. But the outside of these magnificent buildings is often as beautiful as the inside. Moreover, it was amusing enough to watch the congregation assembling, coming in and going out again, busying themselves at the door of the chapel like bees at the mouth of a hive. Many were in cap and gown; some had tufts of fur on their shoulders; others were wheeled in bath-chairs; others, though not past middle age, seemed creased and crushed into shapes so singular that one was reminded of those giant crabs and crayfish who heave with difficulty across the sand of an aquarium. As I leant against the wall the University indeed seemed a sanctuary in which are preserved rare types which would soon be obsolete if left to fight for existence on the pavement of the Strand. Old stories of old deans and old dons came back to mind, but before I had summoned up courage to whistle--it used to be said that at the sound of a whistle old Professor ---- instantly broke into a gallop--the venerable congregation had gone inside. The outside of the chapel remained. As you know, its high domes and pinnacles can be seen, like a sailing-ship always voyaging never arriving, lit up at night and visible for miles, far away across the hills. Once, presumably, this quadrangle with its smooth lawns, its massive buildings and the chapel itself was marsh too, where the grasses waved and the swine rooted. Teams of horses and oxen, I thought, must have hauled the stone in wagons from far countries, and then with infinite labour the grey blocks in whose shade I was now standing were poised in order one on top of another. and then the painters brought their glass for the windows, and the masons were busy for centuries up on that roof with putty and cement, spade and trowel. Every Saturday somebody must have poured gold and silver out of a leathern purse into their ancient fists, for they had their beer and skittles presumably of an evening. An unending stream of gold and silver, I thought, must have flowed into this court perpetually to keep the stones coming and the masons working; to level, to ditch, to dig and to drain. But it was then the age of faith, and money was poured liberally to set these stones on a deep foundation, and when the stones were raised, still more money was poured in from the coffers of kings and queens and great nobles to ensure that hymns should be sung here and scholars taught. Lands were granted; tithes were paid. And when the age of faith was over and the age of reason had come, still the same flow of gold and silver went on; fellowships were founded; lectureships endowed; only the gold and silver flowed now, not from the coffers of the king. but from the chests of merchants and manufacturers, from the purses of men who had made, say, a fortune from industry, and returned, in their wills, a bounteous share of it to endow more chairs, more lectureships, more fellowships in the university where they had learnt their craft. Hence the libraries and laboratories; the observatories; the splendid equipment of costly and delicate instruments which now stands on glass shelves, where centuries ago the grasses waved and the swine rooted. Certainly, as I strolled round the court, the foundation of gold and silver seemed deep enough; the pavement laid solidly over the wild grasses. Men with trays on their heads went busily from staircase to staircase. Gaudy blossoms flowered in window-boxes. The strains of the gramophone blared out from the rooms within. It was impossible not to reflect--the reflection whatever it may have been was cut short. The clock struck. it was time to find one's way to luncheon.

It is a curious fact that novelists have a way of making us believe that luncheon parties are invariably memorable for something very witty that was said, or for something very wise that was done. But they seldom spare a word for what was eaten. It is part of the novelist's convention not to mention soup and salmon and ducklings, as if soup and salmon and ducklings were of no importance whatsoever, as if nobody ever smoked a cigar or drank a glass of wine. Here, however, I shall take the liberty to defy that convention and to tell you that the lunch on this occasion began with soles, sunk in a deep dish, over which the college cook had spread a counterpane of the whitest cream, save that it was branded here and there with brown spots like the spots on the flanks of a doe. After that came the partridges, but if this suggests a couple of bald, brown birds on a plate you are mistaken. The partridges, many and various, came with all their retinue of sauces and salads, the sharp and the sweet, each in its order; their potatoes, thin as coins but not so hard; their sprouts, foliated as rosebuds but more succulent. And no sooner had the roast and its retinue been done with than the silent servingman, the Beadle himself perhaps in a milder manifestation, set before us, wreathed in napkins, a confection which rose all sugar from the waves. To call it pudding and so relate it to rice and tapioca would be an insult. Meanwhile the wineglasses had flushed yellow and flushed crimson; had been emptied; had been filled. And thus by degrees was lit, half-way down the spine, which is the seat of the soul, not that hard little electric light which we call brilliance, as it pops in and out upon our lips, but the more profound, subtle and subterranean glow which is the rich yellow flame of rational intercourse. No need to hurry. No need to sparkle. No need to be anybody but oneself. We are all going to heaven and Vandyck is of the company--in other words, how good life seemed, how sweet its rewards, how trivial this grudge or that grievance, how admirable friendship and the society of one's kind, as, lighting a good cigarette, one sunk among the cushions in the window-seat.

If by good luck there had been an ash-tray handy, if one had not knocked the ash out of the window in default, if things had been a little different from what they were, one would not have seen, presumably, a cat without a tail. The sight of that abrupt and truncated animal padding softly across the quadrangle changed by some fluke of the subconscious intelligence the emotional light for me. It was as if someone had let fall a shade. Perhaps the excellent hock was relinquishing its hold. Certainly, as I watched the Manx cat pause in the middle of the lawn as if it too questioned the universe, something seemed lacking, something seemed different. But what was lacking, what was different, I asked myself, listening to the talk? And to answer that question I had to think myself out of the room, back into the past, before the war indeed, and to set before my eyes the model of another luncheon party held in rooms not very far distant from these; but different. Everything was different. Meanwhile the talk went on among the guests, who were many and young, some of this sex, some of that; it went on swimmingly, it went on agreeably, freely, amusingly. And as it went on I set it against the background of that other talk, and as I matched the two together I had no doubt that one was the descendant, the legitimate heir of the other. Nothing was changed; nothing was different save only here I listened with all my ears not entirely to what was being said, but to the murmur or current behind it. Yes, that was it--the change was there. Before the war at a luncheon party like this people would have said precisely the same things but they would have sounded different, because in those days they were accompanied by a sort of humming noise, not articulate, but musical, exciting, which changed the value of the words themselves. Could one set that humming noise to words? Perhaps with the help of the poets one could.. A book lay beside me and, opening it, I turned casually enough to Tennyson. And here I found Tennyson was singing:

There has fallen a splendid tear
From the passion-flower at the gate.
She is coming, my dove, my dear;
She is coming, my life, my fate;
The red rose cries, 'She is near, she is near';
And the white rose weeps, 'She is late';
The larkspur listens, 'I hear, I hear';
And the lily whispers, 'I wait.'

Was that what men hummed at luncheon parties before the war? And the women?

My heart is like a singing bird
Whose nest is in a water'd shoot;
My heart is like an apple tree
Whose boughs are bent with thick-set fruit,
My heart is like a rainbow shell
That paddles in a halcyon sea;
My heart is gladder than all these
Because my love is come to me.

Was that what women hummed at luncheon parties before the war?

There was something so ludicrous in thinking of people humming such things even under their breath at luncheon parties before the war that I burst out laughing. and had to explain my laughter by pointing at the Manx cat, who did look a little absurd, poor beast, without a tail, in the middle of the lawn. Was he really born so, or had he lost his tail in an accident? The tailless cat, though some are said to exist in the Isle of Man, is rarer than one thinks. It is a queer animal, quaint rather than beautiful. It is strange what a difference a tail makes--you know the sort of things one says as a lunch party breaks up and people are finding their coats and hats.

This one, thanks to the hospitality of the host, had lasted far into the afternoon. The beautiful October day was fading and the leaves were falling from the trees in the avenue as I walked through it. Gate after gate seemed to close with gentle finality behind me. Innumerable beadles were fitting innumerable keys into well-oiled locks; the treasure-house was being made secure for another night. After the avenue one comes out upon a road--I forget its name--which leads you, if you take the right turning, along to Fernham. But there was plenty of time. Dinner was not till half-past seven. One could almost do without dinner after such a luncheon. It is strange how a scrap of poetry works in the mind and makes the legs move in time to it along the road. Those words----

There has fallen a splendid tear
From the passion-flower at the gate.
She is coming, my dove, my dear----

100

sang in my blood as I stepped quickly along towards Headingley. And then, switching off into the other measure, I sang, where the waters are churned up by the weir:

> My heart is like a singing bird
> Whose nest is in a water'd shoot;
> My heart is like an apple tree...

What poets, I cried aloud, as one does in the dusk, what poets they were!

In a sort of jealousy, I suppose, for our own age, silly and absurd though these comparisons are, I went on to wonder if honestly one could name two living poets now as great as Tennyson and Christina Rossetti were then. Obviously it is impossible, I thought, looking into those foaming waters, to compare them. The very reason why that poetry excites one to such abandonment, such rapture, is that it celebrates some feeling that one used to have (at luncheon parties before the war perhaps), so that one responds easily, familiarly, without troubling to check the feeling, or to compare it with any that one has now. But the living poets express a feeling that is actually being made and torn out of us at the moment. One does not recognize it in the first place; often for some reason one fears it; one watches it with keenness and compares it jealously and suspiciously with the old feeling that one knew. Hence the difficulty of modern poetry; and it is because of this difficulty that one cannot remember more than two consecutive lines of any good modern poet. For this reason--that my memory failed me--the argument flagged for want of material. But why, I continued, moving on towards Headingley, have we stopped humming under our breath at luncheon parties? Why has Alfred ceased to sing

> She is coming, my dove, my dear.

Why has Christina ceased to respond

> My heart is gladder than all these
> Because my love is come to me?

Shall we lay the blame on the war? When the guns fired in August 1914, did the faces of men and women show so plain in each other's eyes that romance was killed? Certainly it was a shock (to women in particular with their illusions about education, and so on) to see the faces of our rulers in the light of the shell-fire. So ugly they looked--German, English, French--so stupid. But lay the blame where one will, on whom one will, the illusion which inspired Tennyson and Christina Rossetti to sing so passionately about the coming of their loves is far rarer now than then. One has only to read, to look, to listen, to remember. But why say 'blame'? Why, if it was an illusion, not praise the catastrophe, whatever it was, that destroyed illusion and put truth in its place? For truth...those dots mark the spot where, in search of truth, I missed the turning up to Fernham. Yes indeed, which was truth and which was illusion? I asked myself. What was the truth about these houses, for example, dim and festive now with their red windows in the dusk, but raw and red and squalid, with their sweets and their bootlaces, at nine o'clock in the morning? And the willows and the river and the gardens that run down to the river, vague now with the mist stealing over them, but gold and red in the sunlight--which was the truth, which was the illusion about them? I spare you the twists and turns of my cogitations, for no conclusion was found on the road to Headingley, and I ask You to suppose that I soon found out my mistake about the turning and retraced my steps to Fernham.

As I have said already that it was an October day, I dare not forfeit your respect and imperil the fair name of fiction by changing the season and describing lilacs hanging over garden walls, crocuses, tulips and other flowers of spring. Fiction must stick to facts, and the truer the facts the better the fiction--so we are told. Therefore it was still autumn and the leaves were still yellow and falling, if anything, a little faster than before, because it was now evening (seven twenty-three to be precise) and a breeze (from the south-west to be exact) had risen. But for all that there was something odd at work:

> My heart is like a singing bird
> Whose nest is in a water'd shoot;
> My heart is like an apple tree
> Whose boughs are bent with thick-set fruit--

perhaps the words of Christina Rossetti were partly responsible for the folly of the fancy--it was nothing of course but a fancy--that the lilac was shaking its flowers over the garden walls, and the brimstone butterflies were scudding hither and thither, and the dust of the pollen was in the air. A wind blew, from what quarter I know not, but it lifted the half-grown leaves so that there was a flash of silver grey in the air. It was the time between the lights when colours undergo their intensification and purples and golds burn in window-panes like the beat of an excitable heart; when for some reason the beauty of the world revealed and yet soon to perish (here I pushed into the garden, for, unwisely, the door was left open and no beadles seemed about), the beauty of the world which is so soon to perish, has two edges, one of laughter, one of anguish, cutting the heart asunder. The gardens of Fernham lay before me in the spring twilight, wild and open, and in the long grass, sprinkled and carelessly flung, were daffodils and bluebells, not orderly perhaps at the best of times, and now wind-blown and waving as they tugged at their roots. The windows of the building, curved like ships' windows among generous waves of red brick, changed from lemon to silver under the flight of the quick spring clouds. Somebody was in a hammock, somebody, but in this light they were phantoms only, half guessed, half seen, raced across the grass--would no one stop her?--and then on the terrace, as if popping out to breathe the air, to glance at the garden, came a bent figure, formidable yet humble, with her great forehead and her shabby dress--could it be the famous scholar, could it be J---- H---- herself? All was dim, yet intense too, as if the scarf which the dusk had flung over the garden were torn asunder by star or sword--the gash of some terrible reality leaping, as its way is, out of the heart of the spring. For youth----

Here was my soup. Dinner was being served in the great dining-hall. Far from being spring it was in fact an evening in October. Everybody was assembled in the big dining-room. Dinner was ready. Here was the soup. It was a plain gravy soup. There was nothing to stir the fancy in that. One could have seen through the transparent liquid any pattern that there might have been on the plate itself. But there was no pattern. The plate was plain. Next came beef with its attendant greens and potatoes--a homely trinity, suggesting the rumps of cattle in a muddy market, and sprouts curled and yellowed at the edge, and bargaining and cheapening and women with string bags on Monday morning. There was no reason to complain of human nature's daily food, seeing that the supply was sufficient and coal-miners doubtless were sitting down to less. Prunes and custard followed. And if anyone complains that prunes, even when mitigated by custard, are an uncharitable vegetable (fruit they are not), stringy as a miser's heart and exuding a fluid such as might run in misers' veins who have denied themselves wine and warmth for eighty years and yet not given to the poor, he should reflect that there are people whose charity embraces even the prune. Biscuits and cheese came next, and here the water-jug was liberally passed round, for it is the nature of biscuits to be dry, and these were biscuits to the core. That was all. The meal was over. Everybody scraped their chairs back; the swing-doors swung violently to and fro; soon the hall was emptied of every sign of food and made ready no doubt for breakfast next morning. Down corridors and up staircases the youth of England went banging and singing. And was it for a guest, a stranger (for I had no more right here in Fernham than in Trinity or Somerville or Girton or Newnham or Christchurch), to say, 'The dinner was not good,' or to say (we were now, Mary Seton and I, in her sitting-room), 'Could we not have dined up here alone?' for if I had said anything of the kind I should have been prying and searching into the secret economies of a house which to the stranger wears so fine a front of gaiety and courage. No, one could say nothing of the sort. Indeed, conversation for a moment flagged. The human frame being what it is, heart, body and brain all mixed together, and not contained in separate compartments as they will be no doubt in another million years, a good dinner is of great importance to good talk. One cannot think well, love well, sleep well, if one has not dined well. The lamp in the spine does not light on beef and prunes. We are all PROBABLY going to heaven, and Vandyck is, we HOPE, to meet us round the next corner--that is the dubious and qualifying state of mind that beef and prunes at the end of the day's work breed between them. Happily my friend, who taught science, had a cupboard where there was a squat bottle and little glasses--(but there should have been sole and partridge to begin with)--so that we were able to draw up to the fire and repair some of the damages of the day's living. In a minute or so we were slipping freely in and out among all those objects of curiosity and interest which form in the mind in the absence of a particular person, and are naturally to be discussed on coming together again--how somebody has married, another has not; one thinks this, another that; one has improved out of all knowledge, the other most amazingly gone to the bad--with all those speculations upon human nature and the character of the amazing world we live in which spring naturally from such beginnings. While these things were being said, however, I became shamefacedly aware of a current setting in of its own accord and carrying everything forward to an end of its own. One might be talking of Spain or Portugal, of book or racehorse, but the real interest of whatever was said was none of those things, but a scene of masons on a high roof some five centuries ago. Kings and nobles brought treasure in huge sacks and poured it under the earth. This scene was for ever coming alive in my mind and placing itself by another of lean cows and a muddy market and withered greens and the stringy hearts of old men--these two pictures, disjointed and disconnected and nonsensical as they were, were for ever coming together and combating each other and had me entirely at their mercy. The best course, unless the whole talk was to be distorted, was to expose what was in my mind to the air, when with good luck it would fade and crumble like the head of the dead king when they opened the coffin at Windsor. Briefly, then, I told Miss Seton about the masons who had been all those years on the roof of the chapel, and about the kings and queens and nobles bearing sacks of gold and silver on their shoulders, which they shovelled into the earth; and then how the great financial magnates of our own time came and laid cheques and bonds, I suppose, where the others had laid ingots and rough lumps of gold. All that lies beneath the colleges down there, I said; but this college, where we are now sitting, what lies beneath its gallant red brick and the wild unkempt grasses of the garden? What force is behind that plain china off which we dined, and (here it popped out of my mouth before I could stop it) the beef, the custard and the prunes?

Well, said Mary Seton, about the year 1860--Oh, but you know the story, she said, bored, I suppose, by the recital. And she told me--rooms were hired. Committees met. Envelopes were addressed. Circulars were drawn up. Meetings were held; letters were read out; so-and-so has promised so much; on the contrary, Mr ---- won't give a penny. The SATURDAY REVIEW has been very rude. How can we raise a fund to pay for offices? Shall we hold a bazaar? Can't we find a pretty girl to sit in the front row? Let us look up what John Stuart Mill said on the subject. Can anyone persuade the editor of the ---- to print a letter? Can we get Lady ---- to sign it? Lady ---- is out of town. That was the way it was done, presumably, sixty years ago, and it was a prodigious effort, and a great deal of time was spent on it. And it was only after a long struggle and with the utmost difficulty that they got thirty thousand pounds together.[1] So obviously we cannot have wine and partridges and servants carrying tin dishes on their heads, she said. We cannot have sofas and separate rooms. 'The amenities,' she said, quoting from some book or other, 'will have to wait.'[2]

At the thought of all those women working year after year and finding it hard to get two thousand pounds together, and as much as they could do to get thirty thousand pounds, we burst out in scorn at the reprehensible poverty of our sex.

---

[1] We are told that we ought to ask for £30,000 at least... It is not a large sum, considering that there is to be but one college of this sort for Great Britain, Ireland and the Colonies, and considering how easy it is to raise immense sums for boys' schools. But considering how few people really wish women to be educated, it is a good deal.'--LADY STEPHEN, EMILY DAVIES AND GIRTON COLLEGE.

[2] Every penny which could be scraped together was set aside for building, and the amenities had to be postponed.--R. STRACHEY, THE CAUSE.

What had our mothers been doing then that they had no wealth to leave us? Powdering their noses? Looking in at shop windows? Flaunting in the sun at Monte Carlo? There were some photographs on the mantelpiece. Mary's mother--if that was her picture--may have been a wastrel in her spare time (she had thirteen children by a minister of the church), but if so her gay and dissipated life had left too few traces of its pleasures on her face. She was a homely body; an old lady in a plaid shawl which was fastened by a large cameo; and she sat in a basket-chair, encouraging a spaniel to look at the camera, with the amused, yet strained expression of one who is sure that the dog will move directly the bulb is pressed. Now if she had gone into business; had become a manufacturer of artificial silk or a magnate on the Stock Exchange; if she had left two or three hundred thousand pounds to Fernham, we could have been sitting at our ease to-night and the subject of our talk might have been archaeology, botany, anthropology, physics, the nature of the atom, mathematics, astronomy, relativity, geography. If only Mrs Seton and her mother and her mother before her had learnt the great art of making money and had left their money, like their fathers and their grandfathers before them, to found fellowships and lectureships and prizes and scholarships appropriated to the use of their own sex, we might have dined very tolerably up here alone off a bird and a bottle of wine; we might have looked forward without undue confidence to a pleasant and honourable lifetime spent in the shelter of one of the liberally endowed professions. We might have been exploring or writing; mooning about the venerable places of the earth; sitting contemplative on the steps of the Parthenon, or going at ten to an office and coming home comfortably at half-past four to write a little poetry. Only, if Mrs Seton and her like had gone into business at the age of fifteen, there would have been--that was the snag in the argument--no Mary. What, I asked, did Mary think of that? There between the curtains was the October night, calm and lovely, with a star or two caught in the yellowing trees. Was she ready to resign her share of it and her memories (for they had been a happy family, though a large one) of games and quarrels up in Scotland, which she is never tired of praising for the fineness of its air and the quality of its cakes, in order that Fernham might have been endowed with fifty thousand pounds or so by a stroke of the pen? For, to endow a college would necessitate the suppression of families altogether. Making a fortune and bearing thirteen children--no human being could stand it. Consider the facts, we said. First there are nine months before the baby is born. Then the baby is born. Then there are three or four months spent in feeding the baby. After the baby is fed there are certainly five years spent in playing with the baby. You cannot, it seems, let children run about the streets. People who have seen them running wild in Russia say that the sight is not a pleasant one. People say, too, that human nature takes its shape in the years between one and five. If Mrs Seton, I said, had been making money, what sort of memories would you have had of games and quarrels? What would you have known of Scotland, and its fine air and cakes and all the rest of it? But it is useless to ask these questions, because you would never have come into existence at all. Moreover, it is equally useless to ask what might have happened if Mrs Seton and her mother and her mother before her had amassed great wealth and laid it under the foundations of college and library, because, in the first place, to earn money was impossible for them, and in the second, had it been possible, the law denied them the right to possess what money they earned. It is only for the last forty-eight years that Mrs Seton has had a penny of her own. For all the centuries before that it would have been her husband's property--a thought which, perhaps, may have had its share in keeping Mrs Seton and her mothers off the Stock Exchange. Every penny I earn, they may have said, will be taken from me and disposed of according to my husband's wisdom--perhaps to found a scholarship or to endow a fellowship in Balliol or Kings, so that to earn money, even if I could earn money, is not a matter that interests me very greatly. I had better leave it to my husband.

At any rate, whether or not the blame rested on the old lady who was looking at the spaniel, there could be no doubt that for some reason or other our mothers had mismanaged their affairs very gravely. Not a penny could be spared for 'amenities'; for partridges and wine, beadles and turf, books and cigars, libraries and leisure. To raise bare walls out of bare earth was the utmost they could do.

So we talked standing at the window and looking, as so many thousands look every night, down on the domes and towers of the famous city beneath us. It was very beautiful, very mysterious in the autumn moonlight. The old stone looked very white and venerable. One thought of all the books that were assembled down there; of the pictures of old prelates and worthies hanging in the panelled rooms; of the painted windows that would be throwing strange globes and crescents on the pavement; of the tablets and memorials and inscriptions; of the fountains and the grass; of the quiet rooms looking across the quiet quadrangles. And (pardon me the thought) I thought, too, of the admirable smoke and drink and the deep armchairs and the pleasant carpets: of the urbanity, the geniality, the dignity which are the offspring of luxury and privacy and space. Certainly our mothers had not provided us with any thing comparable to all this--our mothers who found it difficult to scrape together thirty thousand pounds, our mothers who bore thirteen children to ministers of religion at St Andrews.

So I went back to my inn, and as I walked through the dark streets I pondered this and that, as one does at the end of the day's work. I pondered why it was that Mrs Seton had no money to leave us; and what effect poverty has on the mind; and what effect wealth has on the mind; and I thought of the queer old gentlemen I had seen that morning with tufts of fur upon their shoulders; and I remembered how if one whistled one of them ran; and I thought of the organ booming in the chapel and of the shut doors of the library; and I thought how unpleasant it is to be locked out; and I thought how it is worse perhaps to be locked in; and, thinking of the safety and prosperity of the one sex and of the poverty and insecurity of the other and of the effect of tradition and of the lack of tradition upon the mind of a writer, I thought at last that it was time to roll up the crumpled skin of the day, with its arguments and its impressions and its anger and its laughter, and cast it into the hedge. A thousand stars were flashing across the blue wastes of the sky. One seemed alone with an inscrutable society. All human beings were laid asleep--prone, horizontal, dumb. Nobody seemed stirring in the streets of Oxbridge. Even the door of the hotel sprang open at the touch of an invisible hand--not a boots was sitting up to light me to bed, it was so late.

TWO

The scene, if I may ask you to follow me, was now changed. The leaves were still falling, but in London now, not Oxbridge; and I must ask you to imagine a room, like many thousands, with a window looking across people's hats and vans and motor-cars to other windows, and on the table inside the room a blank sheet of paper on which was written in large letters WOMEN AND FICTION, but no more. The inevitable sequel to lunching and dining at Oxbridge seemed, unfortunately, to be a visit to the British Museum. One must strain off what was personal and accidental in all these impressions and so reach the pure fluid, the essential oil of truth. For that visit to Oxbridge and the luncheon and the dinner had started a swarm of questions. Why did men drink wine and women water? Why was one sex so prosperous and the other so poor? What effect has poverty on fiction? What conditions are necessary for the creation of works of art?--a thousand questions at once suggested themselves. But one needed answers, not questions; and an answer was only to be had by consulting the learned and the unprejudiced, who have removed themselves above the strife of tongue and the confusion of body and issued the result of their reasoning and research in books which are to be found in the British Museum. If truth is not to be found on the shelves of the British Museum, where, I asked myself, picking up a notebook and a pencil, is truth?

Thus provided, thus confident and enquiring, I set out in the pursuit of truth. The day, though not actually wet, was dismal, and the streets in the neighbourhood of the Museum were full of open coal-holes, down which sacks were showering; four-wheeled cabs were drawing up and depositing on the pavement corded boxes containing, presumably, the entire wardrobe of some Swiss or Italian family seeking fortune or refuge or some other desirable commodity which is to be found in the boarding-houses of Bloomsbury in the winter. The usual hoarse-voiced men paraded the streets with plants on barrows. Some shouted; others sang. London was like a workshop. London was like a machine. We were all being shot backwards and forwards on this plain foundation to make some pattern. The British Museum was another department of the factory. The swing-doors swung open; and there one stood under the vast dome, as if one were a thought in the huge bald forehead which is so splendidly encircled by a band of famous names. One went to the counter; one took a slip of paper; one opened a volume of the catalogue, and the five dots here indicate five separate minutes of stupefaction, wonder and bewilderment. Have you any notion of how many books are written about women in the course of one year? Have you any notion how many are written by men? Are you aware that you are, perhaps, the most discussed animal in the universe? Here had I come with a notebook and a pencil proposing to spend a morning reading, supposing that at the end of the morning I should have transferred the truth to my notebook. But I should need to be a herd of elephants, I thought, and a wilderness of spiders, desperately referring to the animals that are reputed longest lived and most multitudinously eyed, to cope with all this. I should need claws of steel and beak of brass even to penetrate the husk. How shall I ever find the grains of truth embedded in all this mass of paper? I asked myself, and in despair began running my eye up and down the long list of titles. Even the names of the books gave me food for thought. Sex and its nature might well attract doctors and biologists; but what was surprising and difficult of explanation was the fact that sex--woman, that is to say--also attracts agreeable essayists, light-fingered novelists, young men who have taken the M.A. degree; men who have taken no degree; men who have no apparent qualification save that they are not women. Some of these books were, on the face of it, frivolous and facetious; but many, on the other hand, were serious and prophetic, moral and hortatory. Merely to read the titles suggested innumerable schoolmasters, innumerable clergymen mounting their platforms and pulpits and holding forth with loquacity which far exceeded the hour usually alloted to such discourse on this one subject. It was a most strange phenomenon; and apparently--here I consulted the letter M--one confined to the male sex. Women do not write books about men--a fact that I could not help welcoming with relief, for if I had first to read all that men have written about women, then all that women have written about men, the aloe that flowers once in a hundred years would flower twice before I could set pen to paper. So, making a perfectly arbitrary choice of a dozen volumes or so, I sent my slips of paper to lie in the wire tray, and waited in my stall, among the other seekers for the essential oil of truth.

What could be the reason, then, of this curious disparity, I wondered, drawing cart-wheels on the slips of paper provided by the British taxpayer for other purposes. Why are women, judging from this catalogue, so much more interesting to men than men are to women? A very curious fact it seemed, and my mind wandered to picture the lives of men who spend their time in writing books about women; whether they were old or young, married or unmarried, red-nosed or hump-backed--anyhow, it was flattering, vaguely, to feel oneself the object of such attention provided that it was not entirely bestowed by the crippled and the infirm--so I pondered until all such frivolous thoughts were ended by an avalanche of books sliding down on to the desk in front of me. Now the trouble began. The student who has been trained in research at Oxbridge has no doubt some method of shepherding his question past all distractions till it runs into his answer as a sheep runs into its pen. The student by my side, for instance, who was copying assiduously from a scientific manual, was, I felt sure, extracting pure nuggets of the essential ore every ten minutes or so. His little grunts of satisfaction indicated so much. But if, unfortunately, one has had no training in a university, the question far from being shepherded to its pen flies like a frightened flock hither and thither, helter-skelter, pursued by a whole pack of hounds. Professors, schoolmasters, sociologists, clergymen, novelists, essayists, journalists, men who had no qualification save that they were not women, chased my simple and single question--Why are some women poor?--until it became fifty questions; until the fifty questions leapt frantically into midstream and were carried away. Every page in my notebook was scribbled over with notes. To show the state of mind I was in, I will read you a few of them, explaining that the page was headed quite simply, WOMEN AND POVERTY, in block letters; but what followed was something like this:

Condition in Middle Ages of,
Habits in the Fiji Islands of,

Worshipped as goddesses by,
Weaker in moral sense than,
Idealism of,
Greater conscientiousness of,
South Sea Islanders, age of puberty among,
Attractiveness of,
Offered as sacrifice to,
Small size of brain of,
Profounder sub-consciousness of,
Less hair on the body of,
Mental, moral and physical inferiority of,
Love of children of,
Greater length of life of,
Weaker muscles of,
Strength of affections of,
Vanity of,
Higher education of,
Shakespeare's opinion of,
Lord Birkenhead's opinion of,
Dean Inge's opinion of,
La Bruyere's opinion of,
Dr Johnson's opinion of,
Mr Oscar Browning's opinion of,...

Here I drew breath and added, indeed, in the margin, Why does Samuel Butler say, 'Wise men never say what they think of women'? Wise men never say anything else apparently. But, I continued, leaning back in my chair and looking at the vast dome in which I was a single but by now somewhat harassed thought, what is so unfortunate is that wise men never think the same thing about women. Here is Pope:

Most women have no character at all.

And here is La Bruyère:

Les femmes sont extrêmes, elles sont meilleures ou pires que les hommes----

a direct contradiction by keen observers who were contemporary. Are they capable of education or incapable? Napoleon thought them incapable. Dr Johnson thought the opposite.[3] Have they souls or have they not souls? Some savages say they have none. Others, on the contrary, maintain that women are half divine and worship

---

[3] 'Men know that women are an overmatch for them, and therefore they choose the weakest or the most ignorant. If they did not think so, they never could be afraid of women knowing as much as themselves."...In justice to the sex, I think it but candid to acknowledge that, in a subsequent conversation, he told me that he was serious in what he said.'--BOSWELL, THE JOURNAL OF A TOUR TO THE HEBRIDES.

them on that account.[4] Some sages hold that they are shallower in the brain; others that they are deeper in the consciousness. Goethe honoured them; Mussolini despises them. Wherever one looked men thought about women and thought differently. It was impossible to make head or tail of it all, I decided, glancing with envy at the reader next door who was making the neatest abstracts, headed often with an A or a B or a C, while my own notebook rioted with the wildest scribble of contradictory jottings. It was distressing, it was bewildering, it was humiliating. Truth had run through my fingers. Every drop had escaped.

I could not possibly go home, I reflected, and add as a serious contribution to the study of women and fiction that women have less hair on their bodies than men, or that the age of puberty among the South Sea Islanders is nine--or is it ninety?--even the handwriting had become in its distraction indecipherable. It was disgraceful to have nothing more weighty or respectable to show after a whole morning's work. And if I could not grasp the truth about W. (as for brevity's sake I had come to call her) in the past, why bother about W. in the future? It seemed pure waste of time to consult all those gentlemen who specialize in woman and her effect on whatever it may be--politics, children, wages, morality--numerous and learned as they are. One might as well leave their books unopened.

But while I pondered I had unconsciously, in my listlessness, in my desperation, been drawing a picture where I should, like my neighbour, have been writing a conclusion. I had been drawing a face, a figure. It was the face and the figure of Professor von X engaged in writing his monumental work entitled THE MENTAL, MORAL, AND PHYSICAL INFERIORITY OF THE FEMALE SEX. He was not in my picture a man attractive to women. He was heavily built; he had a great jowl; to balance that he had very small eyes; he was very red in the face. His expression suggested that he was labouring under some emotion that made him jab his pen on the paper as if he were killing some noxious insect as he wrote, but even when he had killed it that did not satisfy him; he must go on killing it; and even so, some cause for anger and irritation remained. Could it be his wife, I asked, looking at my picture? Was she in love with a cavalry officer? Was the cavalry officer slim and elegant and dressed in astrakhan? Had he been laughed at, to adopt the Freudian theory, in his cradle by a pretty girl? For even in his cradle the professor, I thought, could not have been an attractive child. Whatever the reason, the professor was made to look very angry and very ugly in my sketch, as he wrote his great book upon the mental, moral and physical inferiority of women. Drawing pictures was an idle way of finishing an unprofitable morning's work. Yet it is in our idleness, in our dreams, that the submerged truth sometimes comes to the top. A very elementary exercise in psychology, not to be dignified by the name of psychoanalysis, showed me, on looking at my notebook, that the sketch of the angry professor had been made in anger. Anger had snatched my pencil while I dreamt. But what was anger doing there? Interest, confusion, amusement, boredom--all these emotions I could trace and name as they succeeded each other throughout the morning. Had anger,

---

[4] The ancient Germans believed that there was something holy in women, and accordingly consulted them as oracles.'--FRAZER, GOLDEN BOUGH.

the black snake, been lurking among them? Yes, said the sketch, anger had. It referred me unmistakably to the one book, to the one phrase, which had roused the demon; it was the professor's statement about the mental, moral and physical inferiority of women. My heart had leapt. My cheeks had burnt. I had flushed with anger. There was nothing specially remarkable, however foolish, in that. One does not like to be told that one is naturally the inferior of a little man--I looked at the student next me--who breathes hard, wears a ready-made tie, and has not shaved this fortnight. One has certain foolish vanities. It is only human nature, I reflected, and began drawing cartwheels and circles over the angry professor's face till he looked like a burning bush or a flaming comet--anyhow, an apparition without human semblance or significance. The professor was nothing now but a faggot burning on the top of Hampstead Heath. Soon my own anger was explained and done with; but curiosity remained. How explain the anger of the professors? Why were they angry? For when it came to analysing the impression left by these books there was always an element of heat. This heat took many forms; it showed itself in satire, in sentiment, in curiosity, in reprobation. But there was another element which was often present and could not immediately be identified. Anger, I called it. But it was anger that had gone underground and mixed itself with all kinds of other emotions. To judge from its odd effects, it was anger disguised and complex, not anger simple and open.

Whatever the reason, all these books, I thought, surveying the pile on the desk, are worthless for my purposes. They were worthless scientifically, that is to say, though humanly they were full of instruction, interest, boredom, and very queer facts about the habits of the Fiji Islanders. They had been written in the red light of emotion and not in the white light of truth. Therefore they must be returned to the central desk and restored each to his own cell in the enormous honeycomb. All that I had retrieved from that morning's work had been the one fact of anger. The professors--I lumped them together thus--were angry. But why, I asked myself, having returned the books, why, I repeated, standing under the colonnade among the pigeons and the prehistoric canoes, why are they angry? And, asking myself this question, I strolled off to find a place for luncheon. What is the real nature of what I call for the moment their anger? I asked. Here was a puzzle that would last all the time that it takes to be served with food in a small restaurant somewhere near the British Museum. Some previous luncher had left the lunch edition of the evening paper on a chair, and, waiting to be served, I began idly reading the headlines. A ribbon of very large letters ran across the page. Somebody had made a big score in South Africa. Lesser ribbons announced that Sir Austen Chamberlain was at Geneva. A meat axe with human hair on it had been found in a cellar. Mr justice ---- commented in the Divorce Courts upon the Shamelessness of Women. Sprinkled about the paper were other pieces of news. A film actress had been lowered from a peak in California and hung suspended in mid-air. The weather was going to be foggy. The most transient visitor to this planet, I thought, who picked up this paper could not fail to be aware, even from this scattered testimony, that England is under the rule of a patriarchy. Nobody in their senses could fail to detect the dominance of the professor. His was the power and the money and the influence. He was the proprietor of the paper and its editor and sub-editor. He was the Foreign Secretary and the judge. He was the cricketer; he owned the racehorses and the yachts. He was the director of the company that pays two hundred per cent to its shareholders. He left millions to charities and colleges that were ruled by himself. He suspended the film actress in mid-air. He will decide if the hair on the meat axe is human; he it is who will acquit or convict the murderer, and hang him, or let him go free. With the exception of the fog he seemed to control everything. Yet he was angry. I knew that he was angry by this token. When I read what he wrote about women--I thought, not of what he was saying, but of himself. When an arguer argues dispassionately he thinks only of the argument; and the reader cannot help thinking of the argument too. If he had written dispassionately about women, had used indisputable proofs to establish his argument and had shown no trace of wishing that the result should be one thing rather than another, one would not have been angry either. One would have accepted the fact, as one accepts the fact that a pea is green or a canary yellow. So be it, I should have said. But I had been angry because he was angry. Yet it seemed absurd, I thought, turning over the evening paper, that a man with all this power should be angry. Or is anger, I wondered, somehow, the familiar, the attendant sprite on power? Rich people, for example, are often angry because they suspect that the poor want to seize their wealth. The professors, or patriarchs, as it might be more accurate to call them, might be angry for that reason partly, but partly for one that lies a little less obviously on the surface. Possibly they were not 'angry' at all; often, indeed, they were admiring, devoted, exemplary in the relations of private life. Possibly when the professor insisted a little too emphatically upon the inferiority of women, he was concerned not with their inferiority, but with his own superiority. That was what he was protecting rather hot-headedly and with too much emphasis, because it was a jewel to him of the rarest price. Life for both sexes--and I looked at them, shouldering their way along the pavement--is arduous, difficult, a perpetual struggle. It calls for gigantic courage and strength. More than anything, perhaps, creatures of illusion as we are, it calls for confidence in oneself. Without self-confidence we are as babes in the cradle. And how can we generate this imponderable quality, which is yet so invaluable, most quickly? By thinking that other people are inferior to one self. By feeling that one has some innate superiority--it may be wealth, or rank, a straight nose, or the portrait of a grandfather by Romney--for there is no end to the pathetic devices of the human imagination--over other people. Hence the enormous importance to a patriarch who has to conquer, who has to rule, of feeling that great numbers of people, half the human race indeed, are by nature inferior to himself. It must indeed be one of the chief sources of his power. But let me turn the light of this observation on to real life, I thought. Does it help to explain some of those psychological puzzles that one notes in the margin of daily life? Does it explain my astonishment of the other day when Z, most humane, most modest of men, taking up some book by Rebecca West and reading a passage in it, exclaimed, 'The arrant feminist! She says that men are snobs!' The exclamation, to me so surprising--for why was Miss West an arrant feminist for making a possibly true if uncomplimentary statement about the other sex?--was not merely the cry of wounded vanity; it was a protest against some infringement of his power to believe in himself. Women have served all these centuries as looking-glasses possessing the magic and delicious power of reflecting the figure of man at twice its natural size. Without that power probably the earth would still be swamp and jungle. The glories of all our wars would he unknown. We should still be scratching the outlines of deer on the remains of mutton bones and bartering flints for sheep skins or whatever simple ornament took our unsophisticated taste. Supermen and Fingers of Destiny would never have existed. The Czar and the Kaiser would never have worn crowns or lost them. Whatever may be their use in civilized societies, mirrors are essential to all violent and heroic action. That is why Napoleon and Mussolini both insist so emphatically upon the inferiority of women, for if they were not inferior, they would cease to enlarge. That serves to explain in part the necessity that women so often are to men. And it serves to explain how restless they are under her criticism; how impossible it is for her to say to them this book is bad, this picture is feeble, or whatever it may be, without giving far more pain and rousing far more anger than a man would do who gave the same criticism. For if she begins to tell the truth, the figure in the looking-glass shrinks; his fitness for life is diminished. How is he to go on giving judgement, civilizing natives, making laws, writing books, dressing up and speechifying at banquets, unless he can see himself at breakfast and at dinner at least twice the size he really is? So I reflected, crumbling my bread and stirring my coffee and now and again looking at the people in the street. The looking-glass vision is of supreme importance because it charges the vitality; it stimulates the nervous system. Take it away and man may die, like the drug fiend deprived of his cocaine. Under the spell of that illusion, I thought, looking out of the window, half the people on the pavement are striding to work. They put on their hats and coats in the morning under its agreeable rays. They start the day confident, braced, believing themselves desired at Miss Smith's tea party; they say to themselves as they go into the room, I am the superior of half the people here, and it is thus that they speak with that self-confidence, that self-assurance, which have had such profound consequences in public life and lead to such curious notes in the margin of the private mind.

But these contributions to the dangerous and fascinating subject of the psychology of the other sex--it is one, I hope, that you will investigate when you have five hundred a year of your own--were interrupted by the necessity of paying the bill. It came to five shillings and ninepence. I gave the waiter a ten-shilling note and he went to bring me change. There was another ten-shilling note in my purse; I noticed it, because it is a fact that still takes my breath away the power of my purse to breed ten-shilling notes automatically. I open it and there they are. Society gives me chicken and coffee, bed and lodging, in return for a certain number of pieces of paper which were left me by an aunt, for no other reason than that I share her name.

My aunt, Mary Beton, I must tell you, died by a fall from her horse when she was riding out to take the air in Bombay. The news of my legacy reached me one night about the same time that the act was passed that gave votes to women. A solicitor's letter fell into the post-box and when I opened it I found that she had left me five hundred pounds a year for ever. Of the two--the vote and the money--the money, I own, seemed infinitely the more important. Before that I had made my living by cadging odd jobs from newspapers, by reporting a donkey show here or a wedding there; I had earned a few pounds by addressing envelopes, reading to old ladies, making artificial flowers, teaching the alphabet to small children in a kindergarten. Such were the chief occupations that were open to women before 1918. I need not, I am afraid, describe in any detail the hardness of the work, for you

113

know perhaps women who have done it; nor the difficulty of living on the money when it was earned, for you may have tried. But what still remains with me as a worse infliction than either was the poison of fear and bitterness which those days bred in me. To begin with, always to be doing work that one did not wish to do, and to do it like a slave, flattering and fawning, not always necessarily perhaps, but it seemed necessary and the stakes were too great to run risks; and then the thought of that one gift which it was death to hide--a small one but dear to the possessor--perishing and with it my self, my soul,--all this became like a rust eating away the bloom of the spring, destroying the tree at its heart. However, as I say, my aunt died; and whenever I change a ten-shilling note a little of that rust and corrosion is rubbed off, fear and bitterness go. Indeed, I thought, slipping the silver into my purse, it is remarkable, remembering the bitterness of those days, what a change of temper a fixed income will bring about. No force in the world can take from me my five hundred pounds. Food, house and clothing are mine forever. Therefore not merely do effort and labour cease, but also hatred and bitterness. I need not hate any man; he cannot hurt me. I need not flatter any man; he has nothing to give me. So imperceptibly I found myself adopting a new attitude towards the other half of the human race. It was absurd to blame any class or any sex, as a whole. Great bodies of people are never responsible for what they do. They are driven by instincts which are not within their control. They too, the patriarchs, the professors, had endless difficulties, terrible drawbacks to contend with. Their education had been in some ways as faulty as my own. It had bred in them defects as great. True, they had money and power, but only at the cost of harbouring in their breasts an eagle, a vulture, forever tearing the liver out and plucking at the lungs--the instinct for possession, the rage for acquisition which drives them to desire other people's fields and goods perpetually; to make frontiers and flags; battleships and poison gas; to offer up their own lives and their children's lives. Walk through the Admiralty Arch (I had reached that monument), or any other avenue given up to trophies and cannon, and reflect upon the kind of glory celebrated there. Or watch in the spring sunshine the stockbroker and the great barrister going indoors to make money and more money and more money when it is a fact that five hundred pounds a year will keep one alive in the sunshine. These are unpleasant instincts to harbour, I reflected. They are bred of the conditions of life; of the lack of civilization, I thought, looking at the statue of the Duke of Cambridge, and in particular at the feathers in his cocked hat, with a fixity that they have scarcely ever received before. And, as I realized these drawbacks, by degrees fear and bitterness modified themselves into pity and toleration; and then in a year or two, pity and toleration went, and the greatest release of all came, which is freedom to think of things in themselves. That building, for example, do I like it or not? Is that picture beautiful or not? Is that in my opinion a good book or a bad? Indeed my aunt's legacy unveiled the sky to me, and substituted for the large and imposing figure of a gentleman, which Milton recommended for my perpetual adoration, a view of the open sky.

So thinking, so speculating I found my way back to my house by the river. Lamps were being lit and an indescribable change had come over London since the morning hour. It was as if the great machine after labouring all day had made with our help a few yards of something very exciting and beautiful--a fiery fabric flashing with red eyes, a tawny monster roaring with hot breath. Even the wind seemed flung like a flag as it lashed the houses and rattled the hoardings.

In my little street, however, domesticity prevailed. The house painter was descending his ladder; the nursemaid was wheeling the perambulator carefully in and out back to nursery tea; the coal-heaver was folding his empty sacks on top of each other; the woman who keeps the green grocer's shop was adding up the day's takings with her hands in red mittens. But so engrossed was I with the problem you have laid upon my shoulders that I could not see even these usual sights without referring them to one centre. I thought how much harder it is now than it must have been even a century ago to say which of these em ployments is the higher, the more necessary. Is it better to be a coal-heaver or a nursemaid; is the charwoman who has brought up eight children of less value to the world than, the barrister who has made a hundred thousand pounds? it is useless to ask such questions; for nobody can answer them. Not only do the comparative values of charwomen and lawyers rise and fall from decade to decade, but we have no rods with which to measure them even as they are at the moment. I had been foolish to ask my professor to furnish me with 'indisputable proofs' of this or that in his argument about women. Even if one could state the value of any one gift at the moment, those values will change; in a century's time very possibly they will have changed completely. Moreover, in a hundred years, I thought, reaching my own doorstep, women will have ceased to be the protected sex. Logically they will take part in all the activities and exertions that were once denied them. The nursemaid will heave coal. The shopwoman will drive an engine. All assumptions founded on the facts observed when women were the protected sex will have disappeared--as, for example (here a squad of soldiers marched down the street), that women and clergymen and gardeners live longer than other people. Remove that protection, expose them to the same exertions and activities, make them soldiers and sailors and engine-drivers and dock labourers, and will not women die off so much younger, so much quicker, than men that one will say, 'I saw a woman to-day', as one used to say, 'I saw an aeroplane'. Anything may happen when womanhood has ceased to be a protected occupation, I thought, opening the door. But what bearing has all this upon the subject of my paper, Women and Fiction? I asked, going indoors.

THREE

It was disappointing not to have brought back in the evening some important statement, some authentic fact. Women are poorer than men because--this or that. Perhaps now it would be better to give up seeking for the truth, and receiving on one's head an avalanche of opinion hot as lava, discoloured as dish-water. It would be better to draw the curtains; to shut out distractions; to light the lamp; to narrow the enquiry and to ask the historian, who records not opinions but facts, to describe under what conditions women lived, not throughout the ages, but in England, say, in the time of Elizabeth.

For it is a perennial puzzle why no woman wrote a word of that extraordinary literature when every other man, it seemed, was capable of song or sonnet. What were the conditions in which women lived? I asked myself; for fiction, imaginative work that is, is not dropped like a pebble upon the ground, as science may be; fiction is like a spider's web, attached ever so lightly perhaps, but still attached to life at all four corners. Often the attachment is scarcely perceptible; Shakespeare's plays, for instance, seem to hang there complete by themselves. But when the web is pulled askew, hooked up at the edge, torn in the middle, one remembers that these webs are not spun in mid-air by incorporeal creatures, but are the work of suffering human beings, and are attached to grossly material things, like health and money and the houses we live in.

I went, therefore, to the shelf where the histories stand and took down one of the latest, Professor Trevelyan's HISTORY OF ENGLAND. Once more I looked up Women, found 'position of' and turned to the pages indicated. 'Wife-beating', I read, 'was a recognized right of man, and was practised without shame by high as well as low...Similarly,' the historian goes on, 'the daughter who refused to marry the gentleman of her parents' choice was liable to be locked up, beaten and flung about the room, without any shock being inflicted on public opinion. Marriage was not an affair of personal affection, but of family avarice, particularly in the "chivalrous" upper classes...Betrothal often took place while one or both of the parties was in the cradle, and marriage when they were scarcely out of the nurses' charge.' That was about 1470, soon after Chaucer's time. The next reference to the position of women is some two hundred years later, in the time of the Stuarts. 'It was still the exception for women of the upper and middle class to choose their own husbands, and when the husband had been assigned, he was lord and master, so far at least as law and custom could make him. Yet even so,' Professor Trevelyan concludes, 'neither Shakespeare's women nor those of authentic seventeenth-century memoirs, like the Verneys and the Hutchinsons, seem wanting in personality and character.' Certainly, if we consider it, Cleopatra must have had a way with her; Lady Macbeth, one would suppose, had a will of her own; Rosalind, one might conclude, was an attractive girl. Professor Trevelyan is speaking no more than the truth when he remarks that Shakespeare's women do not seem wanting in personality and character. Not being a historian, one might go even further and say that women have burnt like beacons in all the works of all the poets from the beginning of time--Clytemnestra, Antigone,

Cleopatra, Lady Macbeth, Phedre, Cressida, Rosalind, Desdemona, the Duchess of Malfi, among the dramatists; then among the prose writers: Millamant, Clarissa, Becky Sharp, Anna Karenina, Emma Bovary, Madame de Guermantes--the names flock to mind, nor do they recall women 'lacking in personality and character.' Indeed, if woman had no existence save in the fiction written by men, one would imagine her a person of the utmost importance; very various; heroic and mean; splendid and sordid; infinitely beautiful and hideous in the extreme; as great as a man, some think even greater.[5] But this is woman in fiction. In fact, as Professor Trevelyan points out, she was locked up, beaten and flung about the room.

A very queer, composite being thus emerges. Imaginatively she is of the highest importance; practically she is completely insignificant. She pervades poetry from cover to cover; she is all but absent from history. She dominates the lives of kings and conquerors in fiction; in fact she was the slave of any boy whose parents forced a ring upon her finger. Some of the most inspired words, some of the most profound thoughts in literature fall from her lips; in real life she could hardly read, could scarcely spell, and was the property of her husband.

It was certainly an odd monster that one made up by reading the historians first and the poets afterwards--a worm winged like an eagle; the spirit of life and beauty in a kitchen chopping up suet. But these monsters, however amusing to the imagination, have no existence in fact. What one must do to bring her to life was to think poetically and prosaically at one and the same moment, thus keeping in touch with fact--that she is Mrs Martin, aged thirty-six, dressed in blue, wearing a black hat and brown shoes; but not losing sight of fiction either--that she is a vessel in which all sorts of spirits and forces are coursing and flashing perpetually. The moment, however, that one tries this method with the Elizabethan woman, one branch of illumination fails; one is held up by the scarcity of facts. One knows nothing detailed, nothing perfectly true and substantial about her. History scarcely mentions her. And I turned to Professor Trevelyan again to see what history meant to him. I found by looking at his chapter headings that it meant----

---

[5] 'It remains a strange and almost inexplicable fact that in Athena's city, where women were kept in almost Oriental suppression as odalisques or drudges, the stage should yet have produced figures like Clytemnestra and Cassandra Atossa and Antigone, Phedre and Medea, and all the other heroines who dominate play after play of the "misogynist" Euripides. But the paradox of this world where in real life a respectable woman could hardly show her face alone in the street, and yet on the stage woman equals or surpasses man, has never been satisfactorily explained. In modern tragedy the same predominance exists. At all events, a very cursory survey of Shakespeare's work (similarly with Webster, though not with Marlowe or Jonson) suffices to reveal how this dominance, this initiative of women, persists from Rosalind to Lady Macbeth. So too in Racine; six of his tragedies bear their heroines' names; and what male characters of his shall we set against Hermione and Andromaque, Berenice and Roxane, Phedre and Athalie? So again with Ibsen; what men shall we match with Solveig and Nora, Heda and Hilda Wangel and Rebecca West?'--F. L. LUCAS, TRAGEDY, pp. 114-15.

'The Manor Court and the Methods of Open-field Agriculture...The Cistercians and Sheep-farming...The Crusades...The University ...The House of Commons...The Hundred Years' War...The Wars of the Roses...The Renaissance Scholars...The Dissolution of the Monasteries...Agrarian and Religious Strife...The Origin of English Sea-power...The Armada...' and so on. Occasionally an individual woman is mentioned, an Elizabeth, or a Mary; a queen or a great lady. But by no possible means could middle-class women with nothing but brains and character at their command have taken part in any one of the great movements which, brought together, constitute the historian's view of the past. Nor shall we find her in collection of anecdotes. Aubrey hardly mentions her. She never writes her own life and scarcely keeps a diary; there are only a handful of her letters in existence. She left no plays or poems by which we can judge her. What one wants, I thought--and why does not some brilliant student at Newnham or Girton supply it?--is a mass of information; at what age did she marry; how many children had she as a rule; what was her house like, had she a room to herself; did she do the cooking; would she be likely to have a servant? All these facts lie somewhere, presumably, in parish registers and account books; the life of the average Elizabethan woman must be scattered about somewhere, could one collect it and make a book of it. It would be ambitious beyond my daring, I thought, looking about the shelves for books that were not there, to suggest to the students of those famous colleges that they should rewrite history, though I own that it often seems a little queer as it is, unreal, lop-sided; but why should they not add a supplement to history, calling it, of course, by some inconspicuous name so that women might figure there without impropriety? For one often catches a glimpse of them in the lives of the great, whisking away into the back ground, concealing, I sometimes think, a wink, a laugh, perhaps a tear. And, after all, we have lives enough of Jane Austen; it scarcely seems necessary to consider again the influence of the tragedies of Joanna Baillie upon the poetry of Edgar Allan Poe; as for myself, I should not mind if the homes and haunts of Mary Russell Mitford were closed to the public for a century at least. But what I find deplorable, I continued, looking about the bookshelves again, is that nothing is known about women before the eighteenth century. I have no model in my mind to turn about this way and that. Here am I asking why women did not write poetry in the Elizabethan age, and I am not sure how they were educated; whether they were taught to write; whether they had sitting-rooms to themselves; how many women had children before they were twenty-one; what, in short, they did from eight in the morning till eight at night. They had no money evidently; according to Professor Trevelyan they were married whether they liked it or not before they were out of the nursery, at fifteen or sixteen very likely. It would have been extremely odd, even upon this showing, had one of them suddenly written the plays of Shakespeare, I concluded, and I thought of that old gentleman, who is dead now, but was a bishop, I think, who declared that it was impossible for any woman, past, present, or to come, to have the genius of Shakespeare. He wrote to the papers about it. He also told a lady who applied to him for information that cats do not as a matter of fact go to heaven, though they have, he added, souls of a sort. How much thinking those old gentlemen used to save one! How the borders of ignorance shrank back at their approach! Cats do not go to heaven. Women cannot write the plays of Shakespeare.

Be that as it may, I could not help thinking, as I looked at the works of Shakespeare on the shelf, that the bishop was right at least in this; it would have been impossible, completely and entirely, for any woman to have written the plays of Shakespeare in the age of Shakespeare. Let me imagine, since facts are so hard to come by, what would have happened had Shakespeare had a wonderfully gifted sister, called Judith, let us say. Shakespeare himself went, very probably,--his mother was an heiress--to the grammar school, where he may have learnt Latin--Ovid, Virgil and Horace--and the elements of grammar and logic. He was, it is well known, a wild boy who poached rabbits, perhaps shot a deer, and had, rather sooner than he should have done, to marry a woman in the neighbourhood, who bore him a child rather quicker than was right. That escapade sent him to seek his fortune in London. He had, it seemed, a taste for the theatre; he began by holding horses at the stage door. Very soon he got work in the theatre, became a successful actor, and lived at the hub of the universe, meeting everybody, knowing everybody, practising his art on the boards, exercising his wits in the streets, and even getting access to the palace of the queen. Meanwhile his extraordinarily gifted sister, let us suppose, remained at home. She was as adventurous, as imaginative, as agog to see the world as he was. But she was not sent to school. She had no chance of learning grammar and logic, let alone of reading Horace and Virgil. She picked up a book now and then, one of her brother's perhaps, and read a few pages. But then her parents came in and told her to mend the stockings or mind the stew and not moon about with books and papers. They would have spoken sharply but kindly, for they were substantial people who knew the conditions of life for a woman and loved their daughter--indeed, more likely than not she was the apple of her father's eye. Perhaps she scribbled some pages up in an apple loft on the sly but was careful to hide them or set fire to them. Soon, however, before she was out of her teens, she was to be betrothed to the son of a neighbouring wool-stapler. She cried out that marriage was hateful to her, and for that she was severely beaten by her father. Then he ceased to scold her. He begged her instead not to hurt him, not to shame him in this matter of her marriage. He would give her a chain of beads or a fine petticoat, he said; and there were tears in his eyes. How could she disobey him? How could she break his heart? The force of her own gift alone drove her to it. She made up a small parcel of her belongings, let herself down by a rope one summer's night and took the road to London. She was not seventeen. The birds that sang in the hedge were not more musical than she was. She had the quickest fancy, a gift like her brother's, for the tune of words. Like him, she had a taste for the theatre. She stood at the stage door; she wanted to act, she said. Men laughed in her face. The manager--a fat, looselipped man--guffawed. He bellowed something about poodles dancing and women acting--no woman, he said, could possibly be an actress. He hinted--you can imagine what. She could get no training in her craft. Could she even seek her dinner in a tavern or roam the streets at midnight? Yet her genius was for fiction and lusted to feed abundantly upon the lives of men and women and the study of their ways. At last--for she was very young, oddly like Shakespeare the poet in her face, with the same grey eyes and rounded brows--at last Nick Greene the actor-manager took pity on her; she found herself with child by that gentleman and so--who shall measure the heat and violence of the poet's heart when caught and tangled in a woman's body?--killed herself one winter's night and lies buried at some cross-roads where the omnibuses now stop outside the Elephant and Castle.

That, more or less, is how the story would run, I think, if a woman in Shakespeare's day had had Shakespeare's genius. But for my part, I agree with the deceased bishop, if such he was--it is unthinkable that any woman in Shakespeare's day should have had Shakespeare's genius. For genius like Shakespeare's is not born among labouring, uneducated, servile people. It was not born in England among the Saxons and the Britons. It is not born to-day among the working classes. How, then, could it have been born among women whose work began, according to Professor Trevelyan, almost before they were out of the nursery, who were forced to it by their parents and held to it by all the power of law and custom? Yet genius of a sort must have existed among women as it must have existed among the working classes. Now and again an Emily Brontë or a Robert Burns blazes out and proves its presence. But certainly it never got itself on to paper. When, however, one reads of a witch being ducked, of a woman possessed by devils, of a wise woman selling herbs, or even of a very remarkable man who had a mother, then I think we are on the track of a lost novelist, a suppressed poet, of some mute and inglorious Jane Austen, some Emily Brontë who dashed her brains out on the moor or mopped and mowed about the highways crazed with the torture that her gift had put her to. Indeed, I would venture to guess that Anon, who wrote so many poems without singing them, was often a woman. It was a woman Edward Fitzgerald, I think, suggested who made the ballads and the folk-songs, crooning them to her children, beguiling her spinning with them, or the length of the winter's night.

This may be true or it may be false--who can say?--but what is true in it, so it seemed to me, reviewing the story of Shakespeare's sister as I had made it, is that any woman born with a great gift in the sixteenth century would certainly have gone crazed, shot herself, or ended her days in some lonely cottage outside the village, half witch, half wizard, feared and mocked at. For it needs little skill in psychology to be sure that a highly gifted girl who had tried to use her gift for poetry would have been so thwarted and hindered by other people, so tortured and pulled asunder by her own contrary instincts, that she must have lost her health and sanity to a certainty. No girl could have walked to London and stood at a stage door and forced her way into the presence of actor-managers without doing herself a violence and suffering an anguish which may have been irrational--for chastity may be a fetish invented by certain societies for unknown reasons--but were none the less inevitable. Chastity had then, it has even now, a religious importance in a woman's life, and has so wrapped itself round with nerves and instincts that to cut it free and bring it to the light of day demands courage of the rarest. To have lived a free life in London in the six teenth century would have meant for a woman who was poet and playwright a nervous stress and dilemma which might well have killed her. Had she survived, whatever she had written would have been twisted and deformed, issuing from a strained and morbid imagination. And undoubtedly, I thought, looking at the shelf where there are no plays by women, her work would have gone unsigned. That refuge she would have sought certainly. It was the relic of the sense of chastity that dictated anonymity to women even so late as the nineteenth century. Currer Bell,

George Eliot, George Sand, all the victims of inner strife as their writings prove, sought ineffectively to veil themselves by using the name of a man. Thus they did homage to the convention, which if not implanted by the other sex was liberally encouraged by them (the chief glory of a woman is not to be talked of, said Pericles, himself a much-talked-of man) that publicity in women is detestable. Anonymity runs in their blood. The desire to be veiled still possesses them. They are not even now as concerned about the health of their fame as men are, and, speaking generally, will pass a tombstone or a signpost without feeling an irresistible desire to cut their names on it, as Alf, Bert or Chas. must do in obedience to their instinct, which murmurs if it sees a fine woman go by, or even a dog, Ce chien est a moi. And, of course, it may not be a dog, I thought, remembering Parliament Square, the Sieges Allee and other avenues; it may be a piece of land or a man with curly black hair. It is one of the great advantages of being a woman that one can pass even a very fine negress without wishing to make an Englishwoman of her.

That woman, then, who was born with a gift of poetry in the sixteenth century, was an unhappy woman, a woman at strife against herself. All the conditions of her life, all her own instincts, were hostile to the state of mind which is needed to set free whatever is in the brain. But what is the state of mind that is most propitious to the act of creation? I asked. Can one come by any notion of the state that furthers and makes possible that strange activity? Here I opened the volume containing the Tragedies of Shakespeare. What was Shakespeare's state of mind, for instance, when he wrote LEAR and ANTONY AND CLEOPATRA? It was certainly the state of mind most favourable to poetry that there has ever existed. But Shakespeare himself said nothing about it. We only know casually and by chance that he 'never blotted a line'. Nothing indeed was ever said by the artist himself about his state of mind until the eighteenth century perhaps. Rousseau perhaps began it. At any rate, by the nineteenth century self-consciousness had developed so far that it was the habit for men of letters to describe their minds in confessions and autobiographies. Their lives also were written, and their letters were printed after their deaths. Thus, though we do not know what Shakespeare went through when he wrote LEAR, we do know what Carlyle went through when he wrote the FRENCH REVOLUTION; what Flaubert went through when he wrote MADAME BOVARY; what Keats was going through when he tried to write poetry against the coming death and the indifference of the world.

And one gathers from this enormous modern literature of confession and self-analysis that to write a work of genius is almost always a feat of prodigious difficulty. Everything is against the likelihood that it will come from the writer's mind whole and entire. Generally material circumstances are against it. Dogs will bark; people will interrupt; money must be made; health will break down. Further, accentuating all these difficulties and making them harder to bear is the world's notorious indifference. It does not ask people to write poems and novels and histories; it does not need them. It does not care whether Flaubert finds the right word or whether Carlyle scrupulously verifies this or that fact. Naturally, it will not pay for what it does not want. And so the writer, Keats, Flaubert, Carlyle, suffers, especially in the creative years of youth, every form of distraction and discouragement. A curse, a cry of agony, rises from those books of analysis and confession. 'Mighty poets in their misery dead'--that is the burden of their song. If anything comes through in spite of all this, it is a miracle, and probably no book is born entire and uncrippled as it was conceived.

But for women, I thought, looking at the empty shelves, these difficulties were infinitely more formidable. In the first place, to have a room of her own, let alone a quiet room or a sound-proof room, was out of the question, unless her parents were exceptionally rich or very noble, even up to the beginning of the nineteenth century. Since her pin money, which depended on the goodwill of her father, was only enough to keep her clothed, she was debarred from such alleviations as came even to Keats or Tennyson or Carlyle, all poor men, from a walking tour, a little journey to France, from the separate lodging which, even if it were miserable enough, sheltered them from the claims and tyrannies of their families. Such material difficulties were formidable; but much worse were the immaterial. The indifference of the world which Keats and Flaubert and other men of genius have found so hard to bear was in her case not indifference but hostility. The world did not say to her as it said to them, Write if you choose; it makes no difference to me. The world said with a guffaw, Write? What's the good of your writing? Here the psychologists of Newnham and Girton might come to our help, I thought, looking again at the blank spaces on the shelves. For surely it is time that the effect of discouragement upon the mind of the artist should be measured, as I have seen a dairy company measure the effect of ordinary milk and Grade A milk upon the body of the rat. They set two rats in cages side by side, and of the two one was furtive, timid and small, and the other was glossy, bold and big. Now what food do we feed women as artists upon? I asked, remembering, I suppose, that dinner of prunes and custard. To answer that question I had only to open the evening paper and to read that Lord Birkenhead is of opinion--but really I am not going to trouble to copy out Lord Birkenhead's opinion upon the writing of women. What Dean Inge says I will leave in peace. The Harley Street specialist may be allowed to rouse the echoes of Harley Street with his vociferations without raising a hair on my head. I will quote, however, Mr Oscar Browning, because Mr Oscar Browning was a great figure in Cambridge at one time, and used to examine the students at Girton and Newnham. Mr Oscar Browning was wont to declare 'that the impression left on his mind, after looking over any set of examination papers, was that, irrespective of the marks he might give, the best woman was intellectually the inferior of the worst man'. After saying that Mr Browning went back to his rooms--and it is this sequel that endears him and makes him a human figure of some bulk and majesty--he went back to his rooms and found a stable-boy lying on the sofa--'a mere skeleton, his cheeks were cavernous and sallow, his teeth were black, and he did not appear to have the full use of his limbs... "That's Arthur" [said Mr Browning]. "He's a dear boy really and most high-minded."' The two pictures always seem to me to complete each other. And happily in this age of biography the two pictures often do complete each other, so that we are able to interpret the opinions of great men not only by what they say, but by what they do.

But though this is possible now, such opinions coming from the lips of important people must have been formidable enough even fifty years ago. Let us suppose that a father from the highest motives did not wish his daughter to leave home and become writer, painter or scholar. 'See what Mr Oscar Browning says,' he would say; and there so was not only Mr Oscar Browning; there was the SATURDAY REVIEW; there was Mr Greg--the 'essentials of a woman's being', said Mr Greg emphatically, 'are that THEY ARE SUPPORTED BY, AND THEY MINISTER TO, MEN'--there was an enormous body of masculine opinion to the effect that nothing could be expected of women intellectually. Even if her father did not read out loud these opinions, any girl could read them for herself; and the reading, even in the nineteenth century, must have lowered her vitality, and told profoundly upon her work. There would always have been that assertion--you cannot do this, you are incapable of doing that--to protest against, to overcome. Probably for a novelist this germ is no longer of much effect; for there have been women novelists of merit. But for painters it must still have some sting in it; and for musicians, I imagine, is even now active and poisonous in the extreme. The woman composer stands where the actress stood in the time of Shakespeare. Nick Greene, I thought, remembering the story I had made about Shakespeare's sister, said that a woman acting put him in mind of a dog dancing. Johnson repeated the phrase two hundred years later of women preaching. And here, I said, opening a book about music, we have the very words used again in this year of grace, 1928, of women who try to write music. 'Of Mlle. Germaine Tailleferre one can only repeat Dr Johnson's dictum concerning, a woman preacher, transposed into terms of music. "Sir, a woman's composing is like a dog's walking on his hind legs. It is not done well, but you are surprised to find it done at all."[6] So accurately does history repeat itself.

Thus, I concluded, shutting Mr Oscar Browning's life and pushing away the rest, it is fairly evident that even in the nineteenth century a woman was not encouraged to be an artist. On the contrary, she was snubbed, slapped, lectured and exhorted. Her mind must have been strained and her vitality lowered by the need of opposing this, of disproving that. For here again we come within range of that very interesting and obscure masculine complex which has had so much influence upon the woman's movement; that deep-seated desire, not so much that SHE shall be inferior as that HE shall be superior, which plants him wherever one looks, not only in front of the arts, but barring the way to politics too, even when the risk to himself seems infinitesimal and the suppliant humble and devoted. Even Lady Bessborough, I remembered, with all her passion for politics, must humbly bow herself and write to Lord Granville Leveson-Gower: '...notwithstanding all my violence in politicks and talking so much on that subject, I perfectly agree with you that no woman has any business to meddle with that or any other serious business, farther than giving her opinion (if she is ask'd).' And so she goes on to spend her enthusiasm where it meets with no obstacle whatsoever, upon that immensely important subject, Lord Granville's maiden speech in the House of Commons. The spectacle is certainly a strange one, I thought. The history of men's opposition to women's emancipation is more interesting perhaps than the story of that emancipation itself. An amusing book might be made of it if some young student at Girton or Newnham would

---

[6] A SURVEY OF CONTEMPORARY MUSIC, Cecil Gray, P. 246.

collect examples and deduce a theory,--but she would need thick gloves on her hands, and bars to protect her of solid gold.

But what is amusing now, I recollected, shutting Lady Bessborough, had to be taken in desperate earnest once. Opinions that one now pastes in a book labelled cock-a-doodledum and keeps for reading to select audiences on summer nights once drew tears, I can assure you. Among your grandmothers and great-grandmothers there were many that wept their eyes out. Florence Nightingale shrieked aloud in her agony.[7] Moreover, it is all very well for you, who have got yourselves to college and enjoy sitting-rooms--or is it only bed-sitting-rooms?--of your own to say that genius should disregard such opinions; that genius should be above caring what is said of it. Unfortunately, it is precisely the men or women of genius who mind most what is said of them. Remember Keats. Remember the words he had cut on his tombstone. Think of Tennyson; think but I need hardly multiply instances of the undeniable, if very fortunate, fact that it is the nature of the artist to mind excessively what is said about him. Literature is strewn with the wreckage of men who have minded beyond reason the opinions of others.

And this susceptibility of theirs is doubly unfortunate, I thought, returning again to my original enquiry into what state of mind is most propitious for creative work, because the mind of an artist, in order to achieve the prodigious effort of freeing whole and entire the work that is in him, must be incandescent, like Shakespeare's mind, I conjectured, looking at the book which lay open at ANTONY AND CLEOPATRA. There must be no obstacle in it, no foreign matter unconsumed.

For though we say that we know nothing about Shakespeare's state of mind, even as we say that, we are saying something about Shakespeare's state of mind. The reason perhaps why we know so little of Shakespeare--compared with Donne or Ben Jonson or Milton--is that his grudges and spites and antipathies are hidden from us. We are not held up by some 'revelation' which reminds us of the writer. All desire to protest, to preach, to proclaim an injury, to pay off a score, to make the world the witness of some hardship or grievance was fired out of him and consumed. Therefore his poetry flows from him free and unimpeded. If ever a human being got his work expressed completely, it was Shakespeare. If ever a mind was incandescent, unimpeded, I thought, turning again to the bookcase, it was Shakespeare's mind.

---

[7] See CASSANDRA, by Florence Nightingale, printed in THE CAUSE, by R. Strachey.

FOUR

That one would find any woman in that state of mind in the sixteenth century was obviously impossible. One has only to think of the Elizabethan tombstones with all those children kneeling with clasped hands; and their early deaths; and to see their houses with their dark, cramped rooms, to realize that no woman could have written poetry then. What one would expect to find would be that rather later perhaps some great lady would take advantage of her comparative freedom and comfort to publish something with her name to it and risk being thought a monster. Men, of course, are not snobs, I continued, carefully eschewing 'the arrant feminism' of Miss Rebecca West; but they appreciate with sympathy for the most part the efforts of a countess to write verse. One would expect to find a lady of title meeting with far greater encouragement than an unknown Miss Austen or a Miss Brontë at that time would have met with. But one would also expect to find that her mind was disturbed by alien emotions like fear and hatred and that her poems showed traces of that disturbance. Here is Lady Winchilsea, for example, I thought, taking down her poems. She was born in the year 1661; she was noble both by birth and by marriage; she was childless; she wrote poetry, and one has only to open her poetry to find her bursting out in indignation against the position of women:

> How we are fallen! fallen by mistaken rules,
> And Education's more than Nature's fools;
> Debarred from all improvements of the mind,
> And to be dull, expected and designed;
>
> And if someone would soar above the rest,
> With warmer fancy, and ambition pressed,
> So strong the opposing faction still appears,
> The hopes to thrive can ne'er outweigh the fears.

Clearly her mind has by no means 'consumed all impediments and become incandescent'. On the contrary, it is harassed and distracted with hates and grievances. The human race is split up for her into two parties. Men are the 'opposing faction'; men are hated and feared, because they have the power to bar her way to what she wants to do--which is to write.

> Alas! a woman that attempts the pen,
> Such a presumptuous creature is esteemed,
> The fault can by no virtue be redeemed.
> They tell us we mistake our sex and way;
> Good breeding, fashion, dancing, dressing, play,
> Are the accomplishments we should desire;
> To write, or read, or think, or to enquire,
> Would cloud our beauty, and exhaust our time,
> And interrupt the conquests of our prime.

Whilst the dull manage of a servile house
Is held by some our utmost art and use.

Indeed she has to encourage herself to write by supposing that what she writes will never be published; to soothe herself with the sad chant:

To some few friends, and to thy sorrows sing,
For groves of laurel thou wert never meant;
Be dark enough thy shades, and be thou there content.

Yet it is clear that could she have freed her mind from hate and fear and not heaped it with bitterness and resentment, the fire was hot within her. Now and again words issue of pure poetry:

Nor will in fading silks compose,
Faintly the inimitable rose.

--they are rightly praised by Mr Murry, and Pope, it is thought, remembered and appropriated those others:

Now the jonquille o'ercomes the feeble brain;
We faint beneath the aromatic pain.

It was a thousand pities that the woman who could write like that, whose mind was tuned to nature and reflection, should have been forced to anger and bitterness. But how could she have helped herself? I asked, imagining the sneers and the laughter, the adulation of the toadies, the scepticism of the professional poet. She must have shut herself up in a room in the country to write, and been torn asunder by bitterness and scruples perhaps, though her husband was of the kindest, and their married life perfection. She 'must have', I say, because when one comes to seek out the facts about Lady Winchilsea, one finds, as usual, that almost nothing is known about her. She suffered terribly from melancholy, which we can explain at least to some extent when we find her telling us how in the grip of it she would imagine:

My lines decried, and my employment thought
An useless folly or presumptuous fault:

The employment, which was thus censured, was, as far as one can see, the harmless one of rambling about the fields and dreaming:

My hand delights to trace unusual things,
And deviates from the known and common way,
Nor will in fading silks compose,
Faintly the inimitable rose.

Naturally, if that was her habit and that was her delight, she could only expect to be laughed at; and, accordingly, Pope or Gay is said to have satirized her 'as a blue-stocking with an itch for scribbling'. Also it is thought that she offended Gay by laughing at him. She said that his TRIVIA showed that 'he was more proper to walk before a chair than to ride in one'. But this is all 'dubious gossip' and, says Mr Murry, 'uninteresting'. But there I do not agree with him, for I should have liked to have had more even of dubious gossip so that I might have found out or made up some image of this melancholy lady, who loved wandering in the fields and thinking about unusual things and scorned, so rashly, so unwisely, 'the dull manage of a servile house'. But she became diffuse, Mr Murry says. Her gift is all grown about with weeds and bound with briars. It had no chance of showing itself for the fine distinguished gift it was. And so, putting, her back on the shelf, I turned to the other great lady, the Duchess whom Lamb loved, hare-brained, fantastical Margaret of Newcastle, her elder, but her contemporary. They were very different, but alike in this that both were noble and both childless, and both were married to the best of husbands. In both burnt the same passion for poetry and both are disfigured and deformed by the same causes. Open the Duchess and one finds the same outburst of rage. 'Women live like Bats or Owls, labour like Beasts, and die like Worms...' Margaret too might have been a poet; in our day all that activity would have turned a wheel of some sort. As it was, what could bind, tame or civilize for human use that wild, generous, untutored intelligence? It poured itself out, higgledy-piggledy, in torrents of rhyme and prose, poetry and philosophy which stand congealed in quartos and folios that nobody ever reads. She should have had a microscope put in her hand. She should have been taught to look at the stars and reason scientifically. Her wits were turned with solitude and freedom. No one checked her. No one taught her. The professors fawned on her. At Court they jeered at her. Sir Egerton Brydges complained of her coarseness--'as flowing from a female of high rank brought up in the Courts'. She shut herself up at Welbeck alone.

What a vision of loneliness and riot the thought of Margaret Cavendish brings to mind! as if some giant cucumber had spread itself over all the roses and carnations in the garden and choked them to death. What a waste that the woman who wrote 'the best bred women are those whose minds are civilest' should have frittered her time away scribbling nonsense and plunging ever deeper into obscurity and folly till the people crowded round her coach when she issued out. Evidently the crazy Duchess became a bogey to frighten clever girls with. Here, I remembered, putting away the Duchess and opening Dorothy Osborne's letters, is Dorothy writing to Temple about the Duchess's new book. 'Sure the poore woman is a little distracted, shee could never bee soe rediculous else as to venture at writeing book's and in verse too, if I should not sleep this fortnight I should not come to that.'

And so, since no woman of sense and modesty could write books, Dorothy, who was sensitive and melancholy, the very opposite of the Duchess in temper, wrote nothing. Letters did not count. A woman might write letters while she was sitting by her father's sick-bed. She could write them by the fire whilst the men talked without disturbing them. The strange thing is, I thought, turning over the

127

pages of Dorothy's letters, what a gift that untaught and solitary girl had for the framing of a sentence, for the fashioning of a scene. Listen to her running on:

'After dinner wee sitt and talk till Mr B. com's in question and then I am gon. the heat of the day is spent in reading or working and about sixe or seven a Clock, I walke out into a Common that lyes hard by the house where a great many young wenches keep Sheep and Cow's and sitt in the shades singing of Ballads; I goe to them and compare their voyces and Beauty's to some Ancient Shepherdesses that I have read of and finde a vaste difference there, but trust mee I think these are as innocent as those could bee. I talke to them, and finde they want nothing to make them the happiest People in the world, but the knoledge that they are soe. most commonly when we are in the middest of our discourse one looks aboute her and spyes her Cow's goeing into the Corne and then away they all run, as if they had wing's at theire heels. I that am not soe nimble stay behinde, and when I see them driveing home theire Cattle I think tis time for mee to retyre too. when I have supped I goe into the Garden and soe to the syde of a small River that runs by it where I sitt downe and wish you with mee...'

One could have sworn that she had the makings of a writer in her. But 'if I should not sleep this fortnight I should not come to that'--one can measure the opposition that was in the air to a woman writing when one finds that even a woman with a great turn for writing has brought herself to believe that to write a book was to be ridiculous, even to show oneself distracted. And so we come, I continued, replacing the single short volume of Dorothy Osborne's letters upon the shelf, to Mrs Behn.

And with Mrs Behn we turn a very important corner on the road. We leave behind, shut up in their parks among their folios, those solitary great ladies who wrote without audience or criticism, for their own delight alone. We come to town and rub shoulders with ordinary people in the streets. Mrs Behn was a middle-class woman with all the plebeian virtues of humour, vitality and courage; a woman forced by the death of her husband and some unfortunate adventures of her own to make her living by her wits. She had to work on equal terms with men. She made, by working very hard, enough to live on. The importance of that fact outweighs anything that she actually wrote, even the splendid 'A Thousand Martyrs I have made', or 'Love in Fantastic Triumph sat', for here begins the freedom of the mind, or rather the possibility that in the course of time the mind will be free to write what it likes. For now that Aphra Behn had done it, girls could go to their parents and say, You need not give me an allowance; I can make money by my pen. Of course the answer for many years to come was, Yes, by living the life of Aphra Behn! Death would be better! and the door was slammed faster than ever. That profoundly interesting subject, the value that men set upon women's chastity and its effect upon their education, here suggests itself for discussion, and might provide an interesting book if any student at Girton or Newnham cared to go into the matter. Lady Dudley, sitting in diamonds among the midges of a Scottish moor, might serve for frontispiece. Lord Dudley, THE TIMES said when Lady Dudley died the other day, 'a man of cultivated taste and many accomplishments, was benevolent and bountiful, but whimsically despotic. He insisted upon his wife's wearing full dress, even at the remotest shooting-lodge in the Highlands; he loaded her with gorgeous jewels', and so on, 'he gave her everything--always excepting any measure of responsibility'. Then Lord Dudley had a stroke and she nursed him and ruled his estates with supreme competence for ever after. That whimsical despotism was in the nineteenth century too.

But to return. Aphra Behn proved that money could be made by writing at the sacrifice, perhaps, of certain agreeable qualities; and so by degrees writing became not merely a sign of folly and a distracted mind, but was of practical importance. A husband might die, or some disaster overtake the family. Hundreds of women began as the eighteenth century drew on to add to their pin money, or to come to the rescue of their families by making translations or writing the innumerable bad novels which have ceased to be recorded even in text-books, but are to be picked up in the fourpenny boxes in the Charing Cross Road. The extreme activity of mind which showed itself in the later eighteenth century among women--the talking, and the meeting, the writing of essays on Shakespeare, the translating of the classics--was founded on the solid fact that women could make money by writing. Money dignifies what is frivolous if unpaid for. It might still be well to sneer at 'blue stockings with an itch for scribbling', but it could not be denied that they could put money in their purses. Thus, towards the end of the eighteenth century a change came about which, if I were rewriting history, I should describe more fully and think of greater importance than the Crusades or the Wars of the Roses.

The middle-class woman began to write. For if PRIDE AND PREJUDICE matters, and MIDDLEMARCH and VILLETTE and WUTHERING HEIGHTS matter, then it matters far more than I can prove in an hour's discourse that women generally, and not merely the lonely aristocrat shut up in her country house among her folios and her flatterers, took to writing. Without those forerunners, Jane Austen and the Brontës and George Eliot could no more have written than Shakespeare could have written without Marlowe, or Marlowe without Chaucer, or Chaucer without those forgotten poets who paved the ways and tamed the natural savagery of the tongue. For masterpieces are not single and solitary births; they are the outcome of many years of thinking in common, of thinking by the body of the people, so that the experience of the mass is behind the single voice. Jane Austen should have laid a wreath upon the grave of Fanny Burney, and George Eliot done homage to the robust shade of Eliza Carter--the valiant old woman who tied a bell to her bedstead in order that she might wake early and learn Greek. All women together ought to let flowers fall upon the tomb of Aphra Behn, which is, most scandalously but rather appropriately, in Westminster Abbey, for it was she who earned them the right to speak their minds. It is she--shady and amorous as she was--who makes it not quite fantastic for me to say to you to-night: Earn five hundred a year by your wits.

Here, then, one had reached the early nineteenth century. And here, for the first time, I found several shelves given up entirely to the works of women. But why, I could not help asking, as I ran my eyes over them, were they, with very few exceptions, all novels? The original impulse was to poetry. The 'supreme head of song' was a poetess. Both in France and in England the women poets precede the women novelists. Moreover, I thought, looking at the four famous names, what had George Eliot in common with Emily Brontë? Did not Charlotte Brontë fail entirely to understand Jane Austen? Save for the possibly relevant fact that not one of them had a child, four more incongruous characters could not have met together in a room--so much so that it is tempting to invent a meeting and a dialogue between them. Yet by some strange force they were all compelled when they wrote, to write novels. Had it something to do with being born of the middle class, I asked; and with the fact, which Miss Emily Davies a little later was so strikingly to demonstrate, that the middle-class family in the early nineteenth century was possessed only of a single sitting-room between them? If a woman wrote, she would have to write in the common sitting-room. And, as Miss Nightingale was so vehemently to complain,-- "women never have an half hour...that they can call their own"--she was always interrupted. Still it would be easier to write prose and fiction there than to write poetry or a play. Less concentration is required. Jane Austen wrote like that to the end of her days. 'How she was able to effect all this', her nephew writes in his Memoir, 'is surprising, for she had no separate study to repair to, and most of the work must have been done in the general sitting-room, subject to all kinds of casual interruptions. She was careful that her occupation should not be suspected by servants or visitors or any persons beyond her own family party.[8] Jane Austen hid her manuscripts or covered them with a piece of blotting-paper. Then, again, all the literary training that a woman had in the early nineteenth century was training in the observation of character, in the analysis of emotion. Her sensibility had been educated for centuries by the influences of the common sitting-room. People's feelings were impressed on her; personal relations were always before her eyes. Therefore, when the middle-class woman took to writing, she naturally wrote novels, even though, as seems evident enough, two of the four famous women here named were not by nature novelists. Emily Brontë should have written poetic plays; the overflow of George Eliot's capacious mind should have spread itself when the creative impulse was spent upon history or biography. They wrote novels, however; one may even go further, I said, taking PRIDE AND PREJUDICE from the shelf, and say that they wrote good novels. Without boasting or giving pain to the opposite sex, one may say that PRIDE AND PREJUDICE is a good book. At any rate, one would not have been ashamed to have been caught in the act of writing PRIDE AND PREJUDICE. Yet Jane Austen was glad that a hinge creaked, so that she might hide her manuscript before anyone came in. To Jane Austen there was something discreditable in writing PRIDE AND PREJUDICE. And, I wondered, would PRIDE AND PREJUDICE have been a better novel if Jane Austen had not thought it necessary to hide her manuscript from visitors? I read a page or two to see; but I could not find any signs that her circumstances had harmed her work in the slightest. That, perhaps, was the chief miracle about it. Here was a woman about the year 1800 writing without hate, without bitterness, without fear, without protest, without preaching. That was how Shakespeare wrote, I thought, looking at ANTONY AND CLEOPATRA; and when people compare Shakespeare and Jane Austen, they may mean that the minds of both had consumed all impediments; and

---

[8] MEMOIR OF JANE AUSTEN, by her nephew, James Edward Austen-Leigh.

for that reason we do not know Jane Austen and we do not know Shakespeare, and for that reason Jane Austen pervades every word that she wrote, and so does Shakespeare. If Jane Austen suffered in any way from her circumstances it was in the narrowness of life that was imposed upon her. It was impossible for a woman to go about alone. She never travelled; she never drove through London in an omnibus or had luncheon in a shop by herself. But perhaps it was the nature of Jane Austen not to want what she had not. Her gift and her circumstances matched each other completely. But I doubt whether that was true of Charlotte Brontë, I said, opening JANE EYRE and laying it beside PRIDE AND PREJUDICE.

I opened it at chapter twelve and my eye was caught by the phrase 'Anybody may blame me who likes'. What were they blaming Charlotte Brontë for? I wondered. And I read how Jane Eyre used to go up on to the roof when Mrs Fairfax was making jellies and looked over the fields at the distant view. And then she longed--and it was for this that they blamed her--that 'then I longed for a power of vision which might overpass that limit; which might reach the busy world, towns, regions full of life I had heard of but never seen: that then I desired more of practical experience than I possessed; more of intercourse with my kind, of acquaintance with variety of character than was here within my reach. I valued what was good in Mrs Fairfax, and what was good in Adele; but I believed in the existence of other and more vivid kinds of goodness, and what I believed in I wished to behold.

'Who blames me? Many, no doubt, and I shall he called discontented. I could not help it: the restlessness was in my nature; it agitated me to pain sometimes...

'It is vain to say human beings ought to be satisfied with tranquillity: they must have action; and they will make it if they cannot find it. Millions are condemned to a stiller doom than mine, and millions are in silent revolt against their lot. Nobody knows how many rebellions ferment in the masses of life which people earth. Women are supposed to be very calm generally: but women feel just as men feel; they need exercise for their faculties and a field for their efforts as much as their brothers do; they suffer from too rigid a restraint, too absolute a stagnation, precisely as men would suffer; and it is narrow-minded in their more privileged fellow-creatures to say that they ought to confine themselves to making puddings and knitting stockings, to playing on the piano and embroidering bags. It is thoughtless to condemn them, or laugh at them, if they seek to do more or learn more than custom has pronounced necessary for their sex.

'When thus alone I not unfrequently heard Grace Poole's laugh...'

That is an awkward break, I thought. It is upsetting to come upon Grace Poole all of a sudden. The continuity is disturbed. One might say, I continued, laying the book down beside PRIDE AND PREJUDICE, that the woman who wrote those pages had more genius in her than Jane Austen; but if one reads them over and marks that jerk in them, that indignation, one sees that she will never get her genius expressed whole and entire. Her books will be deformed and twisted. She will write in a rage where she should write calmly. She will write foolishly where she should write wisely. She will write of herself where she should write of her characters. She is at war with her lot. How could she help but die young, cramped and thwarted?

One could not but play for a moment with the thought of what might have happened if Charlotte Brontë had possessed say three hundred a year--but the foolish woman sold the copyright of her novels outright for fifteen hundred pounds; had somehow possessed more knowledge of the busy world, and towns and regions full of life; more practical experience, and intercourse with her kind and acquaintance with a variety of character. In those words she puts her finger exactly not only upon her own defects as a novelist but upon those of her sex at that time. She knew, no one better, how enormously her genius would have profited if it had not spent itself in solitary visions over distant fields; if experience and intercourse and travel had been granted her. But they were not granted; they were withheld; and we must accept the fact that all those good novels, VILLETTE, EMMA, WUTHERING HEIGHTS, MIDDLEMARCH, were written by women without more experience of life than could enter the house of a respectable clergyman; written too in the common sitting-room of that respectable house and by women so poor that they could not afford to buy more than a few quires of paper at a time upon which to write WUTHERING HEIGHTS or JANE EYRE. One of them, it is true, George Eliot, escaped after much tribulation, but only to a secluded villa in St John's Wood. And there she settled down in the shadow of the world's disapproval. 'I wish it to be understood', she wrote, 'that I should never invite anyone to come and see me who did not ask for the invitation'; for was she not living in sin with a married man and might not the sight of her damage the chastity of Mrs Smith or whoever it might be that chanced to call? One must submit to the social convention, and be 'cut off from what is called the world'. At the same time, on the other side of Europe, there was a young man living freely with this gypsy or with that great lady; going to the wars; picking up unhindered and uncensored all that varied experience of human life which served him so splendidly later when he came to write his books. Had Tolstoi lived at the Priory in seclusion with a married lady 'cut off from what is called the world', however edifying the moral lesson, he could scarcely, I thought, have written WAR AND PEACE.

But one could perhaps go a little deeper into the question of novel-writing and the effect of sex upon the novelist. If one shuts one's eyes and thinks of the novel as a whole, it would seem to be a creation owning a certain looking-glass likeness to life, though of course with simplifications and distortions innumerable. At any rate, it is a structure leaving a shape on the mind's eye, built now in squares, now pagoda shaped, now throwing out wings and arcades, now solidly compact and domed like the Cathedral of Saint Sofia at Constantinople. This shape, I thought, thinking back over certain famous novels, starts in one the kind of emotion that is appropriate to it. But that emotion at once blends itself with others, for the 'shape' is not made by the relation of stone to stone, but by the relation of human being to human being. Thus a novel starts in us all sorts of antagonistic and opposed emotions. Life conflicts with something that is not life. Hence the difficulty of coming to any agreement about novels, and the immense sway that our private prejudices have upon us. On the one hand we feel You--John the hero--must live, or I shall be in the depths of despair.

On the other, we feel, Alas, John, you must die, because the shape of the book requires it. Life conflicts with something that is not life. Then since life it is in part, we judge it as life. James is the sort of man I most detest, one says. Or, This is a farrago of absurdity. I could never feel anything of the sort myself. The whole structure, it is obvious, thinking back on any famous novel, is one of infinite complexity, because it is thus made up of so many different judgements, of so many different kinds of emotion. The wonder is that any book so composed holds together for more than a year or two, or can possibly mean to the English reader what it means for the Russian or the Chinese. But they do hold together occasionally very remarkably. And what holds them together in these rare instances of survival (I was thinking of WAR AND PEACE) is something that one calls integrity, though it has nothing to do with paying one's bills or behaving honourably in an emergency. What one means by integrity, in the case of the novelist, is the conviction that he gives one that this is the truth. Yes, one feels, I should never have thought that this could be so; I have never known people behaving like that. But you have convinced me that so it is, so it happens. One holds every phrase, every scene to the light as one reads--for Nature seems, very oddly, to have provided us with an inner light by which to judge of the novelist's integrity or disintegrity. Or perhaps it is rather that Nature, in her most irrational mood, has traced in invisible ink on the walls of the mind a premonition which these great artists confirm; a sketch which only needs to be held to the fire of genius to become visible. When one so exposes it and sees it come to life one exclaims in rapture, But this is what I have always felt and known and desired! And one boils over with excitement, and, shutting the book even with a kind of reverence as if it were something very precious, a stand-by to return to as long as one lives, one puts it back on the shelf, I said, taking WAR AND PEACE and putting it back in its place. If, on the other hand, these poor sentences that one takes and tests rouse first a quick and eager response with their bright colouring and their dashing gestures but there they stop: something seems to check them in their development: or if they bring to light only a faint scribble in that corner and a blot over there, and nothing appears whole and entire, then one heaves a sigh of disappointment and says. Another failure. This novel has come to grief somewhere.

And for the most part, of course, novels do come to grief somewhere. The imagination falters under the enormous strain. The insight is confused; it can no longer distinguish between the true and the false, it has no longer the strength to go on with the vast labour that calls at every moment for the use of so many different faculties. But how would all this be affected by the sex of the novelist, I wondered, looking at JANE EYRE and the others. Would the fact of her sex in any way interfere with the integrity of a woman novelist--that integrity which I take to be the backbone of the writer? Now, in the passages I have quoted from JANE EYRE, it is clear that anger was tampering with the integrity of Charlotte Brontë the novelist. She left her story, to which her entire devotion was due, to attend to some personal grievance. She remembered that she had been starved of her proper due of experience--she had been made to stagnate in a parsonage mending stockings when she wanted to wander free over the world. Her imagination swerved from indignation and we feel it swerve. But there were many more influences than anger tugging at her imagination and deflecting it from its path. Ignorance, for instance.

The portrait of Rochester is drawn in the dark. We feel the influence of fear in it; just as we constantly feel an acidity which is the result of oppression, a buried suffering smouldering beneath her passion, a rancour which contracts those books, splendid as they are, with a spasm of pain.

And since a novel has this correspondence to real life, its values are to some extent those of real life. But it is obvious that the values of women differ very often from the values which have been made by the other sex; naturally, this is so. Yet it is the masculine values that prevail. Speaking crudely, football and sport are 'important'; the worship of fashion, the buying of clothes 'trivial'. And these values are inevitably transferred from life to fiction. This is an important book, the critic assumes, because it deals with war. This is an insignificant book because it deals with the feelings of women in a drawing-room. A scene in a battle-field is more important than a scene in a shop--everywhere and much more subtly the difference of value persists. The whole structure, therefore, of the early nineteenth-century novel was raised, if one was a woman, by a mind which was slightly pulled from the straight, and made to alter its clear vision in deference to external authority. One has only to skim those old forgotten novels and listen to the tone of voice in which they are written to divine that the writer was meeting criticism; she was saying this by way of aggression, or that by way of conciliation. She was admitting that she was 'only a woman', or protesting that she was 'as good as a man'. She met that criticism as her temperament dictated, with docility and diffidence, or with anger and emphasis. It does not matter which it was; she was thinking of something other than the thing itself. Down comes her book upon our heads. There was a flaw in the centre of it. And I thought of all the women's novels that lie scattered, like small pock-marked apples in an orchard, about the second-hand book shops of London. It was the flaw in the centre that had rotted them. She had altered her values in deference to the opinion of others.

But how impossible it must have been for them not to budge either to the right or to the left. What genius, what integrity it must have required in face of all that criticism, in the midst of that purely patriarchal society, to hold fast to the thing as they saw it without shrinking. Only Jane Austen did it and Emily Brontë. It is another feather, perhaps the finest, in their caps. They wrote as women write, not as men write. Of all the thousand women who wrote novels then, they alone entirely ignored the perpetual admonitions of the eternal pedagogue--write this, think that. They alone were deaf to that persistent voice, now grumbling, now patronizing, now domineering, now grieved, now shocked, now angry, now avuncular, that voice which cannot let women alone, but must be at them, like some too-conscientious governess, adjuring them, like Sir Egerton Brydges, to be refined; dragging even into the criticism of poetry criticism of sex;[9] admonishing them, if they would be good and win, as I suppose, some shiny prize, to keep within certain limits which the

---

[9] She] has a metaphysical purpose, and that is a dangerous obsession, especially with a woman, for women rarely possess men's healthy love of rhetoric. It is a strange lack in the sex which is in other things more primitive and more materialistic.'--NEW CRITERION, June 1928.

gentleman in question thinks suitable--'... female novelists should only aspire to excellence by courageously acknowledging the limitations of their sex'.[10] That puts the matter in a nutshell, and when I tell you, rather to your surprise, that this sentence was written not in August 1828 but in August 1928, you will agree, I think, that however delightful it is to us now, it represents a vast body of opinion--I am not going to stir those old pools; I take only what chance has floated to my feet--that was far more vigorous and far more vocal a century ago. It would have needed a very stalwart young woman in 1828 to disregard all those snubs and chidings and promises of prizes. One must have been something of a firebrand to say to oneself, Oh, but they can't buy literature too. Literature is open to everybody. I refuse to allow you, Beadle though you are, to turn me off the grass. Lock up your libraries if you like; but there is no gate, no lock, no bolt, that you can set upon the freedom of my mind.

But whatever effect discouragement and criticism had upon their writing--and I believe that they had a very great effect--that was unimportant compared with the other difficulty which faced them (I was still considering those early nineteenth-century novelists) when they came to set their thoughts on paper--that is that they had no tradition behind them, or one so short and partial that it was of little help. For we think back through our mothers if we are women. It is useless to go to the great men writers for help, however much one may go to them for pleasure. Lamb, Browne, Thackeray, Newman, Sterne, Dickens, De Quincey--whoever it may be-- never helped a woman yet, though she may have learnt a few tricks of them and adapted them to her use. The weight, the pace, the stride of a man's mind are too unlike her own for her to lift anything substantial from him successfully. The ape is too distant to be sedulous. Perhaps the first thing she would find, setting pen to paper, was that there was no common sentence ready for her use. All the great novelists like Thackeray and Dickens and Balzac have written a natural prose, swift but not slovenly, expressive but not precious, taking their own tint without ceasing to be common property. They have based it on the sentence that was current at the time. The sentence that was current at the beginning of the nineteenth century ran something like this perhaps: 'The grandeur of their works was an argument with them, not to stop short, but to proceed. They could have no higher excitement or satisfaction than in the exercise of their art and endless generations of truth and beauty. Success prompts to exertion; and habit facilitates success.' That is a man's sentence; behind it one can see Johnson, Gibbon and the rest. It was a sentence that was unsuited for a woman's use. Charlotte Brontë, with all her splendid gift for prose, stumbled and fell with that clumsy weapon in her hands. George Eliot committed atrocities with it that beggar description. Jane Austen looked at it and laughed at it and devised a perfectly natural, shapely sentence proper for her own use and never departed from it. Thus, with less genius for writing than Charlotte Brontë, she got infinitely more said. Indeed, since freedom and fullness of expression are of

---

[10] 'If, like the reporter, you believe that female novelists should only aspire to excellence by courageously acknowledging the limitations of their sex (Jane Austen [has] demonstrated how gracefully this gesture can be accomplished...).'--LIFE AND LETTERS, August 1928.

the essence of the art, such a lack of tradition, such a scarcity and inadequacy of tools, must have told enormously upon the writing of women. Moreover, a book is not made of sentences laid end to end, but of sentences built, if an image helps, into arcades or domes. And this shape too has been made by men out of their own needs for their own uses. There is no reason to think that the form of the epic or of the poetic play suit a woman any more than the sentence suits her. But all the older forms of literature were hardened and set by the time she became a writer. The novel alone was young enough to be soft in her hands another reason, perhaps, why she wrote novels. Yet who shall say that even now 'the novel' (I give it inverted commas to mark my sense of the words' inadequacy), who shall say that even this most pliable of all forms is rightly shaped for her use? No doubt we shall find her knocking that into shape for herself when she has the free use of her limbs; and providing some new vehicle, not necessarily in verse, for the poetry in her. For it is the poetry that is still denied outlet. And I went on to ponder how a woman nowadays would write a poetic tragedy in five acts. Would she use verse?--would she not use prose rather?

But these are difficult questions which lie in the twilight of the future. I must leave them, if only because they stimulate me to wander from my subject into trackless forests where I shall be lost and, very likely, devoured by wild beasts. I do not want, and I am sure that you do not want me, to broach that very dismal subject, the future of fiction. so that I will only pause here one moment to draw your attention to the great part which must be played in that future so far as women are concerned by physical conditions. The book has somehow to be adapted to the body, and at a venture one would say that women's books should be shorter, more concentrated, than those of men, and framed so that they do not need long hours of steady and uninterrupted work. For interruptions there will always be. Again, the nerves that feed the brain would seem to differ in men and women, and if you are going to make them work their best and hardest, you must find out what treatment suits them--whether these hours of lectures, for instance, which the monks devised, presumably, hundreds of years ago, suit them--what alternations of work and rest they need, interpreting rest not as doing nothing but as doing something but something that is different; and what should that difference be? All this should be discussed and discovered; all this is part of the question of women and fiction. And yet, I continued, approaching the bookcase again, where shall I find that elaborate study of the psychology of women by a woman? If through their incapacity to play football women are not going to be allowed to practise medicine--

Happily my thoughts were now given another turn.

FIVE

I had come at last, in the course of this rambling, to the shelves which hold books by the living; by women and by men; for there are almost as many books written by women now as by men. Or if that is not yet quite true, if the male is still the voluble sex, it is certainly true that women no longer write novels solely. There are Jane Harrison's books on Greek archaeology; Vernon Lee's books on aesthetics; Gertrude Bell's books on Persia. There are books on all sorts of subjects which a generation ago no woman could have touched. There are poems and plays and criticism; there are histories and biographies, books of travel and books of scholarship and research; there are even a few philosophies and books about science and economics. And though novels predominate, novels themselves may very well have changed from association with books of a different feather. The natural simplicity, the epic age of women's writing, may have gone. Reading and criticism may have given her a wider range, a greater subtlety. The impulse towards autobiography may be spent. She may be beginning to use writing as an art, not as a method of selfexpression. Among these new novels one might find an answer to several such questions.

I took down one of them at random. It stood at the very end of the shelf, was called LIFE'S ADVENTURE, or some such title, by Mary Carmichael, and was published in this very month of October. It seems to be her first book, I said to myself, but one must read it as if it were the last volume in a fairly long series, continuing all those other books that I have been glancing at--Lady Winchilsea's poems and Aphra Behn's plays and the novels of the four great novelists. For books continue each other, in spite of our habit of judging them separately. And I must also consider her--this unknown woman--as the descendant of all those other women whose circumstances I have been glancing at and see what she inherits of their characteristics and restrictions. So, with a sigh, because novels so often provide an anodyne and not an antidote, glide one into torpid slumbers instead of rousing one with a burning brand, I settled down with a notebook and a pencil to make what I could of Mary Carmichael's first novel, LIFE'S ADVENTURE.

To begin with, I ran my eye up and down the page. I am going to get the hang of her sentences first, I said, before I load my memory with blue eyes and brown and the relationship that there may be between Chloe and Roger. There will be time for that when I have decided whether she has a pen in her hand or a pickaxe. So I tried a sentence or two on my tongue. Soon it was obvious that something was not quite in order. The smooth gliding of sentence after sentence was interrupted. Something tore, something scratched; a single word here and there flashed its torch in my eyes. She was 'unhanding' herself as they say in the old plays. She is like a person striking a match that will not light, I thought. But why, I asked her as if she were present, are Jane Austen's sentences not of the right shape for you? Must they all be scrapped because Emma and Mr Woodhouse are dead? Alas, I sighed, that it should be so. For while Jane Austen breaks from melody to melody as Mozart from song to song, to read this writing was like being out at sea in an open boat. Up one went, down one sank. This terseness, this short-windedness, might mean that she was afraid of something; afraid of being called 'sentimental' perhaps; or she remembers that women's writing has been called flowery and so provides a superfluity of thorns; but until I have read a scene with some care, I cannot be surewhether she is being herself or someone else. At any rate, she does not lower one's vitality, I thought, reading more carefully. But she is heaping up too many facts. She will not be able to use half of them in a book of this size. (It was about half the length of JANE EYRE.) However, by some means or other she succeeded in getting us all--Roger, Chloe, Olivia, Tony and Mr Bigham--in a canoe up the river. Wait a moment, I said, leaning back in my chair, I must consider the whole thing more carefully before I go any further.

I am almost sure, I said to myself, that Mary Carmichael is playing a trick on us. For I feel as one feels on a switchback railway when the car, instead of sinking, as one has been led to expect, swerves up again. Mary is tampering with the expected sequence. First she broke the sentence; now she has broken the sequence. Very well, she has every right to do both these things if she does them not for the sake of breaking, but for the sake of creating. Which of the two it is I cannot be sure until she has faced herself with a situation. I will give her every liberty, I said, to choose what that situation shall be; she shall make it of tin cans and old kettles if she likes; but she must convince me that she believes it to be a situation; and then when she has made it she must face it. She must jump. And, determined to do my duty by her as reader if she would do her duty by me as writer, I turned the page and read...I am sorry to break off so abruptly. Are there no men present? Do you promise me that behind that red curtain over there the figure of Sir Charles Biron is not concealed? We are all women you assure me? Then I may tell you that the very next words I read were these--'Chloe liked Olivia...' Do not start. Do not blush. Let us admit in the privacy of our own society that these things sometimes happen. Sometimes women do like women.

'Chloe liked Olivia,' I read. And then it struck me how immense a change was there. Chloe liked Olivia perhaps for the first time in literature. Cleopatra did not like Octavia. And how completely ANTONY AND CLEOPATRA would have been altered had she done so! As it is, I thought, letting my mind, I am afraid, wander a little from LIFE'S ADVENTURE, the whole thing is simplified, conventionalized, if one dared say it, absurdly. Cleopatra's only feeling about Octavia is one of jealousy. Is she taller than I am? How does she do her hair? The play, perhaps, required no more. But how interesting it would have been if the relationship between the two women had been more complicated. All these relationships between women, I thought, rapidly recalling the splendid gallery of fictitious women, are too simple. So much has been left out, unattempted. And I tried to remember any case in the course of my reading where two women are represented as friends. There is an attempt at it in DIANA OF THE CROSSWAYS. They are confidantes, of course, in Racine and the Greek tragedies. They are now and then mothers and daughters. But almost without exception they are shown in their relation to men. It was strange to think that all the great women of fiction were, until Jane Austen's day, not only seen by the other sex, but seen only in relation to the other sex. And how small a part of a woman's life is that; and how little can a man know even of that when he observes it through the black or rosy spectacles which sex puts upon his nose. Hence, perhaps, the peculiar nature of woman in fiction; the astonishing extremes of her beauty and horror; her alternations between heavenly goodness and hellish depravity--for so a lover would see her as his love rose or sank, was prosperous or unhappy. This is not so true of the nineteenth-century novelists, of course. Woman becomes much more various and complicated there. Indeed it was the desire to write about women perhaps that led men by degrees to abandon the poetic drama which, with its violence, could make so little use of them, and to devise the novel as a more fitting receptacle. Even so it remains obvious, even in the writing of Proust, that a man is terribly hampered and partial in his knowledge of women, as a woman in her knowledge of men.

Also, I continued, looking down at the page again, it is becoming evident that women, like men, have other interests besides the perennial interests of domesticity. 'Chloe liked Olivia. They shared a laboratory together...' I read on and discovered that these two young women were engaged in mincing liver, which is, it seems, a cure for pernicious anaemia; although one of them was married and had--I think I am right in stating--two small children. Now all that, of course, has had to be left out, and thus the splendid portrait of the fictitious woman is much too simple and much too monotonous. Suppose, for instance, that men were only represented in literature as the lovers of women, and were never the friends of men, soldiers, thinkers, dreamers; how few parts in the plays of Shakespeare could be allotted to them; how literature would suffer! We might perhaps have most of Othello; and a good deal of Antony; but no Caesar, no Brutus, no Hamlet, no Lear, no Jaques--literature would be incredibly impoverished, as indeed literature is impoverished beyond our counting by the doors that have been shut upon women. Married against their will, kept in one room, and to one occupation, how could a dramatist give a full or interesting or truthful account of them? Love was the only possible interpreter. The poet was forced to be passionate or bitter, unless indeed he chose to 'hate women', which meant more often than not that he was unattractive to them.

Now if Chloe likes Olivia and they share a laboratory, which of itself will make their friendship more varied and lasting because it will be less personal; if Mary Carmichael knows how to write, and I was beginning to enjoy some quality in her style; if she has a room to herself, of which I am not quite sure; if she has five hundred a year of her own--but that remains to be proved--then I think that something of great importance has happened.

For if Chloe likes Olivia and Mary Carmichael knows how to express it she will light a torch in that vast chamber where nobody has yet been. It is all half lights and profound shadows like those serpentine caves where one goes with a candle peering up and down, not knowing where one is stepping. And I began to read the book again, and read how Chloe watched Olivia put a jar on a shelf and say how it was time to go home to her children. That is a sight that has never been seen since the world began, I exclaimed. And I watched too, very curiously. For I wanted to see how Mary Carmichael set to work to catch those unrecorded gestures, those unsaid or half-said words, which form themselves, no more palpably than the shadows of moths on the ceiling, when women are alone, unlit by the capricious and coloured light of the other sex. She will need to hold her breath, I said, reading on, if she is to do it; for women are so suspicious of any interest that has not some obvious motive behind it, so terribly accustomed to concealment and suppression, that they are off at the flicker of an eye turned observingly in their direction. The only way for you to do it, I thought, addressing Mary Carmichael as if she were there, would be to talk of something else, looking steadily out of the window, and thus note, not with a pencil in a notebook, but in the shortest of shorthand, in words that are hardly syllabled yet, what happens when Olivia--this organism that has been under the shadow of the rock these million years--feels the light fall on it, and sees coming her way a piece of strange food--knowledge, adventure, art. And she reaches out for it, I thought, again raising my eyes from the page, and has to devise some entirely new combination of her resources, so highly developed for other purposes, so as to absorb the new into the old without disturbing the infinitely intricate and elaborate balance of the whole.

But, alas, I had done what I had determined not to do; I had slipped unthinkingly into praise of my own sex. 'Highly developed'--'infinitely intricate'--such are undeniably terms of praise, and to praise one's own sex is always suspect, often silly; moreover, in this case, how could one justify it? One could not go to the map and say Columbus discovered America and Columbus was a woman; or take an apple and remark, Newton discovered the laws of gravitation and Newton was a woman; or look into the sky and say aeroplanes are flying overhead and aeroplanes were invented by women. There is no mark on the wall to measure the precise height of women. There are no yard measures, neatly divided into the fractions of an inch, that one can lay against the qualities of a good mother or the devotion of a daughter, or the fidelity of a sister, or the capacity of a housekeeper. Few women even now have been graded at the universities; the great trials of the professions, army and navy, trade, politics and diplomacy have hardly tested them. They remain even at this moment almost unclassified. But if I want to know all that a human being can tell me about Sir Hawley Butts, for instance, I have only to open Burke or Debrett and I shall find that he took such and such a degree; owns a hall; has an heir; was Secretary to a Board; represented Great Britain in Canada; and has received a certain number of degrees, offices, medals and other distinctions by which his merits are stamped upon him indelibly. Only Providence can know more about Sir Hawley Butts than that.

When, therefore, I say 'highly developed', 'infinitely intricate' of women, I am unable to verify my words either in Whitaker, Debrett or the University Calendar. In this predicament what can I do? And I looked at the bookcase again. There were the biographies: Johnson and Goethe and Carlyle and Sterne and Cowper and Shelley and Voltaire and Browning and many others. And I began thinking of all those great men who have for one reason or another admired, sought out, lived with, confided in, made love to, written of, trusted in, and shown what can only be described as some need of and dependence upon certain persons of the opposite sex. That all these relationships were absolutely Platonic I would not affirm, and Sir William Joynson Hicks would probably deny. But we should wrong these illustrious men very greatly if we insisted that they got nothing from these alliances but comfort, flattery and the pleasures of the body. What they got, it is obvious, was something that their own sex was unable to supply; and it would not be rash, perhaps, to define it further, without quoting the doubtless rhapsodical words of the poets, as some stimulus; some renewal of creative power which is in the gift only of the opposite sex to bestow. He would open the door of drawing-room or nursery, I thought, and find her among her children perhaps, or with a piece of embroidery on her knee--at any rate, the centre of some different order and system of life, and the contrast between this world and his own, which might be the law courts or the House of Commons, would at once refresh and invigorate; and there would follow, even in the simplest talk, such a natural difference of opinion that the dried ideas in him would be fertilized anew; and the sight of her creating in a different medium from his own would so quicken his creative power that insensibly his sterile mind would begin to plot again, and he would find the phrase or the scene which was lacking when he put on his hat to visit her. Every Johnson has his Thrale, and holds fast to her for some such reasons as these, and when the Thrale marries her Italian music master Johnson goes half mad with rage and disgust, not merely that he will miss his pleasant evenings at Streatham, but that the light of his life will be 'as if gone out'.

And without being Dr Johnson or Goethe or Carlyle or Voltaire, one may feel, though very differently from these great men, the nature of this intricacy and the power of this highly developed creative faculty among women. One goes into the room--but the resources of the English language would he much put to the stretch, and whole flights of words would need to wing their way illegitimately into existence before a woman could say what happens when she goes into a room. The rooms differ so completely; they are calm or thunderous; open on to the sea, or, on the contrary, give on to a prison yard; are hung with washing; or alive with opals and silks; are hard as horsehair or soft as feathers--one has only to go into any room in any street for the whole of that extremely complex force of femininity to fly in one's face. How should it be otherwise? For women have sat indoors all these millions of years, so that by this time the very walls are permeated by their creative force, which has, indeed, so overcharged the capacity of bricks and mortar that it must needs harness itself to pens and brushes and business and politics. But this creative power differs greatly from the creative power of men. And one must conclude that it would be a thousand pities if it were hindered or wasted, for it was won by centuries of the most drastic discipline, and there is nothing to take its place. It would be a thousand pities if women wrote like men, or lived like men, or looked like men, for if two sexes are quite inadequate, considering the vastness and variety of the world, how should we manage with one only? Ought not education to bring out and fortify the differences rather than the similarities? For we have too much likeness as it is, and if an explorer should come back and bring word of other sexes looking through the branches of other trees at other skies, nothing would he of greater service to humanity; and we should have the immense pleasure into the bargain of watching Professor X rush for his measuring-rods to prove himself 'superior'.

Mary Carmichael, I thought, still hovering at a little distance above the page, will have her work cut out for her merely as an observer. I am afraid indeed that she will be tempted to become, what I think the less interesting branch of the species--the naturalist-novelist, and not the contemplative. There are so many new facts for her to observe. She will not need to limit herself any longer to the respectable houses of the upper middle classes. She will go without kindness or condescension, but in the spirit of fellowship, into those small, scented rooms where sit the courtesan, the harlot and the lady with the pug dog. There they still sit in the rough and ready-made clothes that the male writer has had perforce to clap upon their shoulders. But Mary Carmichael will have out her scissors and fit them close to every hollow and angle. It will be a curious sight, when it comes, to see these women as they are, but we must wait a little, for Mary Carmichael will still be encumbered with that self-consciousness in the presence of 'sin' which is the legacy of our sexual barbarity. She will still wear the shoddy old fetters of class on her feet.

However, the majority of women are neither harlots nor courtesans; nor do they sit clasping pug dogs to dusty velvet all through the summer afternoon. But what do they do then? and there came to my mind's eye one of those long streets somewhere south of the river whose infinite rows are innumerably populated. With the eye of the imagination I saw a very ancient lady crossing the street on the arm of a middle-aged woman, her daughter, perhaps, both so respectably booted and furred that their dressing in the afternoon must be a ritual, and the clothes themselves put away in cupboards with camphor, year after year, throughout the summer months. They cross the road when the lamps are being lit (for the dusk is their favourite hour), as they must have done year after year. The elder is close on eighty; but if one asked her what her life has meant to her, she would say that she remembered the streets lit for the battle of Balaclava, or had heard the guns fire in Hyde Park for the birth of King Edward the Seventh. And if one asked her, longing to pin down the moment with date and season, but what were you doing on the fifth of April 1868, or the second of November 1875, she would look vague and say that she could remember nothing. For all the dinners are cooked; the plates and cups washed; the children sent to school and gone out into the world. Nothing remains of it all. All has vanished. No biography or history has a word to say about it. And the novels, without meaning to, inevitably lie.

All these infinitely obscure lives remain to be recorded, I said, addressing Mary Carmichael as if she were present; and went on in thought through the streets of London feeling in imagination the pressure of dumbness, the accumulation of unrecorded life, whether from the women at the street corners with their arms akimbo, and the rings embedded in their fat swollen fingers, talking with a gesticulation like the swing of Shakespeare's words; or from the violet-sellers and match-sellers and old crones stationed under doorways; or from drifting girls whose faces, like waves in sun and cloud, signal the coming of men and women and the flickering lights of shop windows. All that you will have to explore, I said to Mary Carmichael, holding your torch firm in your hand. Above all, you must illumine your own soul with its profundities and its shallows, and its vanities and its generosities, and say what your beauty means to you or your plainness, and what is your relation to the everchanging and turning world of gloves and shoes and stuffs swaying up and down among the faint scents that come through chemists' bottles down arcades of dress material over a floor of pseudo-marble. For in imagination I had gone into a shop; it was laid with black and white paving; it was hung, astonishingly beautifully, with coloured ribbons. Mary Carmichael might well have a look at that in passing, I thought, for it is a sight that would lend itself to the pen as fittingly as any snowy peak or rocky gorge in the Andes. And there is the girl behind the counter too--I would as soon have her true history as the hundred and fiftieth life of Napoleon or seventieth study of Keats and his use of Miltonic inversion which old Professor Z and his like are now inditing. And then I went on very warily, on the very tips of my toes (so cowardly am I, so afraid of the lash that was once almost laid on my own shoulders), to murmur that she should also learn to laugh, without bitterness, at the vanities--say rather at the peculiarities, for it is a less offensive word--of the other sex. For there is a spot the size of a shilling at the back of the head which one can never see for oneself. It is one of the good offices that sex can discharge for sex--to describe that spot the size of a shilling at the back of the head. Think how much women have profited by the comments of Juvenal; by the criticism of Strindberg. Think with what humanity and brilliancy men, from the earliest ages, have pointed out to women that dark place at the back of the head! And if Mary were very brave and very honest, she would go behind the other sex and tell us what she found there. A true picture of man as a whole can never be painted until a woman has described that spot the size of a shilling. Mr Woodhouse and Mr Casuabon are spots of that size and nature. Not of course that anyone in their senses would counsel her to hold up to scorn and ridicule of set purpose--literature shows the futility of what is written in that spirit. Be truthful, one would say, and the result is bound to be amazingly interesting. Comedy is bound to be enriched. New facts are bound to be discovered.

However, it was high time to lower my eyes to the page again. It would be better, instead of speculating what Mary Carmichael might write and should write, to see what in fact Mary Carmichael did write. So I began to read again. I remembered that I had certain grievances against her. She had broken up Jane Austen's sentence, and thus given me no chance of pluming myself upon my impeccable taste, my fastidious ear. For it was useless to say, 'Yes, yes, this is very nice; but Jane Austen wrote much better than you do', when I had to admit that there was no point of likeness between them. Then she had gone further and broken the sequence--the expected order. Perhaps she had done this unconsciously, merely giving things their natural order, as a woman would, if she wrote like a woman. But the effect was somehow baffling; one could not see a wave heaping itself, a crisis coming round the next corner. Therefore I could not plume myself either upon the depths of my feelings and my profound knowledge of the human heart. For whenever I was about to feel the usual things in the usual places, about love, about death, the annoying creature twitched me away, as if the important point were just a little further on. And thus she made it impossible for me to roll out my sonorous phrases about 'elemental feelings', the 'common stuff of humanity', 'the depths of the human heart', and ail those other phrases which support us in our belief that, however clever we may be on top, we are very serious, very profound and very humane underneath. She made me feel, on the contrary, that instead of being serious and profound and humane, one might be--and the thought was far less seductive--merely lazy minded and conventional into the bargain.

But I read on, and noted certain other facts. She was no 'genius' that was evident. She had nothing like the love of Nature, the fiery imagination, the wild poetry, the brilliant wit, the brooding wisdom of her great predecessors, Lady Winchilsea, Charlotte Brontë, Emily Brontë, Jane Austen and George Eliot; she could not write with the melody and the dignity of Dorothy Osborne--indeed she was no more than a clever girl whose books will no doubt be pulped by the publishers in ten years' time. But, nevertheless, she had certain advantages which women of far greater gift lacked even half a century ago. Men were no longer to her 'the opposing faction'; she need not waste her time railing against them; she need not climb on to the roof and ruin her peace of mind longing for travel, experience and a knowledge of the world and character that were denied her. Fear and hatred were almost gone, or traces of them showed only in a slight exaggeration of the joy of freedom, a tendency to the caustic and satirical, rather than to the romantic, in her treatment of the other sex. Then there could be no doubt that as a novelist she enjoyed some natural advantages of a high order. She had a sensibility that was very wide, eager and free. It responded to an almost imperceptible touch on it. It feasted like a plant newly stood in the air on every sight and sound that came its way. It ranged, too, very subtly and curiously, among almost unknown or unrecorded things; it lighted on small things and showed that perhaps they were not small after all. It brought buried things to light and made one wonder what need there had been to bury them. Awkward though she was and without the unconscious bearing of long descent which makes the least turn of the pen of a Thackeray or a Lamb delightful to the ear, she had--I began to think--mastered the first great lesson; she wrote as a woman, but as a woman who has forgotten that she is a woman, so that her pages were full of that curious sexual quality which comes only when sex is unconscious of itself.

All this was to the good. But no abundance of sensation or fineness of perception would avail unless she could build up out of the fleeting and the personal the lasting edifice which remains unthrown. I had said that I would wait until she faced herself with 'a situation'. And I meant by that until she proved by summoning, beckoning and getting together that she was not a skimmer of surfaces merely, but had looked beneath into the depths. Now is the time, she would say to herself at a certain moment, when without doing anything violent I can show the meaning of all this. And she would begin--how unmistakable that quickening is!--beckoning and summoning, and there would rise up in memory, half forgotten, perhaps quite trivial things in other chapters dropped by the way. And she would make their presence felt while someone sewed or smoked a pipe as naturally as possible, and one would feel, as she went on writing, as if one had gone to the top of the world and seen it laid out, very majestically, beneath.

At any rate, she was making the attempt. And as I watched her lengthening out for the test, I saw, but hoped that she did not see, the bishops and the deans, the doctors and the professors, the patriarchs and the pedagogues all at her shouting warning and advice. You can't do this and you shan't do that! Fellows and scholars only allowed on the grass! Ladies not admitted without a letter of introduction! Aspiring and graceful female novelists this way! So they kept at her like the crowd at a fence on the racecourse, and it was her trial to take her fence without looking to right or to left. If you stop to curse you are lost, I said to her; equally, if you stop to laugh. Hesitate or fumble and you are done for. Think only of the jump, I implored her, as if I had put the whole of my money on her back; and she went over it like a bird. But there was a fence beyond that and a fence beyond that. Whether she had the staying power I was doubtful, for the clapping and the crying were fraying to the nerves. But she did her best. Considering that Mary Carmichael was no genius, but an unknown girl writing her first novel in a bed-sitting-room, without enough of those desirable things, time, money and idleness, she did not do so badly, I thought.

Give her another hundred years, I concluded, reading the last chapter--people's noses and bare shoulders showed naked against a starry sky, for someone had twitched the curtain in the drawing-room--give her a room of her own and five hundred a year, let her speak her mind and leave out half that she now puts in, and she will write a better book one of these days. She will be a poet, I said, putting LIFE'S ADVENTURE, by Mary Carmichael, at the end of the shelf, in another hundred years' time.

SIX

Next day the light of the October morning was falling in dusty shafts through the uncurtained windows, and the hum of traffic rose from the street. London then was winding itself up again; the factory was astir; the machines were beginning. It was tempting, after all this reading, to look out of the window and see what London was doing on the morning of the 26th of October 1928. And what was London doing? Nobody, it seemed, was reading ANTONY AND CLEOPATRA. London was wholly indifferent, it appeared, to Shakespeare's plays. Nobody cared a straw-- and I do not blame them--for the future of fiction, the death of poetry or the development by the average woman of a prose style completely expressive of her mind. If opinions upon any of these matters had been chalked on the pavement, nobody would have stooped to read them. The nonchalance of the hurrying feet would have rubbed them out in half an hour. Here came an errand-boy; here a woman with a dog on a lead. The fascination of the London street is that no two people are ever alike; each seems bound on some private affair of his own. There were the business-like, with their little bags; there were the drifters rattling sticks upon area railings; there were affable characters to whom the streets serve for clubroom, hailing men in carts and giving information without being asked for it. Also there were funerals to which men, thus suddenly reminded of the passing of their own bodies, lifted their hats. And then a very distinguished gentleman came slowly down a doorstep and paused to avoid collision with a bustling lady who had, by some means or other, acquired a splendid fur coat and a bunch of Parma violets. They all seemed separate, self-absorbed, on business of their own.

At this moment, as so often happens in London, there was a complete lull and suspension of traffic. Nothing came down the street; nobody passed. A single leaf detached itself from the plane tree at the end of the street, and in that pause and suspension fell. Somehow it was like a signal falling, a signal pointing to a force in things which one had overlooked. It seemed to point to a river, which flowed past, invisibly, round the corner, down the street, and took people and eddied them along, as the stream at Oxbridge had taken the undergraduate in his boat and the dead leaves. Now it was bringing from one side of the street to the other diagonally a girl in patent leather boots, and then a young man in a maroon overcoat; it was also bringing a taxi-cab; and it brought all three together at a point directly beneath my window; where the taxi stopped; and the girl and the young man stopped; and they got into the taxi; and then the cab glided off as if it were swept on by the current elsewhere.

The sight was ordinary enough; what was strange was the rhythmical order with which my imagination had invested it; and the fact that the ordinary sight of two people getting into a cab had the power to communicate something of their own seeming satisfaction. The sight of two people coming down the street and meeting at the corner seems to ease the mind of some strain, I thought, watching the taxi turn and make off. Perhaps to think, as I had been thinking these two days, of one sex as distinct from the other is an effort. It interferes with the unity of the mind. Now that effort had ceased and that unity had been restored by seeing two people come together and get into a taxicab. The mind is certainly a very mysterious organ, I reflected, drawing my head in from the window, about which nothing whatever is known, though we depend upon it so completely. Why do I feel that there are severances and oppositions in the mind, as there are strains from obvious causes on the body? What does one mean by 'the unity of the mind'? I pondered, for clearly the mind has so great a power of concentrating at any point at any moment that it seems to have no single state of being. It can separate itself from the people in the street, for example, and think of itself as apart from them, at an upper window looking down on them. Or it can think with other people spontaneously, as, for instance, in a crowd waiting to hear some piece of news read out. it can think back through its fathers or through its mothers, as I have said that a woman writing thinks back through her mothers. Again if one is a woman one is often surprised by a sudden splitting off of consciousness, say in walking down Whitehall, when from being the natural inheritor of that civilization, she becomes, on the contrary, outside of it, alien and critical. Clearly the mind is always altering its focus, and bringing the world into different perspectives. But some of these states of mind seem, even if adopted spontaneously, to be less comfortable than others. In order to keep oneself continuing in them one is unconsciously holding something back, and gradually the repression becomes an effort. But there may be some state of mind in which one could continue without effort because nothing is required to be held back. And this perhaps, I thought, coming in from the window, is one of them. For certainly when I saw the couple get into the taxicab the mind felt as if, after being divided, it had come together again in a natural fusion. The obvious reason would be that it is natural for the sexes to co-operate. One has a profound, if irrational, instinct in favour of the theory that the union of man and woman makes for the greatest satisfaction, the most complete happiness. But the sight of the two people getting into the taxi and the satisfaction it gave me made me also ask whether there are two sexes in the mind corresponding to the two sexes in the body, and whether they also require to be united in order to get complete satisfaction and happiness? And I went on amateurishly to sketch a plan of the soul so that in each of us two powers preside, one male, one female; and in the man's brain the man predominates over the woman, and in the woman's brain the woman predominates over the man. The normal and comfortable state of being is that when the two live in harmony together, spiritually co-operating. If one is a man, still the woman part of his brain must have effect; and a woman also must have intercourse with the man in her. Coleridge perhaps meant this when he said that a great mind is androgynous. It is when this fusion takes place that the mind is fully fertilized and uses all its faculties. Perhaps a mind that is purely masculine cannot create, any more than a mind that is purely feminine, I thought. But it would he well to test what one meant by man-womanly, and conversely by woman-manly, by pausing and looking at a book or two.

Coleridge certainly did not mean, when he said that a great mind is androgynous, that it is a mind that has any special sympathy with women; a mind that takes up their cause or devotes itself to their interpretation. Perhaps the androgynous mind is less apt to make these distinctions than the single-sexed mind. He meant, perhaps, that the androgynous mind is resonant and porous; that it transmits emotion without impediment; that it is naturally creative, incandescent and undivided. In fact one goes back to Shakespeare's mind as the type of the androgynous, of the man-womanly mind, though it would be impossible to say what Shakespeare thought of women. And if it be true that it is one of the tokens of the fully developed mind that it does not think specially or separately of sex, how much harder it is to attain that condition now than ever before. Here I came to the books by living writers, and there paused and wondered if this fact were not at the root of something that had long puzzled me. No age can ever have been as stridently sex-conscious as our own; those innumerable books by men about women in the British Museum are a proof of it. The Suffrage campaign was no doubt to blame. It must have roused in men an extraordinary desire for self-assertion; it must have made them lay an emphasis upon their own sex and its characteristics which they would not have troubled to think about had they not been challenged. And when one is challenged, even by a few women in black bonnets, one retaliates, if one has never been challenged before, rather excessively. That perhaps accounts for some of the characteristics that I remember to have found here, I thought, taking down a new novel by Mr A, who is in the prime of life and very well thought of, apparently, by the reviewers. I opened it. Indeed, it was delightful to read a man's writing again. It was so direct, so straightforward after the writing of women. It indicated such freedom of mind, such liberty of person, such confidence in himself. One had a sense of physical well-being in the presence of this well-nourished, well-educated, free mind, which had never been thwarted or opposed, but had had full liberty from birth to stretch itself in whatever way it liked. All this was admirable. But after reading a chapter or two a shadow seemed to lie across the page. it was a straight dark bar, a shadow shaped something like the letter 'I'. One began dodging this way and that to catch a glimpse of the landscape behind it. Whether that was indeed a tree or a woman walking I was not quite sure. Back one was always hailed to the letter 'I'. One began to be tired of 'I'. Not but what this 'I' was a most respectable 'I'; honest and logical; as hard as a nut, and polished for centuries by good teaching and good feeding. I respect and admire that 'I' from the bottom of my heart. But--here I turned a page or two, looking for something or other--the worst of it is that in the shadow of the letter 'I' all is shapeless as mist. Is that a tree? No, it is a woman. But...she has not a bone in her body, I thought, watching Phoebe, for that was her name, coming across the beach. Then Alan got up and the shadow of Alan at once obliterated Phoebe. For Alan had views and Phoebe was quenched in the flood of his views. And then Alan, I thought, has passions; and here I turned page after page very fast, feeling that the crisis was approaching, and so it was. It took place on the beach under the sun. It was done very openly. It was done very vigorously. Nothing could have been more indecent. But...I had said 'but' too often. One cannot go on saying 'but'. One must finish the sentence somehow, I rebuked myself. Shall I finish it, 'But--I am bored!' But why was I bored? Partly because of the dominance of the letter 'I' and the aridity, which, like the giant beech tree, it casts within its shade. Nothing will grow there. And partly for some more obscure reason. There seemed to be some obstacle, some impediment in Mr A's mind which blocked the fountain of creative energy and shored it within narrow limits. And remembering the lunch party at Oxbridge, and the cigarette ash and the Manx cat and Tennyson and Christina Rossetti all in a bunch, it seemed possible that the impediment lay there. As he no longer hums under his breath, 'There has fallen a splendid tear from the passion-flower at the gate', when Phoebe crosses the beach, and she no longer replies, 'My heart is like a singing bird whose nest is in a water'd shoot', when Alan approaches what can he do? Being honest as the day and logical as the sun, there is only one thing he can do. And that he does, to do him justice, over and over (I said turning the pages) and over again. And that, I added, aware of the awful nature of the confession, seems somehow dull. Shakespeare's indecency uproots a thousand other things in one's mind, and is far from being dull. But Shakespeare does it for pleasure; Mr A, as the nurses say, does it on purpose. He does it in protest. He is protesting against the equality of the other sex by asserting his own superiority. He is therefore impeded and inhibited and self-conscious as Shakespeare might have been if he too had known Miss Clough and Miss Davies. Doubtless Elizabethan literature would have been very different from what it is if the women's movement had begun in the sixteenth century and not in the nineteenth.

What, then, it amounts to, if this theory of the two sides of the mind holds good, is that virility has now become self-conscious--men, that is to say, are now writing only with the male side of their brains. It is a mistake for a woman to read them, for she will inevitably look for something that she will not find. It is the power of suggestion that one most misses, I thought, taking Mr B the critic in my hand and reading, very carefully and very dutifully, his remarks upon the art of poetry. Very able they were, acute and full of learning; but the trouble was that his feelings no longer communicated; his mind seemed separated into different chambers; not a sound carried from one to the other. Thus, when one takes a sentence of Mr B into the mind it falls plump to the ground--dead; but when one takes a sentence of Coleridge into the mind, it explodes and gives birth to all kinds of other ideas, and that is the only sort of writing of which one can say that it has the secret of perpetual life.

But whatever the reason may be, it is a fact that one must deplore. For it means--here I had come to rows of books by Mr Galsworthy and Mr Kipling--that some of the finest works of our greatest living writers fall upon deaf ears. Do what she will a woman cannot find in them that fountain of perpetual life which the critics assure her is there. It is not only that they celebrate male virtues, enforce male values and describe the world of men; it is that the emotion with which these books are permeated is to a woman incomprehensible. It is coming, it is gathering, it is about to burst on one's head, one begins saying long before the end. That picture will fall on old Jolyon's head; he will die of the shock; the old clerk will speak over him two or three obituary words; and all the swans on the Thames will simultaneously burst out singing. But one will rush away before that happens and hide in the gooseberry bushes, for the emotion which is so deep, so subtle, so symbolical to a man moves a woman to wonder. So with Mr Kipling's officers who turn their Backs; and his Sowers who sow the Seed; and his Men who are alone with their Work; and the Flag--one blushes at all these capital letters as if one had been caught eavesdropping at some purely masculine orgy. The fact is that neither Mr Galsworthy nor Mr Kipling has a spark of the woman in him. Thus all their qualities seem to a woman, if one may generalize, crude and immature. They lack suggestive power. And when a book lacks suggestive power, however hard it hits the surface of the mind it cannot penetrate within.

And in that restless mood in which one takes books out and puts them back again without looking at them I began to envisage an age to come of pure, of self-assertive virility, such as the letters of professors (take Sir Walter Raleigh's letters, for instance) seem to forebode, and the rulers of Italy have already brought into being. For one can hardly fail to be impressed in Rome by the sense of unmitigated masculinity; and whatever the value of unmitigated masculinity upon the state, one may question the effect of it upon the art of poetry. At any rate, according to the newspapers, there is a certain anxiety about fiction in Italy. There has been a meeting of academicians whose object it is 'to develop the Italian novel'. 'Men famous by birth, or in finance, industry or the Fascist corporations' came together the other day and discussed the matter, and a telegram was sent to the Duce expressing the hope 'that the Fascist era would soon give birth to a poet worthy of it'. We may all join in that pious hope, but it is doubtful whether poetry can come of an incubator. Poetry ought to have a mother as well as a father. The Fascist poem, one may fear, will be a horrid little abortion such as one sees in a glass jar in the museum of some county town. Such monsters never live long, it is said; one has never seen a prodigy of that sort cropping grass in a field. Two heads on one body do not make for length of life.

However, the blame for all this, if one is anxious to lay blame, rests no more upon one sex than upon the other. All seducers and reformers are responsible: Lady Bessborough when she lied to Lord Granville; Miss Davies when she told the truth to Mr Greg. All who have brought about a state of sex-consciousness are to blame, and it is they who drive me, when I want to stretch my faculties on a book, to seek it in that happy age, before Miss Davies and Miss Clough were born, when the writer used both sides of his mind equally. One must turn back to Shakespeare then, for Shakespeare was androgynous; and so were Keats and Sterne and Cowper and Lamb and Coleridge. Shelley perhaps was sexless. Milton and Ben Jonson had a dash too much of the male in them. So had Wordsworth and Tolstoi. In our time Proust was wholly androgynous, if not perhaps a little too much of a woman. But that failing is too rare for one to complain of it, since without some mixture of the kind the intellect seems to predominate and the other faculties of the mind harden and become barren. However, I consoled myself with the reflection that this is perhaps a passing phase; much of what I have said in obedience to my promise to give you the course of my thoughts will seem out of date; much of what flames in my eyes will seem dubious to you who have not yet come of age.

Even so, the very first sentence that I would write here, I said, crossing over to the writing-table and taking up the page headed Women and Fiction, is that it is fatal for anyone who writes to think of their sex. It is fatal to be a man or woman pure and simple; one must be woman-manly or man-womanly. It is fatal for a woman to lay the least stress on any grievance; to plead even with justice any cause; in any way to speak consciously as a woman. And fatal is no figure of speech; for anything written with that conscious bias is doomed to death. It ceases to be fertilized. Brilliant and effective, powerful and masterly, as it may appear for a day or two, it must wither at nightfall; it cannot grow in the minds of others. Some collaboration has to take place in the mind between the woman and the man before the art of creation can be accomplished. Some marriage of opposites has to be consummated. The whole of the mind must lie wide open if we are to get the sense that the writer is communicating his experience with perfect fullness. There must be freedom and there must be peace. Not a wheel must grate, not a light glimmer. The curtains must be close drawn. The writer, I thought, once his experience is over, must lie back and let his mind celebrate its nuptials in darkness. He must not look or question what is being done. Rather, he must pluck the petals from a rose or watch the swans float calmly down the river. And I saw again the current which took the boat and the under-graduate and the dead leaves; and the taxi took the man and the woman, I thought, seeing them come together across the street, and the current swept them away, I thought, hearing far off the roar of London's traffic, into that tremendous stream.

Here, then, Mary Beton ceases to speak. She has told you how she reached the conclusion--the prosaic conclusion--that it is necessary to have five hundred a year and a room with a lock on the door if you are to write fiction or poetry. She has tried to lay bare the thoughts and impressions that led her to think this. She has asked you to follow her flying into the arms of a Beadle, lunching here, dining there, drawing pictures in the British Museum, taking books from the shelf, looking out of the window. While she has been doing all these things, you no doubt have been observing her failings and foibles and deciding what effect they have had on her opinions. You have been contradicting her and making whatever additions and deductions seem good to you. That is all as it should be, for in a question like this truth is only to be had by laying together many varieties of error. And I will end now in my own person by anticipating two criticisms, so obvious that you can hardly fail to make them.

No opinion has been expressed, you may say, upon the comparative merits of the sexes even as writers. That was done purposely, because, even if the time had come for such a valuation--and it is far more important at the moment to know how much money women had and how many rooms than to theorize about their capacities--even if the time had come I do not believe that gifts, whether of mind or character, can be weighed like sugar and butter, not even in Cambridge, where they are so adept at putting people into classes and fixing caps on their heads and letters after their names. I do not believe that even the Table of Precedency which you will find in Whitaker's ALMANAC represents a final order of values, or that there is any sound reason to suppose that a Commander of the Bath will ultimately walk in to dinner behind a Master in Lunacy. All this pitting of sex against sex, of quality against quality; all this claiming of superiority and imputing of inferiority, belong to the private-school stage of human existence where there are 'sides', and it is necessary for one side to beat another side, and of the utmost importance to walk up to a platform and receive from the hands of the Headmaster himself a highly ornamental pot. As people mature they cease to believe in sides or in Headmasters or in highly ornamental pots. At any rate, where books are concerned, it is notoriously difficult to fix labels of merit in such a way that they do not come off. Are not reviews of current literature a perpetual illustration of the difficulty of judgement? 'This great book', 'this worthless book', the same book is called by both names. Praise and blame alike mean nothing. No, delightful as the pastime of measuring may be, it is the most futile of all occupations, and to submit to the decrees of the measurers the most servile of attitudes. So long as you write what you wish to write, that is all that matters; and whether it matters for ages or only for hours, nobody can say. But to sacrifice a hair of the head of your vision, a shade of its colour, in deference to some Headmaster with a silver pot in his hand or to some professor with a measuring-rod up his sleeve, is the most abject treachery, and the sacrifice of wealth and chastity which used to be said to be the greatest of human disasters, a mere flea-bite in comparison.

Next I think that you may object that in all this I have made too much of the importance of material things. Even allowing a generous margin for symbolism, that five hundred a year stands for the power to contemplate, that a lock on the door means the power to think for oneself, still you may say that the mind should rise above such things; and that great poets have often been poor men. Let me then quote to you the words of your own Professor of Literature, who knows better than I do what goes to the making of a poet. Sir Arthur Quiller-Couch writes:'[11]

'What are the great poetical names of the last hundred years or so? Coleridge, Wordsworth, Byron, Shelley, Landor, Keats, Tennyson, Browning, Arnold, Morris, Rossetti, Swinburne--we may stop there. Of these, all but Keats, Browning, Rossetti were University men, and of these three, Keats, who died young, cut off in his prime, was the only one not fairly well to do. It may seem a brutal thing to say, and it is a sad thing to say: but, as a matter of hard fact, the theory that poetical genius bloweth where it listeth, and equally in poor and rich, holds little truth. As a matter of hard fact, nine out of those twelve were University men: which means that somehow or other they procured the means to get the best education England can give. As a matter of hard fact, of the remaining three you know that Browning was well to do, and I challenge you that, if he had not been well to do, he would no more have attained to write SAUL or THE RING AND THE BOOK than Ruskin would have attained to writing MODERN PAINTERS if his father had not dealt prosperously in business. Rossetti had a small private income; and, moreover, he painted. There remains but Keats; whom Atropos slew young, as she slew John Clare in a mad-house, and James Thomson by the laudanum he took to drug disappointment. These are dreadful facts, but let us face them. It is--however dishonouring to us as a nation--certain that, by some fault in our commonwealth, the poor poet has not in these days, nor has had for two hundred years, a dog's chance. Believe me--and I have spent a great part of ten years in watching some three hundred and twenty elementary schools, we may prate of democracy, but actually, a poor child in England has little more hope than had the son of an Athenian slave to be emancipated into that intellectual freedom of which great writings are born.'

---

[11] THE ART OF WRITING, by Sir Arthur Quiller-Couch.

Nobody could put the point more plainly. 'The poor poet has not in these days, nor has had for two hundred years, a dog's chance...a poor child in England has little more hope than had the son of an Athenian slave to be emancipated into that intellectual freedom of which great writings are born.' That is it. Intellectual freedom depends upon material things. Poetry depends upon intellectual freedom. And women have always been poor, not for two hundred years merely, but from the beginning of time. Women have had less intellectual freedom than the sons of Athenian slaves. Women, then, have not had a dog's chance of writing poetry. That is why I have laid so much stress on money and a room of one's own. However, thanks to the toils of those obscure women in the past, of whom I wish we knew more, thanks, curiously enough to two wars, the Crimean which let Florence Nightingale out of her drawing-room, and the European War which opened the doors to the average woman some sixty years later, these evils are in the way to be bettered. Otherwise you would not be here tonight, and your chance of earning five hundred pounds a year, precarious as I am afraid that it still is, would be minute in the extreme.

Still, you may object, why do you attach so much importance to this writing of books by women when, according to you, it requires so much effort, leads perhaps to the murder of one's aunts, will make one almost certainly late for luncheon, and may bring one into very grave disputes with certain very good fellows? My motives, let me admit, are partly selfish. Like most uneducated Englishwomen, I like reading--I like reading books in the bulk. Lately my diet has become a trifle monotonous; history is too much about wars; biography too much about great men; poetry has shown, I think, a tendency to sterility, and fiction but I have sufficiently exposed my disabilities as a critic of modern fiction and will say no more about it. Therefore I would ask you to write all kinds of books, hesitating at no subject however trivial or however vast. By hook or by crook, I hope that you will possess yourselves of money enough to travel and to idle, to contemplate the future or the past of the world, to dream over books and loiter at street corners and let the line of thought dip deep into the stream. For I am by no means confining you to fiction. If you would please me--and there are thousands like me--you would write books of travel and adventure, and research and scholarship, and history and biography, and criticism and philosophy and science. By so doing you will certainly profit the art of fiction. For books have a way of influencing each other. Fiction will be much the better for standing cheek by jowl with poetry and philosophy. Moreover, if you consider any great figure of the past, like Sappho, like the Lady Murasaki, like Emily Brontë, you will find that she is an inheritor as well as an originator, and has come into existence because women have come to have the habit of writing naturally; so that even as a prelude to poetry such activity on your part would be invaluable.

But when I look back through these notes and criticize my own train of thought as I made them, I find that my motives were not altogether selfish. There runs through these comments and discursions the conviction--or is it the instinct?--that good books are desirable and that good writers, even if they show every variety of human depravity, are still good human beings. Thus when I ask you to write more books I am urging you to do what will be for your good and for the good of the world at large. How to justify this instinct or belief I do not know, for philosophic words, if one has not been educated at a university, are apt to play one false. What is meant by 'reality'? It would seem to be something very erratic, very undependable--now to be found in a dusty road, now in a scrap of newspaper in the street, now a daffodil in the sun. It lights up a group in a room and stamps some casual saying. It overwhelms one walking home beneath the stars and makes the silent world more real than the world of speech--and then there it is again in an omnibus in the uproar of Piccadilly. Sometimes, too, it seems to dwell in shapes too far away for us to discern what their nature is. But whatever it touches, it fixes and makes permanent. That is what remains over when the skin of the day has been cast into the hedge; that is what is left of past time and of our loves and hates. Now the writer, as I think, has the chance to live more than other people in the presence of this reality. It is his business to find it and collect it and communicate it to the rest of us. So at least I infer from reading LEAR or EMMA or LA RECHERCHE DU TEMPS PERDU. For the reading of these books seems to perform a curious couching operation on the senses; one sees more intensely afterwards; the world seems bared of its covering and given an intenser life. Those are the enviable people who live at enmity with unreality; and those are the pitiable who are knocked on the head by the thing done without knowing or caring. So that when I ask you to earn money and have a room of your own, I am asking you to live in the presence of reality, an invigorating life, it would appear, whether one can impart it or not.

Here I would stop, but the pressure of convention decrees that every speech must end with a peroration. And a peroration addressed to women should have something, you will agree, particularly exalting and ennobling about it. I should implore you to remember your responsibilities, to be higher, more spiritual; I should remind, you how much depends upon you, and what an influence you can exert upon the future. But those exhortations can safely, I think, be left to the other sex, who will put them, and indeed have put them, with far greater eloquence than I can compass. When I rummage in my own mind I find no noble sentiments about being companions and equals and influencing the world to higher ends. I find myself saying briefly and prosaically that it is much more important to be oneself than anything else. Do not dream of influencing other people, I would say, if I knew how to make it sound exalted. Think of things in themselves.

And again I am reminded by dipping into newspapers and novels and biographies that when a woman speaks to women she should have something very unpleasant up her sleeve. Women are hard on women. Women dislike women. Women--but are you not sick to death of the word? I can assure you that I am. Let us agree, then, that a paper read by a woman to women should end with something particularly disagreeable.

But how does it go? What can I think of? The truth is, I often like women. I like their unconventionality. I like their completeness. I like their anonymity. I like--but I must not run on in this way. That cupboard there,--you say it holds clean table-napkins only; but what if Sir Archibald Bodkin were concealed among them? Let me then adopt a sterner tone. Have I, in the preceding words, conveyed to you sufficiently the warnings and reprobation of mankind? I have told you the very low opinion in which you were held by Mr Oscar Browning. I have indicated what Napoleon once thought of you and what Mussolini thinks now. Then, in case any of you aspire to fiction, I have copied out for your benefit the advice of the critic about courageously acknowledging the limitations of your sex. I have referred to Professor X and given prominence to his statement that women are intellectually, morally and physically inferior to men. I have handed on all that has come my way without going in search of it, and here is a final warning--from Mr John Langdon Davies.[12] Mr John Langdon Davies warns women 'that when children cease to be altogether desirable, women cease to be altogether necessary'. I hope you will make a note of it.

How can I further encourage you to go about the business of life? Young women, I would say, and please attend, for the peroration is beginning, you are, in my opinion, disgracefully ignorant. You have never made a discovery of any sort of importance. You have never shaken an empire or led an army into battle. The plays of Shakespeare are not by you, and you have never introduced a barbarous race to the blessings of civilization. What is your excuse? It is all very well for you to say, pointing to the streets and squares and forests of the globe swarming with black and white and coffee-coloured inhabitants, all busily engaged in traffic and enterprise and love-making, we have had other work on our hands. Without our doing, those seas would be unsailed and those fertile lands a desert. We have borne and bred and washed and taught, perhaps to the age of six or seven years, the one thousand six hundred and twenty-three million human beings who are, according to statistics, at present in existence, and that, allowing that some had help, takes time.

There is truth in what you say--I will not deny it. But at the same time may I remind you that there have been at least two colleges for women in existence in England since the year 1866; that after the year 1880 a married woman was allowed by law to possess her own property; and that in 1919--which is a whole nine years ago she was given a vote? May I also remind you that most of the professions have been open to you for close on ten years now? When you reflect upon these immense privileges and the length of time during which they have been enjoyed, and the fact that there must be at this moment some two thousand women capable of earning over five hundred a year in one way or another, you will agree that the excuse of lack of opportunity, training, encouragement, leisure and money no longer holds good. Moreover, the economists are telling us that Mrs Seton has had too many children. You must, of course, go on bearing children, but, so they say, in twos and threes, not in tens and twelves.

Thus, with some time on your hands and with some book learning in your brains--you have had enough of the other kind, and are sent to college partly, I suspect, to be uneducated--surely you should embark upon another stage of your very long, very laborious and highly obscure career. A thousand pens are ready to suggest what you should do and what effect you will have. My own suggestion is a little fantastic, I admit; I prefer, therefore, to put it in the form of fiction.

---

[12] A SHORT HISTORY OF WOMEN, by John Langdon Davies.

I told you in the course of this paper that Shakespeare had a sister; but do not look for her in Sir Sidney Lee's life of the poet. She died young--alas, she never wrote a word. She lies buried where the omnibuses now stop, opposite the Elephant and Castle. Now my belief is that this poet who never wrote a word and was buried at the cross-roads still lives. She lives in you and in me, and in many other women who are not here to-night, for they are washing up the dishes and putting the children to bed. But she lives; for great poets do not die; they are continuing presences; they need only the opportunity to walk among us in the flesh. This opportunity, as I think, it is now coming within your power to give her. For my belief is that if we live another century or so--I am talking of the common life which is the real life and not of the little separate lives which we live as individuals--and have five hundred a year each of us and rooms of our own; if we have the habit of freedom and the courage to write exactly what we think; if we escape a little from the common sitting-room and see human beings not always in their relation to each other but in relation to reality; and the sky, too, and the trees or whatever it may be in themselves; if we look past Milton's bogey, for no human being should shut out the view; if we face the fact, for it is a fact, that there is no arm to cling to, but that we go alone and that our relation is to the world of reality and not only to the world of men and women, then the opportunity will come and the dead poet who was Shakespeare's sister will put on the body which she has so often laid down. Drawing her life from the lives of the unknown who were her forerunners, as her brother did before her, she will be born. As for her coming without that preparation, without that effort on our part, without that determination that when she is born again she shall find it possible to live and write her poetry, that we cannot expect, for that would he impossible. But I maintain that she would come if we worked for her, and that so to work, even in poverty and obscurity, is worth while.

THE END.

Also from Benediction Books ...
Wandering Between Two Worlds: Essays on Faith and Art
Anita Mathias
Benediction Books, 2007
152 pages
ISBN: 0955373700

Available from www.amazon.com, www.amazon.co.uk

In these wide-ranging lyrical essays, Anita Mathias writes, in lush, lovely prose, of her naughty Catholic childhood in Jamshedpur, India; her large, eccentric family in Mangalore, a sea-coast town converted by the Portuguese in the sixteenth century; her rebellion and atheism as a teenager in her Himalayan boarding school, run by German missionary nuns, St. Mary's Convent, Nainital; and her abrupt religious conversion after which she entered Mother Teresa's convent in Calcutta as a novice. Later rich, elegant essays explore the dualities of her life as a writer, mother, and Christian in the United States-- Domesticity and Art, Writing and Prayer, and the experience of being "an alien and stranger" as an immigrant in America, sensing the need for roots.

About the Author

Anita Mathias is the author of *Wandering Between Two Worlds: Essays on Faith and Art.* She has a B.A. and M.A. in English from Somerville College, Oxford University, and an M.A. in Creative Writing from the Ohio State University, USA. Anita won a National Endowment of the Arts fellowship in Creative Nonfiction in 1997. She lives in Oxford, England with her husband, Roy, and her daughters, Zoe and Irene.

Visit Anita at http://www.anitamathias.com.

The Church Thad Had Too Much
Anita Mathias
Benediction Books, 2010
52 pages
ISBN: 9781849026567

Available from www.amazon.com, www.amazon.co.uk

The Church That Had Too Much was very well-intentioned. She wanted to love God, she wanted to love people, but she was both hampered by her muchness and the abundance of her possessions, and beset by ambition, power struggles and snobbery. Read about the surprising way The Church That Had Too Much began to resolve her problems in this deceptively simple and enchanting fable.

About the Author

Anita Mathias is the author of *Wandering Between Two Worlds: Essays on Faith and Art.* She has a B.A. and M.A. in English from Somerville College, Oxford University, and an M.A. in Creative Writing from the Ohio State University, USA. Anita won a National Endowment of the Arts fellowship in Creative Nonfiction in 1997. She lives in Oxford, England with her husband, Roy, and her daughters, Zoe and Irene.

Visit Anita at http://www.anitamathias.com

Francesco, Artist of Florence: The Man Who Gave Too Much
Anita Mathias
Benediction Books, 2014
52 pages (full colour)
ISBN:978-1781394175

In this lavishly illustrated book by Anita Mathias, Francesco, artist of Florence, creates magic in pietre dure, inlaying precious stones in marble in life-like "paintings." While he works, placing lapis lazuli birds on clocks, and jade dragonflies on vases, he is purely happy. However, he must sell his art to support his family. Francesco, who is incorrigibly soft-hearted, cannot stand up to his haggling customers. He ends up almost giving away an exquisite jewellery box to Signora Farnese's bambina, who stands, captivated, gazing at a jade parrot nibbling a cherry. Signora Stallardi uses her daughter's wedding to cajole him into discounting his rainbowed marriage chest. His old friend Girolamo bullies him into letting him have the opulent table he hoped to sell to the Medici almost at cost. Carrara is raising the price of marble; the price of gems keeps rising. His wife is in despair. Francesco fears ruin.

* * *

Sitting in the church of Santa Maria Novella at Mass, very worried, Francesco hears the words of Christ. The lilies of the field and the birds of the air do not worry, yet their Heavenly Father looks after them. As He will look after us. He resolves not to worry. And as he repeats the prayer the Saviour taught us, Francesco resolves to forgive the friends and neighbours who repeatedly put their own interests above his. But can he forgive himself for his own weakness, as he waits for the eternal city of gold whose walls are made of jasper, whose gates are made of pearls, and whose foundations are sapphire, emerald, ruby and amethyst? There time and money shall be no more, the lion shall live with the lamb, and we shall dwell trustfully together. Francesco leaves Santa Maria Novella, resolving to trust the One who told him to live like the lilies and the birds, deciding to forgive those who haggled him into bad bargains--while making a little resolution for the future